Penguin Books
The Birds on the Trees

50

KU-739-437

Nina Bawden was born in London, and educated at a local
grammar school and Somerville College Oxford. Her
first novel was published in 1952. Since then she has
written eleven others, among them *Devil by the Sea*,
Tortoise by Candlelight, *A Little Love, A Little Learning*,
A Woman of My Age and *The Grain of Truth*. She has also
written six books for children, four of which, *A Handful of
Thieves*, *The Witch's Daughter*, *On The Run* and *The
White Horse Gang*, are available in Puffins. She is married
to Austen Kark of the BBC European Service and lives at
Weybridge, Surrey.

'The author is observing life as she sees it, centering on an entirely believable middle-class family, with children who puzzle and dismay their parents, because these are the people she sees every day and these are the children who interest and baffle her, too. That she is English and the setting is the London suburbs won't disorient the American reader, for everything in the novel can and does happen here.' – *Saturday Review*

'Here is a book that will delight many readers : young people who do not understand their parents; parents who do not understand their children; even grandparents who, perhaps, didn't do a very good job with their own children but are convinced they know what to do for their grandchildren.' – *Greenboro Daily News*

'Although generation gap stories can easily drown in a sea of cliches, *The Birds on the Trees* is a marvel of buoyancy. Miss Bawden beautifully captures the capricious intensity of sibling love, rivalry and loyalty. She is reluctant to pin blame and quick to display compassion. She is also logical enough to offer no easy solutions, but sufficiently warm-hearted to include realistic sprinklings of hope. The combination is excellent; her book is a joy to read.' – *Christian Science Monitor*

Nina Bawden

The Birds on the Trees

Penguin Books

Penguin Books Ltd, Harmondsworth,
Middlesex, England
Penguin Books Australia Ltd, Ringwood,
Victoria, Australia

First published by Longman 1970
Published in Penguin Books 1972

Copyright © Nina Bawden, 1970

Made and printed in Great Britain by
Richard Clay (The Chaucer Press) Ltd, Bungay, Suffolk
Set in Linotype Pilgrim

To John Guest
with affection and gratitude

Prologue

'I hope we've done right,' Clara Tilney said. From her, this was an unusual remark – she seldom doubted her actions, nor expected her husband to share the responsibility when she did – but the occasion was exceptional. An hour earlier, ten o'clock on Christmas Eve, she had opened the back door to clear the steam from her kitchen and found the child outside. How long he had been there was anyone's guess : his little hands were cold as toads and his striped, knitted hat beaded with moisture, although the rain had stopped some time before, leaving a clear, seasonal, carolling night. Certainly he hadn't knocked – busy at the stove with mince pies and turkey stuffing, Mrs Tilney would have heard him – and all he would say, once coaxed inside and comforted, was that Mummy and Daddy had gone away for Christmas and left him behind, alone.

Although shocking, the situation was not entirely beyond belief. The family had moved into the house at the bottom of the Tilneys' garden nine months ago and the boy had become an accepted visitor some time in the middle of the summer, infiltrating so unobtrusively that it was hard to say, exactly, when he had ceased to be a small, anonymous figure standing silently at the broken fence, and begun to appear regularly, weekend mornings when the Tilneys were sitting down to their enormous breakfast, to watch from the back door with huge, dark famine eyes. Looking at those eyes, it was easy to believe him when he said Mummy had given him nothing to eat, but Clara Tilney was not one to choose the easy road. Nobody's fool, she took most of what she heard with a pinch of salt. But if the child was a persistent liar – for the complaint, or statement, was frequently repeated – he was not one of a kind she was accustomed to, being neither bold nor sly; having, on the contrary, a steady if wistful gaze and gentle manners, saying *if you please*, and *thank you so much*, with a solemn, old-fashioned air. Accepting, then, that he spoke the truth, Mrs Tilney looked for other signs of ill-treatment but found none. 'Not a mark on his little body,' she said to her husband, after she had seen him stripped one hot afternoon, playing with her own children under the garden hose. Though not disappointed (she wasn't a morbid woman), she could not help feeling a little at a loss. Blows she could comprehend and would have dealt with : Clara had been brought up in the slums and knew the proper channels. But what was wrong here was something not only harder to deal with, but to place. You couldn't call the child really neglected. Thin he might be, but some people are like that, all scrag and muscle, and he was always decently, if sometimes oddly, clothed. Mrs Tilney had seen him at the bus-stop with his mother, dressed neatly enough in the uniform of the local private school but wearing, on his head, a towering pink velvet toque with a tattered, trailing veil. His mother had smiled, but Mrs Tilney hadn't liked to speak.

Her inhibition was to some extent social. Not – in spite of the private school – a question of money, for the little boy's parents were visibly shabby. They had no television set, so the Tilney children reported, and no car; only an ancient, high-seated bicycle which the tall young mother rode, that had a carrier behind for the boy and a cradle in front for the baby. Nor was it old-fashioned snobbery. Mrs Tilney had no ear for accents and no interest, anyway, in ladies-and-gentlemen non-sense. It was power that impressed her; not Dukes, but Captains of Industry, Presidents of the United States. No – as far as class went, what divided her from the children's mother was simply a difference of *approach*. Except in moments of brutal necessity, it was not Clara's habit to come straight out with things, especially if they were of a delicate nature. And the only time she had actually had an opportunity was once in the launderette; she was folding her sheets, warmly crinkled from the tumbler-drier, when the younger woman came up with a bundle of wet washing and said, without any preamble, 'I meant to ask you before – I *do* hope he isn't a nuisance, run-ning in and out all the time.' It was said breathlessly – all that bicycling, perhaps, and heaving the fat baby about – but with such a clear, confident ring that 'No, of course not, it's a pleasure,' was the only possible answer. No lead in for a comfortable discussion of childish habits, fads and fancies – *mine won't touch cornflakes, or meat roll, or dripping toast* – which might have made it possible, after a reasonable length of time, to cautiously bring up the business of the breakfasts.

'Not that I grudge the child,' Mrs Tilney often said, either to her husband or aloud to herself, holding an imagined conversation with the mother. Perhaps that was, really, what held her back from going round to the house and coming out with it: the fear that she might be thought inhospitable. Clara's childhood had been hungry and miserable, her parents being both poor, and mean by nature, so that even the food they could afford to put on the table was jealously watched, mouthful by mouthful. (Marge *and* jam; Money no object, I suppose! When you grow up, my girl, you can put two spoons of sugar in your tea, but while you're under this roof, you'll toe the chalk line!) From this sour soil, Mrs Tilney had flowered remarkably, large-hearted and generous. 'Eat,' she said to her children. 'Eat. Have butter on that potato. Can't you really manage another piece of pie?' Using, always, thick cream and butter, best meat not scrag end, fresh vegetables, the biggest eggs, stone-ground flour. Mr Tilney earned good money working for a hire firm that ran a fleet of school buses, but even if he had not, she would have served up good bean stews, home-made soups. She often lay awake at night devising cheap, nourishing meals, so that if the worst should happen she could still feed her family with a flourish.

Having grown strong and sturdy, happy and casually greedy, they now had almost ceased to need her. The little boy was, therefore, both a replacement, and a challenge. Clara longed to put colour in that milk-pale face, flesh on the bony limbs. She kept back the brownest, most speckled eggs, bought jars of expensive honey. 'That'll keep you going for a bit,' she said as the child tucked in. 'There's my pet, my lambkin-pie.' Her own children had grown out of such endearments, as they had grown out of caresses and lap-sitting: if she reached out to touch them, they jerked their heads like ponies.

In fact, though, the boy preferred Mr Tilney's lap to his

wife's, perhaps because he sat still for longer. Mr Tilney was a quiet, lethargic man who suffered with his stomach. (Boiled fish and skim milk was what he needed, but never got.) His role in the household was negligible, but he never complained, only gazed, occasionally, at his lusty wife and children as if wondering how he had ever had the energy. This imported child was a better match for his temperament. He would sit on the tired man's lap, watching television, sucking his thumb. From time to time he would glance up at the underside of the scraggy, tortoise neck; sigh, and snuggle closer.

It was Mr Tilney who put him to bed on Christmas Eve while Clara went round to his parents' house – a big, run-down place in half an acre of neglected garden. By the time she got back to report that the house was dark and empty and that all she had been able to do was push a note through the door to say where the child was, he was already asleep, tucked up on the divan in the Tilneys' bedroom and Mr Tilney was filling a stocking for him with small things from the tree.

It was hard to know what to do for the best. In the first flush of outrage, Mrs Tilney was all for going to the police, but her husband talked her out of it. They would come and ask questions which would only upset the poor little bugger without getting anyone any further: since he wouldn't – or couldn't – tell them what had happened, he was hardly likely to talk to a stranger. Best to wait twenty-four hours and let him enjoy his Christmas. 'The bird's big enough to go round an extra one, isn't it, mother?' Mr Tilney not-so-innocently asked. A convinced procrastinator, he was also tired.

Once in bed, though, he couldn't sleep. There was no sound from the divan. He found himself – foolishly, he knew – holding his breath to listen for the child's, but all he could hear was his wife breathing beside him with little, fussy, puffs and snorts like a steam-engine. After a while, he got out of bed and went over to the divan. Enough light came in from the street lamp outside to show the child, lying on his back as a young baby sometimes lies, both hands palm upwards on either side of his face, the fingers loosely curled. Mr Tilney stood, looking down, his feet cold on the cold linoleum. It was some seconds before he realized that the boy was awake and looking up at him, and it shocked him, momentarily; those large, dark eyes, wide open and fathomless. His own children only lay so still when fast asleep. He said nervously, 'All right, are you?' The child did not answer. Mr Tilney touched the palm of one hand, very gently, and the fingers curled over his like tentacles, and gripped tight. Mr Tilney felt a curious, uneasy emotion; as if he were being asked a question he didn't know how to answer. He said, 'It's all right, you know. I expect your Mum and Dad will turn up tomorrow.'

'Mummy and Daddy are dead,' the child said, softly but distinctly so that Mr Tilney could not pretend he hadn't heard. Not that he wished to: after the first chill, the sad little statement opened doors in his mind that had been closed for a long time. All he said was, 'Oh, come on now,' but he sat down on the divan and gathered the boy into his arms, pressing the small head into the bony hollow of his neck and shoulder. After a brief resistance the child began to weep silently, and Mr Tilney rocked him, stroking the limp, silky hair, and felt his throat constrict with tenderness. Even when they were small, his own children had never needed him like this. He loved them dutifully, admired them, as he admired his wife, for their marvellous vitality, their unthinking good humour, but they were strangers to him; they rocketed about his house like foreign, billeted troops, shouting, banging doors, swilling milk, needing no more from anyone than food and discipline, which his wife could easily supply. His own, gentler offers were unnecessary, and disregarded.

Mr Tilney was cold and in an awkward position that increased the pain of his ulcer, but the discomfort was suddenly sweet. 'Quiet,' he murmured, 'quiet, now. It's all right. Uncle's here. Uncle knows...'

After lunch on Christmas Day, while his wife and eldest girl washed up the mammoth meal, Mr Tilney took the other children and the little boy for a walk on the common. A white sun shone and the heather was furred with frost. His own children ran and hollered and stamped in puddles: their shouts cracked the thin air as their boots splintered the frail skim of ice. The boy walked with Mr Tilney, holding his hand. From time to time he ran to join the others but always returned, after a very brief foray, to the shelter of Mr Tilney's side, smiling up at him with a kind of shy flirtatiousness – it was indeed, Mr Tilney felt, almost as if there were a burgeoning love affair between them. Certainly he felt strongly drawn towards the child; the more so, perhaps, because he knew he must betray him. He had promised his wife that he would telephone the police this evening; although this was the sensible course, Mr Tilney found it hard to respond to that happy, cozening smile. The memory came to him of a tale heard at school : a young, imprisoned prince whose eyes were to be put out by the order of his uncle, the king. There had been a picture in the history book of the pretty, trusting boy, and the kindly jailer, weeping . . .

Mr Tilney's imagination, once the flood gates were opened, was a sentimental one. Once or twice, as he did his best to amuse the child and encourage the rare, high laugh, his own eyes filled.

But he was spared his Judas role. When they got back, the parents were already there, sitting by the fire Clara had banked up so high against her family's return that the heat struck like a furnace as Mr Tilney opened the door. In that instant their faces, turned towards him, seemed curiously alike – brother and sister was his first, bemused thought – but on second look the similarity lay only in their expressions which were so shocked and bewildered as to be robbed of individuality, like the expressions of people caught in a road accident, and in their pallor, though when the woman saw the little boy, pressed close to Mr Tilney's side, the colour flooded her face. She said, 'Darling.'

The child made a grunting sound and fled down the passage to the kitchen.

The woman – girl, rather – half rose. Her husband said 'No,' rather sharply, and she sank back again, though her hands still gripped the arms of the chair. She looked up at Mr Tilney with eyes like her son's : enormous, dark and sad. He saw her throat move as she swallowed.

She said, 'I'm so terribly, terribly sorry.'

And so you should be, was on the tip of Mr Tilney's tongue. Unlike his wife, he was slow to anger, but now, faced with this wicked pair, outrage swelled within him. His hands had begun to shake; he pushed them deep into his trouser pockets and took a step into the room.

His wife said, flatly, 'Apparently he ran away, the naughty boy. After everyone was fast asleep.'

Her broad face was blank. She sat stiffly on a hard, high-backed chair.

The girl said, 'We went to my husband's sister for Christmas. It's not far, just a few streets, but she likes to see the children open their stockings on Christmas morning. I think he's frightened of his grandmother. She lives there. She's got Parkinson's, and shakes . . .'

The husband sighed, not loudly but definitely.

The girl said, 'Well, she will *kiss* him.' Her pleading eyes met Mr Tilney's. He felt only anger.

'Darling.' Her husband sighed again, perhaps reproachfully. He was looking at Mr Tilney, too. 'We're afraid it may not be so much my poor Mum, as the associated memory that's upset him. At least, it's all we can think of. We left him with my sister when the baby was born. Put him to bed and left him . . .'

'For Christ's sake, what could I *do*; I was in *labour*,' the young woman said, shocking Mr Tilney who hated to hear a woman swear. She seemed to be trembling with anger.

Her husband was massaging the side of his face, dragging the flesh downwards. He said evenly, 'Look, we can't know, and of course it wasn't your fault, but it's an explanation. Whenever he's put to bed there, he's afraid the same thing will happen again. Mummy will tuck him up and when he wakes, Auntie will be there instead. No Mum, no Dad . . .'

'You *said* you'd go and see him every night!'

'It seemed to upset him. You agreed it was best . . .' He began to rub at his eyes with the heel of his hand as if he were very tired. 'Lord above, we've gone over and over . . . I don't even believe it. *You* don't believe it. Do we have to go on?'

'You started it,' she said, like a child.

Mr Tilney looked at his wife. He assumed, from her tight-lipped look that she felt the same way as he did, but she said, suddenly and loudly, lifting her jaw, 'Poor souls, they've been half out of their minds with worry.'

The girl blushed, very deeply. 'It has been pretty awful,' the husband admitted, taking a crushed pack of cigarettes out of his pocket and extending it in Mr Tilney's direction. Mr Tilney shook his head. He was amazed. Not so much by the couple's behaviour (though that they should quarrel in front of strangers seemed extraordinary to him) but by his wife's attitude. She had given them sherry and was getting up now to fetch the bottle from the sideboard. "All's well that ends well, look at it that way, dear,' she said, as she re-filled the girl's empty glass. Turning her head she shot Mr Tilney a challenging look. 'Offer the biscuits, father.'

Mr Tilney stared. Had she forgotten; She was behaving as if this were an isolated incident. As if all that had happened was that a little boy had run away from his Auntie's house and upset his poor parents. A naughty child. Not a neglected child, a starved child . . .

He said hoarsely, 'There have been other things.'

'All lies,' Mrs Tilney said, meeting his eyes. 'We've had it all out.'

'You should have told us,' the girl said. 'Really.'

'Well.' Mrs Tilney offered biscuits, sighed, sat down.

'Oh, I know. Frightfully *embarrassing*, I can see that!' The girl gave a little kind, understanding laugh, though Mr Tilney guessed that she could not really see at all and found it, indeed, almost unbelievable that one neighbour should suspect another of keeping a young child hungry, and not say so. 'I mean,' the girl went on, wrinkling her forehead in a nervous effort to comprehend such bizarre behaviour, 'what would one *say*?' She laughed again – giggled. 'Oh dear! you must have thought us *monsters*!' She looked helpless: this was, presumably, what they *had* thought. She said. 'I really am so terribly sorry about it all.'

'Well, you can't say fairer than that,' the man said in a suddenly assumed cockney accent that sounded to Mr Tilney like mockery. Perhaps the man sensed this; he clapped his hands on his knees and stood up, reverting rather too loudly to his normal voice. 'Honestly, we can't thank you enough, you've been marvellously kind, but we better get on now, I think. Ring the police and tell them to call off the tracker dogs!' He put out his hand to his wife, smiling, and pulled her to her feet. They stood together, fingers clasped. She was taller than he was; a gangling girl in a darned jersey.

'I'll get him,' Mrs Tilney said.

When she had gone, the three left in the room stood still, almost at attention. The smile had gone from the man's face and Mr Tilney thought, *if he lays a finger on him* . . .

The child was there, in the doorway, pushed forward by Mrs Tilney, her bulk solid behind him. He walked across the small, hot room, straight to the place, on the floor in the window bay, where he had left the pile of presents from his stocking. He knelt and began to examine them.

The girl said, 'Hallo, there,' and he lifted his head, briefly, weaving it round in a blind way, like a mole.

His father cleared his throat. There were red patches, like burns, on his cheekbones. He was standing under the naked glare of the hanging central light. He said, 'Well, you gave us quite a fright, old man.'

The child had spread out his toys in a neat circle round him. He selected a puzzle and began to tip it carefully from side to side, holding it with both hands. The room was silent except for the tiny, sliding, rattling sound as he tried to persuade a plastic mouse into its hole.

The parents looked at each other. They seemed uncertain, almost afraid. Finally the father said, in a loud, cheerful voice, 'I suppose we'd better be going, Mrs Tilney.'

She preceded them. They shook hands with Mr Tilney, smiling elaborately, like actors. He wanted to stop them, to say, *this is terrible, what you are doing is terrible*, but he couldn't say it. He didn't even know what he meant.

The child sat quite still, head bent sideways like a blind child listening. Then, when the front door opened, he staggered to his feet and ran after them, screaming: agonized cries of rage and loss that made Mr Tilney sit down and put his head in his hands.

'It isn't natural,' he said later.

Mrs Tilney folded coloured wrapping paper on her lap. 'I'd have knocked him into the middle of next week.'

'Or hugged him,' Mr Tilney said. His wife's bark was worse

than her bite. 'Either would have been...' He paused; there seemed no word for what he wanted to say. 'More natural,' he ended. 'Poor little chap.'

'It's the parents I'm sorry for,' Mrs Tilney said.

Mr Tilney mended the fence between the two gardens. Towards the end of the afternoon, the little boy came out of the house with his mother. They ran about, playing ball. He missed a catch. 'Fetch it, darling,' his mother called.

But he was watching Mr Tilney. Colour was draining from the day. His face was indistinct, a pale flower at dusk, but what Mr Tilney could not see his guilt supplied: the wide, patient, dark, sad eyes, the hurt, rejected mouth. His mother laughed and struck her hands together. 'Come *on*, stir your aged stumps.' Mr Tilney banged in the last nail and got down from the fence.

Chapter One

At school we had to write an essay called 'My Favourite Relation'. I got a good mark but Miss Climper spoiled it by saying, 'You really do think your brother is wonderful, don't you, Lucy?' with that bright, sideways, sneery smile that is her speciality when she wants to make someone feel a fool.

I hated Miss Climper. That was a time when I hated a lot of people whom I quite like now, but what I felt for Miss Climper stayed. She's one of those people who think it a degrading weakness to like or admire anyone, and I think people like that do a great deal of harm in the world.

She kept things up, too. Later that same term, one snapping-cold winter afternoon when Toby came to fetch me from school, she passed us in the yard and said, 'So this is your famous brother, is it, Lucy? Well, well.' She rolled her pale, marbly eyes, as if she and the rest of the world knew something that I was too stupid to have grasped yet, and looked at Toby with her sneery smile. Not that she looked at him very differently from the way other grown-ups did. Even some of the bigger girls at school, when they saw him for the first time, giggled and whispered behind their hands because he was different from their rotten brothers, I suppose, wild hair like a brush and queer clothes, sometimes. Like a tramp, not a hippie. But when people looked at him like that, I wanted to kill them.

I often wanted to kill people. Sometimes I had a terrible dream that I really had done it and was going to be hanged. I was locked in a room with cold, tiled walls, and no way out. One night I woke up screaming and Toby came and said that a lot of children felt as I did, but it wore off as they got older. After that, I went on feeling the same way, but knowing that other people did too, made it less frightening.

One of the people I wanted to kill that year was my grandfather. He and my grandmother live in a cottage on the edge of a wood; two houses knocked into one but still small, two rooms downstairs and three bedrooms up. Whenever we went to see them my grandfather would take Greg and me into the garden and show us the rabbits he was breeding to make his fortune, beautiful rabbits with blue, silky hair, and then we would go in and have lunch and everything would be fine for a while, my father talking and making jokes, until we got to the pudding when my grandfather would start looking at Toby, just looking at first and raising his eyebrows which were like squashed toothbrushes and clearing his throat and then in the end he would say something like, 'For God's sake, boy, why don't you get your hair cut? You look like a girl. D'you want to look like a girl? Or a nancy boy?'

Toby never said anything, just smiled, but what was really awful was that my mother and father never said anything either. My mother said once that my grandfather was so old and set in his ideas it would be unkind to argue with him, but I knew this wasn't why they said nothing: the truth was, they were against Toby, too, and they were glad when other people said the things they would like to say but were afraid to. When I'm grown up, if people say things against my children I won't sit and say nothing, I can tell you.

That Sunday, as on so many Sundays before, her father said, 'Must you make all this fuss, Maggie? It's only Phoebe, coming to lunch.'

Her mother sighed as she always did. 'I like to make a fuss. People are always making single women eat in the kitchen and not bothering to give them a decent bottle of wine. I want your sister to feel welcome when she comes here, not a lonely old woman to be given charity to!'

Her father laughed. Yawned and stretched and laughed in the chair by the window while her mother laid the table. 'Do you really see old Phoebe in that tragic light?'

'I don't see why you always have to *argue*, Charlie,' her mother said. 'Phoebe has been coming to lunch approximately every third Sunday since we've been married. Which is going on for nineteen years now, so you can work out for yourself just about how many times we've had this *argument*.'

Although there was irritation in her voice there was laughter, too, so that Lucy knew this was just a joke between them, one of their mock battles that had scared her when she was younger, sitting on the stairs or lying in bed with the door open and their voices floating up. But she was not quite comforted: beneath the irritation and the laughter, familiar and accepted now, there was something else hidden. Something new.

Once, she had seen a picture in a book of a woman running across a bridge; a reproduction, her father told her, of a famous painting called *The Scream*. The woman's face was red and twisted and her mouth open in a small, round O that could have been surprise, but was not. 'She's afraid,' Lucy had said, and her father smiled and turned the page, saying lightly, 'I expect someone's chasing her, don't you?' But Lucy had known this wasn't true. The woman wasn't frightened of someone coming behind, but of something cold and dark, hidden inside her.

Although it was like an ordinary Sunday, Aunt Phoebe coming, and the table being laid, and the smell of roast from the kitchen, and her father reading the newspapers, and the sun coming in, Lucy thought of the picture now. Her mother was looking at her father with her forehead wrinkled and her eyes screwed up and her bottom lip caught between her teeth making a plump, pink cushion on one side, as if she wanted to stop something, some sound, coming out.

Her father said, 'Maggie.' Then he got up and began to open a bottle, holding it between his knees and grunting. The cork came out with a damp plop, like a frog in a pond; he set the bottle down on the table in a patch of yellow sunshine and said, 'All the wine in the world won't keep her quiet, I'm afraid. You know Phoebe. She likes to have things out.' He put his hand on the back of his wife's neck and stroked it with his thumb.

She leaned against him. Strong and stocky, an inch or so shorter than she was, he seemed to support her like a prop a young tree.

She said, 'But *today*! Can't we just say he's ill? Or got a few days out of school, for Hugh's twenty-first?'

Lucy said, 'I thought Toby *was* ill. I mean, you said last night you were taking him to Dr Henry.'

They both looked at her, considering.

'Not Dr Henry, dear,' her mother said. 'He's not ill in that way.'

'There's no point in putting it off,' her father said. 'And, really, rather unkind. She's fond of Toby.'

Her mother sighed. She moved away from her father and began to put knives and forks on the table, rubbing them on her apron and placing them, very slowly and exactly on either side of the flowered mats.

Lucy said, 'She's fonder of Greg. She likes him best.'

'Rubbish,' her father said, but kindly and smiling. Then his smile went; he stood, looking at Lucy and pulling at his upper lip with his thumb and bent forefinger, the way he did when he was troubled. The skin on his face was loose and baggy: he was always folding and pleating it, as if it was an ill-fitting garment he happened to be wearing. He said, 'Lucy, darling, when Aunt Phoebe comes, could you keep Greg out of the way for a bit? While we explain about Toby?'

'Whispering behind my back,' Lucy said. 'I don't like it.'

'Lucy,' her mother said, putting down the last fork, fiercely. 'Please,' her father said.

Lucy wished she could say, 'Of course I don't mind,' but pleasant words stuck in her throat like apologies, or pills. She said, 'I haven't got any choice, have I?'

As she went – stumped – from the room out into the humming, summer garden, and down to the river where she knew Greg would be, crouched in a damp shadow on the steep, weedy bank, racing sticks in the current, her mother called after her, through the window, 'And try to get Toby up in time to get dressed before lunch, will you darling, and ask him to *please* comb his hair.'

Lucy shouted back, automatically, 'Why can't you?' but did not wait for the answer, which she knew anyway; as she knew that her mother would never have given it. Not the true answer, certainly, which was that her mother was frightened of Toby, too frightened to ask him the everyday things she asked of her younger children: combing hair, washing hands, sitting up straight at table. Lucy did not understand why this was, she simply saw it and felt it, knowing it as she knew a great many things; directly, without any intervening process of reason or deduction. That her mother was often afraid for no very obvious reason was something Lucy had accepted long ago as part of the scenery of her life, but sometimes it made her uneasy and bad-tempered.

She went through the squeaky gate, on to the rotting landing-stage, trod carefully to the end and said, 'You're not getting your clean clothes dirty Greg, I do hope.'

The water runs at the end of the garden, deep and fast flowing. Once, I ran from my mother and hid on the bank in a secret, green hiding-place, smelling the sour, tangy river smell, mixed with the musty smell of the nettles, and watching the river, pale as tea where the sun touched it, dark and silk-smooth in the shade. There were insects trailing legs like black cotton over the top of the water, and spiders' webs on the bank that I couldn't see, only feel, when my face touched them. The baby cried in his pram and my mother called me. I didn't answer, to tease her, and then later, when she had begun to sound angry, I didn't go because I was frightened. My feet slipped and squeaked on the wet bank and I was afraid I would fall and drown. I began to cry, very loudly, so she would hear and be sorry and come to find me. But when she did come, she wasn't kind; she dragged me off the bank, through the nettles, and slapped my face, only once, but hard. I said, 'It's not fair, I wasn't being bad, just playing,' and she said, 'Oh darling, I'm a pig, I was just so frightened,' and started to kiss the place where she had hit me and stroke back my hair. But I went stiff and turned my face away; I wouldn't speak to her, not all the rest of that day, not even when she put me to bed and said could she read me a story. I pulled the bedclothes over my head. When my father came home, he pulled them off me and tickled my stomach and said, 'What's all this, chicken?' I said, 'She hit me because SHE was frightened,' and he laughed and laughed and pulled me on his lap and rasped his chin into my neck to make me laugh too, and said, 'Well, at least you've learned something today,' and called my mother to come and read us both a story.

Her brother said, 'Time for lunch.'

Lucy looked up and saw Toby on the landing-stage. She said, indignantly, 'I was supposed to call *you*.'

He laughed and held out his hand to help them across the tricky bit where the bank had crumbled. Greg swung on his arm suddenly, almost jerking him off balance, and Toby cuffed him lightly.

'Has she come?' Lucy asked. She thought Toby nodded, but

since he was covered from head to foot in a black, Arab burnous, only his nose showing, it was hard to say.

They went up the garden, clinging to his robe, wet feet squeaking on the dry, cropped lawn. Toby said, 'Change your shoes, they stink. And Greg, don't lick Aunt Phoebe when you kiss her.'

Aunt Phoebe used a face powder that smelled like icing sugar, which was why Greg had once licked it. It lay in pale drifts at the sides of her cheeks and in the creases of her prominent, beautiful eyes. Her face was handsome in a formidable, bony way, the flesh having receded with age like sand from a wind-swept shore, leaving her high-ridged nose somehow naked and stranded, like a proud, wrecked ship on a beach. This was the Flower nose. Toby had inherited it, but his version was still soft with youth, still delicately beaky: it was a feature, his father said, that only reached its full glory with age. In Aunt Phoebe, fifty-seven years old, it had come to maturity: beneath it, her darkly painted, rosebud mouth seemed absurd, as if Genghis Khan had worn lipstick. Greg ducked his head as she kissed him and her lips touched his hair; Lucy endured them on her cheek.

Her father, carving the joint, said, 'What have you been up to? Your mother, yelling her head off!'

Aunt Phoebe said, 'I was afraid I wasn't going to see you today.'

'We were racing sticks,' Lucy said.

Aunt Phoebe smiled. But her eyes were fixed on Toby who had sat down opposite her, his face almost hidden by the hood of his burnous.

Lucy was frightened. She said quickly, 'The river's terribly fast, like rapids. We'd have been swept over the weir, if we'd fallen in.'

Aunt Phoebe's attention was usually to be caught with tales of physical danger, but not today. All she said was, 'Lucky you can both swim, dear.'

Toby began to hum softly.

Lucy said, 'Whether Greg could swim well enough, I don't know! He shouldn't really have been down there on his own!'

Greg went scarlet. 'I got my swimmer's badge hundreds of years ago.'

'This summer,' Lucy said.

'Don't speak with your mouth full,' her mother said.

Aunt Phoebe helped herself to beans. She said, 'Toby, do look at me.' She laughed her trilling laugh. 'I'm not an ogre you know.'

'Ogress,' Lucy said.

Her father frowned at her.

'You correct *me*,' Lucy said.

Toby had raised his head a little. But the hood still covered the upper part of his face.

Aunt Phoebe said, 'Toby, your parents have told me what happened at school. It's a terrible disappointment for you and for them, but what's done is done and I don't intend to dwell on it. I just want to say one thing. I hope you'll treat this, not as a disaster, but a challenge! When something like this happens, it is often the moment to change direction! Lots of great men have had setbacks, worse ones than being expelled from school! But they haven't sat down under them, nor retreated into self-pity. Not stagnated, but gone on to climb the heights. Failure was often just what they needed to set them on the path of success. A timely spur! Grasp the nettle, Toby, grasp the nettle!'

'Suppose it stings me,' Toby said, but so softly that only sharp, young ears could catch it. Lucy pursed her mouth and breathed deeply but Greg spluttered a quantity of roast beef on to the polished table.

'Greg,' his mother said. 'Oh Greg!' And got up quickly to fetch a cloth from the kitchen.

But once Greg had started, he couldn't stop. Aunt Phoebe often set him off – not the things she said, but the way she looked when she said them. For one thing, she always kept her hat on during lunch, and today she was wearing a stranger decoration than usual; what seemed to be two tropical birds, intertwined in death, their blue and purple wings brushing her lined, ivory forehead. When she ate or talked, her scalp moved, so that the bright birds' wings quivered.

Eyes fixed on the hat, Greg started banging with his fork

and hiccuping, mouth wide open, showing what was left inside.

Toby took the fork away, cracked him lightly over the knuckles and said, 'Shut up this minute.'

Greg stopped at once. He gave Toby a baleful look and stared at his plate. Two enormous tears splashed down.

Lucy saw that Aunt Phoebe had coloured up in a curious way: her cheeks had brownish patches, like iron mould, and the end of her nose had gone white. She drew a deep breath, patted the collar of her blouse with her thin, ringed hand, and said, 'Toby, do you really think it your place to teach little Gregory good behaviour?'

She stood, laying her napkin by her plate; went round the table and put one arm lovingly round Gregory's shoulders, drawing him to her. When his sobs subsided, she held a lace handkerchief to his nose with her free hand and said, 'Blow.' Greg blew; then smiled up at her, very sweetly. A kind child, he did, whenever possible what was expected of him. 'Poor lamb,' Aunt Phoebe said, and returned to her own place.

Toby sat still, his face hidden again by the black hood.

His father said, 'Phoebe, Toby was perfectly right, you know.'

He was smiling calmly, almost merrily, as if all that was under discussion was a simple issue of manners. Perhaps he was pretending, but Lucy thought it unlikely. She had noticed before that her father seemed only to see the surface of things, to hear just the words spoken, not what lay beneath them. He could never scent trouble as she could. As her mother could . . .

She had come back into the room and was rubbing at the mess Greg had made round his plate. 'Mucky little rat,' she muttered, and then looked at Aunt Phoebe. 'Right about what?' she said, speaking slowly and somehow reluctantly, as if, although she knew she must ask, she didn't really want to know.

Lucy said, 'Nothing. Just Toby slapped Greg because he couldn't stop laughing.'

'It wasn't nothing, Lucy,' Aunt Phoebe said. Her eyes shone and she lifted her face with that proud, great nose – like a general, Lucy thought, half-admiring, half-fearful, a general, going into battle. 'You have to earn the right to correct others, Toby. And a boy who indulges in the sort of filthy habit – *vice*, if we are to speak plainly, and it is a moment to speak plainly, I think – that has got you expelled from the school your parents have worked and slaved to send you to, has no right to anything until he has tried to re-establish himself. Certainly no right at all to make his innocent little brother cry!'

Lucy looked at her father. *Oh, please.* He smiled at her, apparently naturally. 'For heaven's sake, Phoebe. There's only one way to stop an hysterical child!'

'That's not what she's talking about.' Lucy transferred her gaze to her mother, who was polishing away as she spoke, hard and resentfully as if she really cared about marks on her table. Then she stopped, heaved a deep, deep sigh, and looked at Aunt Phoebe, although Lucy knew she was really speaking to her father. 'I told you it was stupid to tell her, that she couldn't possibly understand, that she'd just go on and on as if the child should be punished. As if he were some sort of criminal . . .'

'In the eyes of the law, he is a criminal, Margaret.' Aunt Phoebe's voice rang out like a bugle; a call to battle. 'You're deceiving yourself if you think otherwise. And harming the boy. Oh, I've seen things before and kept quiet for the sake of peace, but you can't go on, not and keep your self respect! You've been too easy. Why, I've been here weekend after weekend and seen Charlie mowing the lawn and you up to your eyes in the kitchen and not a hand's turn from him – lying in bed till all hours or out on the lawn reading, like a great, idle lout!'

'Idle louts don't read,' Lucy said, and began to tremble with excitement and dread. Forces were being released here like bats from a box: their dark wings beat round her head.

'You never loved him,' her mother said. She spoke quietly, but something in her voice carried like a shout. 'He was born before you thought it was sensible. Do you think I forget? You came to see me in hospital and said – Poor Charlie, what a millstone to hang round his neck!'

Lucy stared at her aunt.

'*Did* you say that, Phoebe?' her father inquired – for form's sake, presumably: remarks of this kind being as natural from his sister as breathing.

'Not that I remember.' Aunt Phoebe spoke in a cold, quick, angry voice. A long pause. Then, quite differently, 'You know I love the child.' She looked down at her plate and touched the knife and fork beside it with hands that had begun to shake a little: there were blue snaking veins on the backs and the knuckles rose in small, soft-seeming bumps, like pink pads.

Toby got up and left the room, tripping once over his robe. He closed the door, not quite slamming it, but hard enough to shake a sliver of paint from the hinge. Lucy saw it fall to the floor, a pale arrow-fleck on the dark carpet.

Her mother said, carefully, brightly, 'Lucy darling, have you finished your meat?'

Lucy put her knife and fork together and nodded without looking.

'*Well*, then! Why don't you and Greg take your fruit and cheese into the garden? It's so stuffy indoors and so lovely outside. We may not have another day like this all summer!'

Greg got off his chair before she had finished speaking. His face was closed. He had shut himself off, Lucy saw, remembering suddenly how she had once been able to do just that, unfocusing her eyes and concentrating hard on something else, and envying him because he was young enough to do it now. Her own legs would scarcely obey her; they felt cold and heavy, tingling pins and needles as if she had been sitting crouched up too long and they had gone to sleep beneath her. By the time she was on her feet, her mother had cut several hunks of pale, crumbly cheese and wrapped them in a napkin. 'Apple or pear?' she asked, hand hovering over the fruit bowl.

'Both,' Greg said.

'Greg, that's not *polite*!'

'Christ, Maggie!' Shocked, Lucy looked at her father. His face had gone pink and puffy. He banged the heel of his hand on the table. 'Must we be so bloody genteel?'

Her mother sat down suddenly, as if hit. She said, 'I suppose not,' in so stumbling and unnatural a tone that Lucy felt instantly protective towards her. 'Take what you like,' she said, and pushed the bowl towards her children with a small, tight, shamed smile: as their hands went out, her own dropped into her lap and laced together.

They went into the garden. Greg ran off without a word, down to the river, tunelessly singing. Toby was lying on the lawn, face down. Lucy squatted beside him.

She said, 'Toby.' He didn't move. She said, 'Don't take any notice of her. She's a silly old fool.' He didn't answer. 'A rotten, awful *bitch*,' she said, biting into her apple and looking up at the sun. There was a skim of cloud across it, making it paler than it had been earlier, and watery round the edges. She said, 'You can have my cheese if you like.'

Toby made a low sound, a grunt, or moan, and got up from the ground in one quick movement, arms flailing like huge, awkward wings as he half-lost his balance; then he ran, stumbling, up the lawn. Watching him, Lucy bit into her apple without looking and her teeth met in slimy mush. She said, 'Eeeeugh,' retching, stiff with disgust, and threw the bad fruit into the rose bushes.

Toby had vanished round the side of the house; when she had finished spitting, and was cleaning her tongue with her handkerchief, he appeared again, hauling the motor mower behind him. Bending over it, he yanked at the starter string; once, twice, three times. It gave an uneasy petulant cough, stammered, roared into life. Toby came down the lawn at full throttle: reaching the rose bed, he arched himself back like a charioteer and hurled the machine round, hardly slowing. Up the lawn and down, up and down; wheels gouging as he turned and curling up fresh earth like a plough. It was as if he were running some terrible race: when he passed close to Lucy, in a wave of exhaust fumes and flying, sweet-scented grass, she could hear his panting breath. She ran after him to stop him, to say their father had cut the lawn only that morning, but as she came near, his hood fell back and she saw his face, streaming with tears. Then he whirled on, past her.

She felt breathless as if she had just swallowed a cup of icy water. Her stomach tightened. She said, aloud, 'Oh, his poor face.'

She turned towards the house. Her legs carried her up the steps to the flagged terrace and along the cool hall to the open door of the dining-room.

They were sitting where she had left them. Her father at the end of the table, facing her; her mother and Aunt Phoebe on his either side, the fruit bowl between them. All three were looking at her. She wanted to shout at them, but her tongue was clumsy and thick in her mouth. She thought she did say something, perhaps just, *Toby is crying*, but perhaps not, because Aunt Phoebe said, quite cheerfully and naturally, 'Goodness me, what an expression to frighten the crows!'

For a second, Lucy stood, frozen: then that foolish, innocent remark seemed to seize and canalize her, pick her up and sweep her forward on a narrow, swift current of rage. There was something bright on the table; bright and cold in her hand. 'I hate you,' she said, and lunged forward. Her aunt's face reared backwards above her; flaring, horse's nostrils, a stretched, taut, red-patched neck. Her father shouted 'Lucy!' but it was her mother's hands that caught her elbows and pinioned them behind her.

Her mother said, 'Darling, Aunt Phoebe wants to say good-bye to you.'

Lucy lay on her bed, staring at the wall. Her face was puffed and hot and her eyes burned. The wallpaper had a yellow and orange pattern, half-moons and stripes; it was bubbly in places and there was one hole where she had pushed her finger through and picked at the plaster. 'She's so upset,' her mother said. 'Not angry. A lot of people would have been, although *we* know you didn't mean to hurt her, but she isn't. She blames herself. She's sorry.'

Lucy stroked the rough hole with her forefinger and began to sing under her breath.

'Be nice to her, chicken,' her mother said.

Aunt Phoebe came. She said 'Lucy' and waited, but Lucy lay silent and still, only rolling her eyes sideways (so far in the sockets that it hurt) to see, in the tilted mirror on the white chest of drawers, exactly where Aunt Phoebe was standing. She couldn't see her face, only part of her tweed-skirted stomach across which a thin hand moved, nervously picking and pluck-ing.

'I didn't mean to make Toby unhappy,' Aunt Phoebe said. 'But I know how you must have felt. If it had been my brother...'

Lucy closed her eyes tight. Circles of red and yellow light whirled against darkness.

Aunt Phoebe said, 'Dear Lucy, I love him too,' and her voice was suddenly so lost and trailingly sad that it brought a lump into Lucy's throat; she felt, not pity for her Aunt but a generalized, elegiac sorrow, as if she had been listening to a sad poem or play.

'Try to forgive me,' Aunt Phoebe said, but Lucy did not move. Fear and shame were equal in her: both held her rigid.

Aunt Phoebe let out breath in a long sigh; then – it seemed hours later – she left, softly closing the door.

Lucy lay, not daring to turn her head. Above the hole she had picked in the plaster, there was a small, wriggly stain she had not noticed before. Like a snake. She put out a finger, timidly, holding her breath, and traced it from its tiny, blob-like head to tapering tail. Blurring vision made it appear to move; she drew in her breath until her chest hurt, to stop herself crying.

Voices outside. Feet crunching on the gravel. The slam of a car door. Her father saying something; her mother – incredibly – laughing. The car engine started, revved, slowed to a gentler sound. 'Good-bye', someone shouted – it seemed from further away. Toby!

She rolled on to her face. They were all outside, talking and laughing. Even Toby. Only she was an outcast, for *his* sake! She wept into the pillow with bitter grief until she was drained and weak; then she must have slept because when she next opened her eyes, the light had changed in the room. She saw, through sticky lashes, a fuzz of gold: the evening sun slanting in.

Toby said, 'Awake?' He was sitting on her bed. He said, 'That was a wicked thing you did, I hope you realize,' and she began to cry again, not despairingly now, but with comfortable, resigned relief: his stern, matter-of-fact tone seemed to take some burden from her.

He let her cry for a little, watching her, then he wiped her hot face with a corner of the sheet and said, 'It's all very well, she's the one should be crying, not you. Lucky it was the grape scissors, not the carving knife. That might really have hurt her.'

'I meant to,' she whispered, suddenly afraid he had not picked up the full weight of her wickedness.

But he said at once, 'I know that, though *they* don't, of course,' adding grimly, after a moment's searching glance, 'Lucky for you!'

'Are they very angry?' she asked, meaning, *Are you?* — speaking in a childish voice, to appease him.

He took her hand, turning it up flat on his own, measuring her stubby fingers against his long ones and thoughtfully tracing the lines on the damp palm. 'They ought to be! *Poor child, she's so loyal!*' A smile flicked briefly at the corners of his mouth as he mimicked his father's voice. 'Even Dad!'

She said, emboldened, 'It was only because she was so foul to you.'

'That's no excuse.'

'It *is*. Going on and on,' she said, beginning to be righteous and loud, and saw him wince and screw up his eyes so that fine lines appeared, fanning out from the corners. 'And making out she's fond of you!' Lucy said.

'She probably is, that's the trouble.' He sighed, folded her hand, and gave it back to her, like a parcel; then tucked his own into the sleeves of his burnous and seemed to bow and shrink his body as if trying to hide himself inside it. 'Families are terrible,' he said.

Chapter Two

All generations face, on the surface, much the same problems; each knows its situation to be unique. Ours, for example. Children before the war, emerging through it into parenthood, Freud in one hand, Spock in the other, into a world where truth is relative, uncertainty a virtue, nothing known ...

Charlie, writing his weekly *Diary* in his head, frowned at himself while he fastened his bow-tie – flick, flick – stretching and lifting his chin.

Except guilt, possibly. That is our hall-mark. Our parents did their duty, knew what was right; our sins were original, no fault of theirs ...

'Prosy,' Charlie said, pushing the knot with his thumb, and easing it over the shirt button. 'Pompous.'

He continued to frown, not at the intended paragraph but because it had become a habit whenever he looked in the mirror: since he rarely saw his own face without this defensive expression, he thought himself an ugly man, and this had lately begun to depress him. Now he glared into his reflected eyes, coldly noting bags, red threads, wrinkles, before he sighed, turned slightly sideways, slapped once and sharply at the underside of his chin, sighed again, pulled his mobile mouth into a comic, resigned grin (all right, old friend, we stagger on together) and emerged from the bathroom into the bedroom where his wife was telephoning her mother.

'Try to understand,' she was saying. 'Toby is ill. Not wicked, not immoral, *ill*. The psychiatrist says it's quite common, this sort of depression in adolescence. The laziness and untidiness are all part of the same syndrome.'

'I never heard of such a thing,' Sara Evans said. 'Taking a boy to a psychiatrist because he refuses to have his hair cut!'

The telephone seemed to crackle with her scorn, but it was merely a bad line. Maggie moved the receiver rest up and down.

'I thought I'd tried to explain. The trouble about the hair is purely incidental. And that was last term, anyway! As a matter of fact, Charlie thinks the school were frightfully silly about that and it may well have contributed to the present crisis – made him extra resentful and difficult!' Catching Charlie's eye in the dressing-table mirror, she grinned at him shyly, acknowledging her deceit: she had quoted his opinion rather than her own because she thought it would impress her mother more. 'I mean, not cutting your hair is a fairly common sort of protest!'

'If any son of mine had protested like that,' Sara said, 'he would have felt the weight of my hand. And I don't want to start an argument about corporal punishment! Now, Margaret . . .'

Maggie lifted her shoulders in a resigned gesture; while her mother's voice quacked on, she licked her finger and smoothed her eyebrows, winked at her husband in the mirror. Her eyes were shining-bright with battle but there was pain there too, Charlie saw. He put his hand on the back of her neck and stroked it in the way she liked, hoping to calm her before she said something she would be sorry for.

But she had already begun to tremble. She said, on a new sharp, defensive note, 'Well, there's one good thing, anyway. Since they've decided to chuck him out, it's just as well they've done it now, instead of waiting until the end of term! At least we can take him to Hugh's twenty-first birthday party!'

Her mother said something Charlie couldn't catch, and the colour rose in her cheeks. 'No, I didn't expect you to understand what's important to him!'

'I understand the boy all right, Margaret! It's you I don't understand!'

'Have you ever?' she answered, but softly, and the crackling, anyway, had returned. Charlie shook his head warningly, and Maggie joggled the receiver rest and wrinkled her nose at him.

'All I see is this charming but spoiled and thoughtless boy,'

Sara continued, 'and that you are not helping him. This frivolous attitude! Making light on one hand, and too much fuss and anxiety on the other. He doesn't need a psychiatrist. He needs guide lines. Discipline. And a good bath once a week if he cannot endure it more frequently. Are you afraid of him, or what? It seems to me . . .'

'Oh, it's easy to be a back-seat driver,' Maggie said.

Charlie felt her neck, cool and smooth under his hand, and sighed. Why should his wife, his competent, sensible wife, be so truculent, so, sometimes, simply *silly* where her mother was concerned? It amazed him – still, after all these years – it amazed and bewildered him. He tried to put his lack of comprehension down to ignorance of this kind of emotional bond (his own parents, dead now, had been elderly and gentle, polite with him, as they were with each other, like strangers) and tried to tread warily: he was a man who respected what he did not know. But it hurt him. He loved them both, his wife and her mother, and it hurt him to have to stand by and see two people he loved tear each other to pieces . . .

When Maggie put the telephone down, she said, 'All she can say is, well, she's glad it's our problem, not hers, but if we want her opinion she thinks its a pity National Service is finished, what he could do with is a spell in the army.'

She looked so distressed and astonished by this predictable response that he almost laughed. She was like a child sometimes, he thought; experimenting, putting her finger in the candle flame. A little like their daughter, Lucy, who wanted to know, always, what was the worst thing that could happen, to get it over with.

He said, 'Darling heart, I told you not to tell her. At least, not tonight, not on the telephone.' He had meant to write himself; a cautious letter.

'I thought she had a right to know at once! Toby's her grandson!' Her voice rose with sudden, adventitious bitterness. 'You'd think she'd be interested, wouldn't you?'

Charlie looked at her face in the mirror: dark eyes, pained, pale face, hair done in a fancy topknot for the party. Several things came into his mind to say. Among them, *you didn't tell her because you thought she'd be interested, but because you wanted comfort.* Or – since the opposite could equally be true – *because you felt guilty and wanted to be blamed.* But neither remark seemed kind. He said, 'Well, I dare say your mother's had her share of trouble!'

A mistake. Her eyes snapped at him. Like Toby's, they were nearer black than brown; in artificial light, almost coaly. 'She doesn't have to go on, living with my father. It's just self-imposed martyrdom – she thinks it virtuous to be unhappy! Oh – I suppose it gives her a good excuse. She can say, don't bring me *your* worries, haven't I enough of my own?'

Near tears, she picked up a hair pin and stabbed severely at a loose curl that had strayed (becomingly, Charlie thought) down the back of her neck. He wanted to say, 'You know it's not like that, she loves you,' but did not: in her present mood, Maggie would find this criticism, not comfort.

He said carefully, 'Perhaps it was a mistake to tell her about the psychiatrist,' and felt, immediately, guilty. Talking about other people, you give yourself away: he had thought it a mistake himself to go at this stage, before other, simpler measures had been tried, but had not said so. He smiled, to cover up. 'I think your mother's generation distrust talk of mental illness. Modern *jargon*. It sounds like an excuse. Or perhaps it's fear. In their day, mad people were locked up, in the asylum up the hill.'

'She should know better. She's lived with a loony for years.' She swung round on the stool and regarded him angrily. 'It's ridiculous. She should have left him years ago.'

'If she'd wanted to, she would have, I think.' Charlie looked at his wife, thinking that he liked her with her hair up, and knowing that what he had just said made hardly any sense to her: for Maggie, the only solution to almost any situation you could name, lay in action. Her father was an impossible old man, so her mother must leave him. Their eldest son was dismissed from school six weeks before his final examination, so they must rush to psychiatrists, find a good crammer at once, get him to have his hair cut. Charlie, in the middle of his weekly editorial conference, must leave and come home within an hour of Toby's arrival, to try to coax him off the gabled roof outside the lavatory window where he was sitting and playing the guitar in the rain, and take him to the barber ...

Charlie usually did what his wife asked: her urgency seemed to rebuke him, perhaps his own caution was laziness? Besides, he had always rather admired her impatience – if a thing was wrong, it had to be put right now, this minute – seeing it as a kind of obsessional, creative energy, a desire for order. Now, for the first time (their first, real crisis?) he saw that what drove her was something much more like fear: she raced through life as over marshy ground, fearing to stand still in case she sank in quagmire.

The image moved him. Caressing her neck, he moved his hand lower and massaged her back. 'Darling, Toby's not mad. Any more than your father is! Just a bit withdrawn. At his age, it's common.'

Was it? At Toby's age, Charlie had been in the navy, in the Pacific: what he chiefly remembered was, each day you stayed alive seemed a bonus. He still felt that sometimes, even now: surprised, grateful. Perhaps when you were young, you needed to live on the edge of something – war, the dole, the Black Death? He thought, *you pompous, middle-aged toot*! He stroked his wife's shoulder blades. They seemed to spring out under the delicate silk of her dress. She was very thin. Too thin. He thought, perhaps she doesn't eat enough? He worried about that for a minute – now Greg was at school she probably didn't eat in the middle of the day, women often didn't when they had no-one to cook for – and then felt ashamed, because he should have been worrying about his son. He smiled at her sad face in the mirror and said, 'You heard what the doctor said!'

We were not to blame ourselves. We had not said we did, but I suppose we looked the sort who were likely to. He said it was a negative approach and could become self-indulgent. He smiled: we were, of course, intelligent enough to know that! He had a gentle, ascetic face on which the smile sat oddly, making him appear insincere, which he had not, until then, appeared to be. Nor was, I think; only shy ... He had a habit of clearing his throat and then, immediately, touching the photograph on his desk. A plump, pretty woman with a dark, plump mouth. His wife? I wondered if she was much younger than he was, or if it was just that the picture had been taken a long time ago.

He was saying that whatever the cause it made no difference to the diagnosis or the treatment. A mild depression of this kind, while extremely disturbing to parents, was not unusual in adolescence. It would probably pass by itself in a year or two but he thought, in the circumstances, it would be a good idea to try chemiotherapy. Toby had his A-levels in June, his university entrance in the autumn. It was important he should be on top of his form.

Charlie said we didn't want to pressurize him. He seemed surprised to find a psychiatrist so practical. Was it a trap? Charlie frowned like an elder statesman and said that Toby had always been an ambitious boy, ambitious for himself, not just to please us, and then glanced at me, wondering if this was protesting too much. We both had the same fear – that everything said here was likely to be given a different meaning from the one we had intended.

The doctor said if Toby was ambitious, then it was important to help him. Not cure, exactly; he was immature and had certain personality problems that only time could set right. But drugs would help. Perk him up. Get him through this sticky patch.

Charlie asked, why was he immature? Anxiety made him speak loudly, almost in a bullying way. The doctor cleared his throat and touched the photograph in front of him, re-aligning it a little. He said he supposed one would say, technically, that at some point or other Toby had failed to make the right transference. No doubt, if we rootled around, we could come up with something, but it would only be guesswork, no practical help. His was a very inexact science. He smiled that incongruous smile and said, if you want theories, ask your wife, she's the novelist.

It sounded as if he thought writing novels a nice game for children. Embarrassed, I began to talk fast and badly, as if disclaiming any special skill with words. I didn't know what he meant about personality problems: until recently Toby had been perfectly normal. Not ordinary – were his children ordinary to him? – but a lively, eager, natural boy. A bit emotional, perhaps, but that wasn't a crime! (His mouth twitched: so I thought mental illness a crime, did I?) Wasn't unusual, I said. After all, we were an emotional family; we quarrelled occasionally and banged doors. I laughed boisterously to convince him that this was entirely normal. I said that if he had asked me a year ago what Toby was like, I could have told him he was much like any other boy his age. Now he had changed, but not in any positive way. Positive – that was the key! It was rather as if we had had a photograph of our son and it had suddenly been replaced by the negative: thin and transparent. And slightly blurred . . .

This seemed to me clumsy, but exact. I looked at the doctor hopefully. He touched his wife's picture with the tip of his finger and said (hinting reproach?) that personally he had found Toby a most gentle and delightful boy. Quite charming, in fact. Of course he was extremely sensitive, some people were born like that, a skin short. And frequently closed up in adolescence; withdrew, to protect themselves. Pot was what drink would have been in our young day, a refuge from the harsh world. We should not worry about it; he was sure it had been no more than an experimental interlude and thought, frankly, that the school had been unfairly precipitate in expelling him for it. He supposed that as there had been a history of other difficulties, non-cooperation, slovenly appearance and so on, they had seized on this as a convenient excuse.

He had an accent, a lilt. Welsh? My father is Welsh, but he speaks Southern English, flat, featureless. I listened to the doctor's voice which was musical and soothing and remembered my father showing me a photograph of some long-dead relation – great-aunt, cousin? – in Welsh national dress, and wished I had not ventured on that flight of fancy about the negative. It was true, in the sense that it was how I had felt at that moment, but perhaps it had sounded overcharged, and therefore false, to him.

He was asking me something. What disturbed me most about Toby? His disorderly room? Bizarre behaviour? The hair?

Pinned down, it was hard to say. I have no composite picture of Toby, only snapshots – a little boy on the beach in the summer time – a list of things done, things said. As a young child, he was valiant and loving. Once, when Charlie was out of a job, he packed up his best toys, weeping, and gave them to us to sell. Always up at first light, a tuneless lark singing. Now it is like waking the dead; he is a bundle of old clothes, sleeping. He sits on the roof in thin, grey needles of rain, refusing to answer us; removed, in danger. Holding us to ransom? For what? My mother wouldn't put up with it from her son. But her son is dead.

I said, we had to defend him all the time.

This seemed to interest him. He leaned forward, long, agile fingers pressed firmly together. Did I resent him for that?

It was hot in the room which was triangular-shaped as if a partition had, at some point, been put up. What was he getting at? Can you resent, where you love? Perhaps he thought I wanted Toby to conform, to shine, be a credit to us. In his book, that would be a sin. I thought why doesn't he ask Charlie these unanswerable questions. Men hang together; it is always the mother's fault!

Charlie said the difficulty was to separate what one felt about the boy from the situation he created round him. Schools demanded certain standards; grandparents thought untidiness a sign of immorality, or, at least, lack of backbone! He smiled – when Charlie smiles, his face lights up like a lamp – and said it was stupid, of course, but so much of one's energy was drawn off in this way. One was always charging uselessly into battle.

The doctor's face cleared, as if he understood something he had not understood before. (Why not? Had he no children, no parents?)

I said I got so angry . . .

It seemed an inadequate word. What possessed me was an uncontrollable, roaring rage, like a sweeping, spring tide, drowning reason. And my own fault, perhaps: I never said to my mother what I wanted to say. Here is my poor child, so hurt, help me to help him, to make the ground firm under his feet. And under mine . . .

She said, in the car, 'I suppose I could have told her the whole truth. About the drugs. It would have sounded less trivial, but I didn't want to upset her more than I had to.'

'What?' Charlie glanced sideways, at a loss for the moment. Then he laughed and groped for her hand.

'What's funny?'

'Just you. The way you brood on a thing.'

She said, stiffly, 'After all, look at the way your sister reacted.'

They spoke in undertones: Toby was in the back seat, though apparently asleep.

'Umm.' Charlie squeezed her hand and released it to steer round a bend. Headlights stabbed dark, wet hedges: there had been a short, summer storm. 'I think you were right to give your mother an edited version. So stop worrying. Eh?' His voice was warm. 'Come on, love. Big girl, now.'

Would she ever feel it, though; feel arrived, *grown up*? What was an adult, anyway? She felt no different, was still a child to her mother; awkward and wayward, always in the wrong. This was something she had to carry around with her. Charlie had no such burden. His relationship with Phoebe was the only comparable thing, and it wasn't comparable at all. When their mother had broken down after his father died – become within weeks, a shambling, sick old woman – and Phoebe had taken charge, both of her and of Charlie, she had been twenty-four years old. But she had never been a mother to him; he was a little boy, away at school, and in the holidays she was his rather bossy playmate. Only since his marriage and her widowhood had she pressed stronger claims, and by then he had been old enough, complete enough, to withstand them. There had been no emotional tugs-of-war in his childhood, nothing to mar his strong, confident growth. The only real, painful love of his early years had been his friend, Roy Honey, whose son's birthday party they were going to now. Poor, dead Roy . . .

She said, 'I can't believe Hugh's twenty-one.'

Charlie grunted.

She turned to the back of the car. 'Toby, wake up. We're almost there.'

He stirred, rubbing his eyes and yawning.

'We'll be there in a minute. Do wake up.'

He groaned, 'Oh God,' and she felt impatient, wanted to shake him.

'Don't you want to go to Hugh's party?'

'Umm.'

'You might be a bit enthusiastic!' She laughed in a forced way.

'I'm sorry,' he said in a blurred, sleepy voice, 'I just don't feel particularly enthusiastically inclined at the moment.'

'Oh, I know. *I'm* sorry. I know how you feel.'

'Do you?' Not rudeness; polite inquiry.

'Well. Shall we say, I have an inkling?' she heard herself give that artificial laugh again, and despaired. Why not be natural? She wanted to put out her hand, to touch him, but was afraid to. There seemed no way to express love. She said, 'Your aged parents were young once! We haven't absolutely forgotten!' Beside her, Charlie stirred uneasily, gave a pointed sigh. To warn her she was on the wrong tack? Oh, it was easy enough to keep silent! She said, 'Everything looks terribly black at the moment. But it won't go on. That's one of the few things you do learn from experience. You come through something and you wonder what all the fuss was about!'

'I'm not fussing,' he said, speaking evenly and pleasantly.

'No. You've been very good about it, Daddy and I have been really rather impressed. Haven't we, Charlie?' That awful, bright voice! How she despised herself for it! She said, 'When one door closes, others open. A boring platitude, but true, you'll find out. This firm of tutors you're going to, is really very good. You may even get better exam results with a bit of extra tuition these next few weeks than if you'd stayed at school! Fewer distractions, no tedious, compulsory games! And then you can concentrate on the Oxford entrance in the autumn. If you put your back into it . . .'

'I don't want to go to Oxford,' Toby said.

'Oh darling, don't start that!' Of course, she should have expected this! She said, in a cheerful voice, 'Well, what do you want to do?'

'Be a bus driver,' he said, promptly.

'Toby!'

Charlie's hand was on her knee, pressing it gently. She looked at his profile and saw he was smiling. 'Good steady job with a pension,' he said. 'Socially useful, too.'

'Or a private hire firm,' Toby said. 'Driving a minibus, taking little kids to school. I'd like that.'

Maggie stopped herself laughing. It was important to respect his feelings. She should have remembered her own childhood better : when you had failed at something, you had to pretend you never wanted it! You had to collect the tattered rags of your pride . . .

She said, 'Darling, if that was really, truly, what you wanted, then of course we'd want it for you. Just don't make up your mind in too much of a rush, that's all. And don't fall into the trap of thinking *it'll pay them out* if you don't take your exam. That's a thoroughly natural feeling – I daresay I'd be feeling it if I were in your place at this moment – but it would, really, be cutting off your nose to spite your face with a vengeance, wouldn't it?' She looked at him hopefully; he was staring out of the window. She said, 'We only want you to be happy, Toby, that's really all.'

'It's asking quite a lot, isn't it?' His voice, so gentle and resigned, seemed to hurt her physically like a blow in the chest. She laid her arm along the back of Charlie's seat, letting her hand dangle, ready to take Toby's should he turn and see it. But he was staring out of the window.

Charlie said, in a loud voice, 'You know, I can't believe Hugh is twenty-one!' He switched his headlamps on full as they turned off the main road and up Elsa Honey's sweeping, overgrown drive. 'Makes me feel old,' he said.

But he sounded young. When he had stopped the car, he hopped out at once and ran round to open Maggie's door, suddenly spruced-up and gay like a young man with an adventurous evening before him.

'You'd better keep an eye on Dad,' Toby said, speaking quite seriously as if his father was a randy young bull to be tethered, and when Maggie laughed, added, 'Well, you know Elsa. And for an older woman, she's really very attractive, isn't she, Dad?'

'She is quite sure of it, which is half the battle,' Maggie said, and Charlie, looking down at her, grinned and touched her cheek.

Most of us give ourselves away when we talk about other people. Elsa can talk about herself – which she does, an endless monologue – and give away nothing. In her stories, she is always the comic, anti-heroine, the butt, the loser. Charlie says this is an act to placate her listeners, particularly the female ones: Elsa is too successful in too many ways for most women not to resent her. At parties, she holds court, magnificent in a terrible old dress dragged out from some attic or other; sometimes, even, smelling of camphor ...

An Empress, in mothballs.

'Dear God, it made me feel old,' Elsa was saying, holding court by the window overlooking the river, and Charlie winked at his wife; partly amusement because he had just said the same thing, and partly to appease the vague sense of guilt he often felt, when he was with Maggie and Elsa together.

'Old and humiliated,' Elsa went on, waving an imperious hand at the Flowers: they must wait to be welcomed until she had finished. It was not, it became apparent, her son's coming of age that made her feel old, but a recent visit to an electrolysis clinic.

She sank her voice to a deep, tragic purr. 'Imagine – there I lay, recumbent, with this gorgeous nymphet in white bending over me. "When did you last interfere with yourself?" she asks, solemn as a young judge. "*What?*" say I, laughing in my coarse way, but no smile back, not a flicker! She writes my name on a card and sits, pencil poised. "When did you last shave, or wax, or pluck" – very stern and hushed, as if these are terrible, sinful orgies I must confess to! "Interfering with yourself means something rather different to my generation," I say, still gallantly trying for some teeny-weeny human response. No luck! She sits there, pure and calm as a television doctor and writes on my card. Dark growth on upper lip, strong single hairs on chin. "How old are you, Mrs Honey? Have you reached the menopause?" Dear God – I felt like a bearded octogenarian! Then she comes at me with the needle – well, you're all my dear, dear friends, so I'll spare you that horror! But I came out – *sneaked*, as if I'd been to some back-street abortionist, and slunk along, collar up, peeping at other women's chins in the street. All smooth as pearls! I tell you, it was the most traumatic thing since my father made a pass at me in the bathroom when I was seven years old. This is what you've come to my girl, I said, the rot's set in. Superfluous hair, varicose veins, false teeth . . .'

Laughing at herself – good old Elsa! – she led her audience's laughter. Only one listener seemed constrained; a small, young-ish woman with delicately blunted features, like a pretty cat. She smiled, but with a certain, wincing dismay, and her hand fluttered shyly towards her mouth.

'Nothing from now on, my dears,' Elsa went on, taking, as it were, her curtain call, 'but endless, boring *maintenance*.'

She laughed again, showing good, strong teeeth (her own) and advanced on the Flowers. 'Darlings . . .' Her cool cheek touched theirs, her lips sucked air. She took Toby in her arms and kissed him on the mouth. 'Sweet Toby, you look marvel-lous in that get-up. The girls will go down like ninepins. Go and take your pick – they're all down in the boat-house.'

Bright red and breathing hard, Toby retreated backwards, as if leaving a royal presence. 'That is the most super boy,' Elsa said. 'I wish I were younger.' She sighed, put her hand on Maggie's arm. 'It really is the most frightful thing about the school. I'm so terribly sorry.'

As she probably was, Maggie thought. Elsa was always really sorry, truly involved, honestly wracked with anguish for her friends in trouble. Maggie smiled, feeling it was cold and un-generous not to like her more; and Elsa said, 'What you need, poor love, is a simply enormous drink. Charlie m'darling, help yourself, it's all there. Maggie, Iris Tate is here, she asked when you were coming, I'll go and find her.'

She moved off, not to find Iris, but because she was always restless at parties. Her retinue followed her like swarming bees;

only the pretty cat remained behind. She said, with sudden, startling belligerence, 'Of course I know who you two are, but you won't know me. I'm Sally Howard.'

Charlie, who often assumed a different accent when embarrassed, said, 'Glad to know you,' in an American voice and poured champagne for them all. Bottle in hand, he looked round, but no one else was near: they had all gathered at the far end of the long room to watch, through the glass wall, the converted Victorian boat-house below where the dancing was taking place and round which the modern house had been built, incorporating it in the design as a focal point, a centre. The idea had been romantic – through glass walls, cunningly placed interior windows, you were to glimpse dark, silken water, rocking boats – but Elsa, who disliked sailing, had floored the place over and except when it was cleared for dancing simply stored garden things there, so that the effect differed markedly from the original intention. This did not stop her telling surprised visitors, peering down from one of many vantage points at what seemed merely a dark junk shed, given over to old bird tables, canvas chairs and rusty lawn mowers, that the house, designed by her first husband, had won several important prizes and been featured in *Country Life*. Elsa had no visual sense, nor even any sense of current taste. She had furnished Roy Honey's charmingly proportioned living-room with squat, solid sofas, elaborate, wrought-iron lamp-stands and cocktail cabinets with lights inside. The period was the worst of the thirties, and there was a reason for that. Generous with food and drink always, Elsa was mean about clothes and furniture – a chair is only something to sit on, if you can get one for five pounds, why pay fifty? – which basic approach led her inexorably to the dreariest of suburban sale-rooms and resulted, also, in a generally eccentric personal appearance: her friends said that she wore her clothes until the safety-pins rusted. This evening, she was wearing what had once been a very grand ball-gown of green, watered silk which still, from a kindly distance, retained some of its former magnificence: only close to was it clear that the artificial rose, roughly tacked to the bosom, barely covered the place where the silk had rotted. And, looking at her from behind as she embraced a new influx of dear old friends at the top of the staircase, you could see the patch where she had, long ago, sat in something.

Sally Howard's eyes were riveted on it. She wrenched them away, smiled timidly at the Flowers and then glanced round the room with a perplexed and almost fearful expression that they both understood. This was the first time she had been here and she was suffering from a sense of disorientation: she could not 'place' Elsa, could not equate this room, so casually and hideously furnished, with the excellent champagne and the Beluga caviar, set out on the long, buffet table. Her nervous survey finished, she said, 'It's a very unusual house, isn't it?' – cautiously feeling her way, as if afraid she might have missed a sudden change in fashion.

This is a story Charlie likes to tell. How Roy built his house. Although it is not really about that, but about two young men, on the river, laughing. I wasn't with them when they found the site, but they took Elsa and me to see it, later on that summer. All four of us in a punt on the river. Elsa in a full, white dress, her tawny hair loose and long round her shoulders. She looks – when I think about that day, I think in the present tense – like something out of a myth. A corn goddess. I watch her – she is so beautiful – and smile at Charlie, behind her. Sun sparkles on water drops as he lifts the punt pole. He is energetic and stocky, with broad shoulders and neat, muscular hips, like a boxer. He looks strong and alive; beside him, Roy is pale. He is ill – dying, in fact – but we don't know that yet. We are happy, the four of us together (although I am a little left out because the other three have known each other so much longer) and we are going to see the place where Roy is going to build his house: an acre of land on an island. There is a marvellous, Victorian boat-house, tumbledown, stagnant with water weed; a nineteenth-century Gothic folly. Roy is very excited; he has just finished his architect's training and he is going to build a house for Elsa and his baby. (They are living, now, in the cold, cavernous house in Clapham that Charlie will buy from him, when we get married.) Roy describes the house he wants to build: something that will be an integral part of the river, taking it into the house, not shutting it out. He explains his plan, making excited, flowing gestures with his hands. Charlie smiles. Elsa smiles too, but at her own thoughts, trailing her hand in the water. She is a big, beautiful, apparently idle girl, but the idleness is only on the surface and is really composure: beneath it she is energetic and competent: she has inherited – and runs – her grandfather's food-importing business, and it is her money Roy will use to build his house. I want to like her, but I am frightened of her. She comes from a different world from mine: rich and careless. I want to like her, I am not jealous of her yet: I love Charlie and she loves Roy, and Roy and Charlie love each other. Elsa and I have only to join hands to make a closed, tight circle into which no harm can come. That is how it seems, that afternoon on the river. Everything is in front of us and is sure to be good; we will love each other and be happy, our children will be beautiful and clever, Roy's house a marvel. One day I will try to hurt Charlie by calling it an example of gimmicky, bourgeois inventiveness, but not yet, not yet . . .

'He wanted to build something that was an integral part of the river, taking it into the house, not shutting it out . . .'

Charlie made flowing gestures with his hands, the way he often did when he was remembering Roy, and being a young man, and it made him look almost like one; more excited, more mobile. But Sally Howard was looking only politely interested: none of this was, really, the answer to the question she had asked. Recognizing this, Charlie smiled. 'Of course, Elsa had to put the finishing touches, furnish it, and so on.'

'Roy Honey died before the house was finished. He had leukemia,' Maggie said. She felt pain, saying this, but it was mostly Charlie's pain. She had not known Roy as he had known him, could only remember him, really, as he had been the months before he died. A pale, bedraggled boy, with bleeding gums. Not so very much older than his son was now.

'How terrible.' Sally Howard paused delicately, then frowned. 'Honey? I thought . . .'

Charlie said, 'She's been married twice since, but neither *took* you might say, so she went back to the first name.'

'Less embarrassing for Hugh, I suppose? Children find that sort of thing so difficult, don't they, explaining at school and so on?' Her gaze wandered to where Elsa was standing now, by the buffet table, deep in conversation with a tall man whose profile was bent, absorbed and lover-like towards her. Sally Howard said, 'I know Edward and I couldn't make up our minds about my boys for simply ages. We decided to let them keep their father's name in the end – Edward thought it might

48

create problems of identity for them if we changed it. After all, it's not as if they were girls. Or there had been a divorce.'

The assumption that the Flowers knew her history made it difficult to reply. Both merely smiled.

At the table, Elsa was looking into the tall man's eyes. Her strong, beautiful neck and shoulders gleamed palely under the light and her expression was serious, rather emotional. An emotional moment, Maggie thought, one's son's twenty-first, no husband, no father; trust Elsa to make the most of it, fling herself into this good, meaty part . . .

Sally Howard said, 'She must have so much self-confidence.' She glanced at the Flowers and added – quickly, as if afraid they might think she meant *taking my husband away like that*! – 'to tell that story about her moustache.' She gave a nervous, crowing laugh. 'And about her father! Do you think that was *true*?'

'Hardly,' Charlie said. 'I believe he cleared off before she was born.'

'How odd of her to say that, then!' Sally sighed. 'She's awfully attractive.' She looked down at her empty glass. Tears were not far away.

'Mmm. On rather a grand scale for someone my size,' Charlie clowned, shrinking inside his clothes.

Sally blinked and said, earnestly, 'I think you're just a nice height for a man,'

Charlie laughed. 'As a reward for that kindly remark, you may dance with me. Women queue up for the honour.'

'Charlie *dancing*?'

He was forcing his way through the press in a brisk military trot, one arm round Sally, the other extended and sawing the air, like Hitler. He had learned this step at a dancing class when he was nine years old. Around him, the young swayed separately; shut off from each other like autistic children. Another generation; an alien army with soft, absorbed faces. Chalk swirled round their feet, like mist.

'Once every ten years,' Maggie answered, unsure who had spoken. There were so many guests on the staircase that led down to the boat-house, crushed thigh to thigh, breast to back, like strap-hangers in a tube. Watching their children.

She looked for Toby. She couldn't see him. She saw Hugh Honey, dancing with – opposite – Hermia Tate, Iris's daughter; a fair girl with a dazed expression, rather fat. She was wearing a short, silver dress that looked as if it were made of metal. Her bare arms worked at her sides, like pumps.

When had she last seen Iris? Maggie tried to remember. Could it really be a year ago, the last time Elsa had given a party? The Tates had a house on the other side of the river; it had a big garden with a sloping lawn down which Hermia and Toby had once rolled, shrieking. Maggie half-closed her eyes and saw the scene like a clip from an old film: the children – three years old, four? – and their parents watching from the terrace, mugs of beer in their hands. Charlie in a pink shirt, laughing. Iris's husband in a suit. A psychiatrist who looked, Charlie said, like a successful banker – not that Charlie, at that date, knew any. But he was plump and prosperous, Iris's husband, inclined to stand legs slightly apart, thumbs tucked in waistcoat, while he analysed the iniquities of the tax system or the disgraceful workmanship in his new, expensive car. A boring man, supposed to be clever. He's so mature, Iris had said, when they got engaged, six months after she and Maggie came down from Oxford: at their age, at that time, maturity was accounted a virtue. Born old, Charlie said. Charlie had never liked him, and they quarrelled, one evening, over Suez. Charlie had banged a wine glass down on the table and broken the stem. It didn't matter a bit, Iris had said, even though it was an antique, one of a set given them as a wedding present . . .

Had Iris really said that, Maggie wondered. So many myths grew up, over the years . . .

She turned and saw Iris, wriggling towards her, laughing, her champagne glass held high, like a chalice.

She said, 'Iris, how marvellous to see you,' meaning it, but conscious that it sounded false: people always said *how marvellous to see you* at parties.

'You look wonderful, Maggie.'

'So do you.' Iris seemed hardly to have changed since girlhood; sweet, peaky face, hair caught back in velvet bow.

'I see your name in the papers. My famous friend! I tell people – I know her!'

The high-pitched, ecstatic voice, the breathless, mock admiration. Iris hadn't changed. Real success would have been passed over in silence. Or perhaps she would have said, 'Have you been writing lately?'

She said, 'Of course I suppose Charlie is helpful. He must know so many useful people.'

'Not really. He's a political journalist.' She had forgotten Iris's habit of giving with one hand and snatching back with the other, and it affected her the way the prospect of a good bout in the gym with an old sparring partner must affect a boxer: she felt stretched and cheerful, on her toes.

The flat, button eyes sparkled. 'Don't mind me, duckie. I'm only jealous. We hausfraus, you know. How's Charlie?'

'Down there.'

Maggie pointed; close beside her, Iris peered down. On the top of her head, the blonde roots were dark.

'Dear Charlie, just the same! A crumpled *gnome*. Toby here?'

'Somewhere.' *Where?* Maggie said, 'Hermia looks fine.'

'Too fat.' Iris straightened up. 'Dragon's teeth,' Maggie thought she said.

'What?' Above the thrum of the music, they were shrieking at each other like parrots.

Iris said, 'They spring up overnight. Can't we sit down somewhere? Lord above, don't you hate parties? Yes, the weight is a problem, poor lambie. She sticks to the diet in public and eats in private – night raids on the larder, toffee papers under the mattress. Secret eating, like an alcoholic. Exams, of course. She was thin as a twig until she failed her A-levels last year. Angus says she's feeding her sense of inadequacy.'

She laughed proudly at this prime example of her husband's wit.

'How is Angus?'

'Not here, of course. He says, all these boring, middle-class people, broadcasting their repulsive opinions, why should he waste his time? Oh, he's working too hard and it makes him uncharitable.' Iris giggled. 'He makes me take tranquillizers so *he* can be bad-tempered with impunity! Has Toby taken his A-levels yet? Poor Hermia took them a year early, which was a mistake, we see now. She's not bright like Griselda which is hard on her, having a younger sister coming up fast on the outside rail! Sibling rivalry, etc, though I must say she seems a most unjealous child, it quite worries Angus! She's too nice, he says, there must be some basic insecurity there. How are your younger two. Lucy and George, isn't it?'

'Gregory.' Maggie felt as if she were drowning. She and Iris had been at school together, shared sweets and secrets, formed a society, *The Grey Sisters*, pricking fingers and mingling blood; at college they had joined the same societies, borrowed each other's clothes, argued about politics and God. Now it seemed all they could talk about was their children. It was all most of their friends talked about most of the time, tenderly inquiring after Tom, or Jane, or Joe, as older people might ask about each other's chronic ailments . . .

The music seemed to have got much louder. Maggie felt it was inside her head, pushing the bones outwards.

Elsa shouted, 'For Christ's sake, Hugh. Turn that bloody noise down!'

She was on the staircase above them, leaning over. Her hair was coming down. Hugh looked up, hands cupped round his ears, though he must have heard her, He wore high boots, black jeans, and a frilled, lace blouse with feminine bust darts.

'Don't you adore this jumble sale gear?' Iris said. 'Though I must say I'm glad Hermia still pays some attention to Mummy! With her shape, she has to be careful!'

'I said, *turn it down*,' Elsa trumpeted, producing silence on the staircase, at least. All turned to look.

Iris whispered. 'Do you know what Angus calls her? Born free!' She laughed at Maggie's blank expression. 'The *name*, dear, and that lioness's hair!'

Hugh was staring at his mother. Then he turned and began to push his way off the floor. Abandoned, Hermia went on dancing alone, exaggerating the movements of her arms and generous hips, face dreamily uplifted as if lost to the world. But she had gone scarlet.

Iris drew a sharp, hissing breath. 'Can you remember the absolute *agony*? One would rather have been *shot at dawn* than left in the middle of the dance floor!'

The music quietened. 'Thank God for that, keep it that way,' Elsa said. Coming down the staircase, she laughed over her shoulder at the man behind her. Sally Howard's Edward.

'The latest victim,' Iris said when they had gone by, edging closer, like a little girl with a secret. 'New neighbours. They moved in last month and she's nabbed him already. Mends the lawn mower, pours drinks. I don't know if he's been promoted to what Angus calls the Highest Honour yet.'

'I don't think so, she's too nice to him.' Maggie found herself bubbling with inner hilarity. She was by nature cautious, tightly wound; Iris seemed to release some spring in her of cheerful silliness. A lightening agent, like yeast in a pudding, Maggie thought, and said, 'I think his wife's upset, she had her eye on them earlier.'

'No avail, though, not if Elsa fancies him. I must say, I hope there isn't a scene tonight. Poor Hugh's party! Though I don't know, he must be used to Mama by now. But one wonders. I'm afraid I'm frightfully thin-skinned where the young are concerned. Watching them suffer. I feel it in my *bowels*, Mag, I really do.' Her eyes moistened: sensibility, always her stock-in-trade, was heightened by drink.

'I don't suppose it's any worse for them than it was for us,' Maggie said.

Elsa and Edward Howard were dancing. Elsa with curious, stately movements, rather like a long distance swimmer. The man kept a foot away from her, very upright, his body shimmering with an unexpected, almost professional precision.

Iris said, 'Thank God for *that* strange mercy, anyway.' Following the direction of her besotted gaze, Maggie saw that Hermia had been joined by a familiar, shrouded figure in a black burnous that hid the face and reached the ankles. He jigged loosely, out of rhythm, and waggled his wide sleeves, clowning. Maggie smiled. Like Charlie, Toby hated dancing; like Charlie, he was kind.

Hermia was laughing. Toby put his feet together and twisted from side to side, as if ski-ing fast downhill. Hermia laughed more loudly, inviting everyone to see how much she was enjoying herself.

'She worships Hugh, of course,' Iris said.

Charlie was coming up the stairs, trailing Sally behind him. Catching Maggie's eye, he turned his eyes up, acting exhaustion, puffing like an old man.

'Charlie!' Iris held out both arms.

'Iris.' They embraced. At this point in a party, even old enemies could kiss like friends. Over her shoulder, Charlie winked at his wife. 'How are you, *ma vielle hollandaise?*'

Iris gave a shout of laughter. 'The same old Charlie!' she said.

Hermia said, 'This is my parent's house. It's absolutely awful, isn't it?'

The Tate's drawing-room, polished and comfortable, was unexceptional. A few good, modern paintings on the walls; a long, low bookcase in natural wood; an artistic arrangement of dried beech leaves and silk roses in the grate.

'Everything out of magazines,' Hermia said, in tones of exaggerated despair. 'My mother spent hundreds of years making these ghastly flowers. I think it's *futile*. I mean, she could be doing a job, like looking after blind old people, or something. It's not as if she was stupid, she's got a *degree*, for God's sake, but her mind's just addled with doing nothing. It's my father's fault, really, he's *feudal*. He thinks that if women don't stay at home, their children grow up delinquent. It's all right for him. I mean, he doesn't have to keep on telling her things to make her feel she's still useful because she hasn't any life of her own. It's a terrible responsibility for *us*.'

Toby said nothing. From the hood of his black burnous, he smiled, like a shy animal.

Hermia was afraid he had noticed the spot on her chin. When she had last examined it, it had looked quite small, but now she was sure it had grown into a huge, swollen lump, disfiguring one side of her face. She put up her hand to hide it, pretending to fiddle with her hair. 'Would you like some whisky?' Toby shook his head. 'Do you smoke pot, then? I'm afraid I'm old-fashioned, I just stick to alcohol.'

Toby said, 'I don't drink, I think drunkenness is disgusting. Besides, I'm sufficiently out of contact with reality as it is. Hugh says I'm basically a bit schizophrenic.'

'I'm more of a depressive, myself.' Hermia sighed and shook her head so that her hair swung forward in a soft, shining curtain. If she kept her head at this angle, tilted slightly to the right, the spot would remain concealed. 'I used to think Hugh was fabulous, but I've grown out of him this last year. I mean, I still like him but one grows sort of *past* people.'

She wished she could put that better – she had a rather frightening feeling, much of the time now, that she was moving somewhere very fast while the rest of the world was standing still, and would have liked to share it with someone – but Toby's eyes, watching her steadily from the dark folds of his cumbersome garment, unnerved her. She said, 'Aren't you hideously hot in that?'

'No.'

'Do you want to go back to the party?'

'No.'

Hermia wanted to yawn. She had a good appetite for life, and though easily hurt, healed quickly. Humiliated by Hugh, she had meant not to return to the party; now she had begun to be afraid she might be missing something.

But Toby stood there, hands folded in his sleeves, waiting.

She said, 'Well, now you're here, you might as well see round the family mansion.'

At the bottom of the stairs she stood back, so he should go up ahead of her. The backs of her knees were fat. She said, 'You go first. I want to see what that thing looks like from behind. Where'd you get it?'

'Tunisia. My Aunt took Lucy and me last year.' He went up the stairs in front of her and it swirled out behind him.

Hermia said, 'This is my sister's room. She's gone to stay with a friend for a night.'

The faces of pop stars stared down from the wall. 'What's your sister like?' Toby asked.

For Hermia, at this point of time, the most important thing about Griselda was her figure: in that graceful, coltish presence, she felt like a stuffed bolster. But to say 'She's thin,' seemed trivial. She said, 'How do you know what anyone is like?'

'That's lazy,' Toby said. 'It sounds philosophical, but it's just lazy, really.'

He smiled, kindly.

'Prig,' Hermia said. 'What's your sister like then?'

'Lucy? Well, that's harder because she's younger than yours. So she's not settled into a fixed personality yet. She switches, like changing clothes – grubby ten-year-old boy one minute, sophisticated woman of the world the next.'

'How old is she?' Hermia asked, mystified.

'Twelve. What I mean is, she's always arranging her room. This week, she's been labelling all the drawers in her chest – listing what's in them exactly. She wrote one marvellous label, Brassières, Talcum Powder, False Scabs and Stink Bombs. I thought that was marvellous. She was so serious about it, sitting on the floor and writing with her tongue sticking out. Then my mother brought someone in to show them, and they laughed about it.'

'Did Lucy mind?'

'I don't think so, really. She quite likes it, in fact, when people laugh at her. She likes to be noticed. But I minded for her. I was furious with my mother.'

'Your mother's a friend of my mother's.' Hermia said. 'They were at school together before the Boer War.'

'Do we have to talk about them?'

Snubbed, Hermia turned and crossed the passage into her own room. Toby put his hand on her arm. 'I'm sorry. It's just that I have a difficult relationship with my parents. It's a painful topic. I only really stay at home because of Lucy. She's at a tricky stage in her development and they're handling it badly. They're far too permissive and it's bad for her. I like your room.'

'Oh, it's grotty, really.' But she looked round with pride, at the orange walls, the posters, the sociological paperbacks. Hermia lived through other people's eyes: whenever she left her room, she arranged it to impress a possible visitor; suitable books lying open on chairs and bed as evidence of careless scholarship; make-up tidied away in case anyone should think she cared about her appearance; messages or injunctions written on the mirror with lipstick. Today's read, *Moderation in All Things*.

Toby was looking at it. Hermia laughed stagily and

said, 'I just have to remind myself! I'm such an extreme person, up in the air one minute, down in the dumps the next!'

Toby's expression was grave. His intent, dark eyes looked, Hermia felt, straight through her pretensions into the shallow waters of her soul.

She said, in terrible despair, 'Oh, it's not true, of course. I'm so ordinary!' She plumped on the bed, her weight creaking the bedsprings, and looked up at him pleadingly but his eyes, though kind, would not let her off the hook. She said. 'It's nothing to do with not being clever; stupid people aren't always ordinary, but I am. There's nothing special about me, I'll never do anything that no one else can do. When I die, it'll be as if I'd never lived at all!'

Toby said, 'Actually, you can't be very stupid if you know that.' He sat in a basket chair, facing her, and arranged his skirts over his knees. 'Dostoevsky says something about that in *The Idiot*.' He paused, but Hermia had not read Dostoevsky. 'About clever, ordinary people,' he went on. 'How terrible it is for them to know that there is nothing different about them that will set them apart from the rest.'

Hermia felt nervous. 'I'm in good company, anyway.'

His eyes rebuked her. 'Dostoevsky wasn't writing about himself.'

She said timidly, 'You're not ordinary, are you? I mean, you're not like most boys. I mean you don't ...' *Try to kiss people*, was what she had been going to say, but faced with this monkish figure, it seemed a crass and clumsy comment. She lowered her gaze to her lap, plump hands folded on plump knees, and thought, suddenly and longingly, of food: fudge, powdered drinking chocolate spooned straight out of the tin, bread and butter sprinkled with hundreds and thousands. She had had so little to eat today; nothing really since lunch except caviar at the party and she had eaten very little of that. And she had only had three pieces of toast for breakfast. Three pieces of toast, steak and salad for lunch, and only half a baked potato – why, she had only had about three-quarters of the calories necessary to keep a sedentary invalid alive, and she had been dancing all evening ...

She said, 'What are you going to do? I mean, when you leave school?'

He said, with a kind smile, 'I have left school. But I haven't made up my mind. Eventually, I expect, I shall go into something interesting and creative, like publishing or films. Or perhaps the theatre, though the standard's so terrifyingly low at the moment, one would have to be careful. I mean, it would be so easy to write a play just for commercial success, one would have to watch out that one wasn't corrupted. The most important thing is to develop one's full potential. And to do that, one has to lie fallow, to explore oneself.'

'That might be all right for you,' Hermia said, 'but it would be boring for me. I mean, because *I* am boring.'

'No you're not.' Toby cleared his throat. 'I don't think you're boring. I think you're clever and beautiful.' Hermia looked at him, amazed and fearful, but he wasn't laughing at her. He smiled, shyly, and went on, 'It's so hard to know what one is like. *I* can only see myself in relation to other people. My parents, for example. As their son, I have a function. I mean, by the time most people are thirty, they have no real motive to go on living other than their children. But when I try to see myself apart from them, I feel as if I were alone, on a swaying bridge over a chasm. I have to cross it to find myself and I'm not sure I can manage it. It's so dark all round me.'

'Oh Toby, how absolutely awful,' Hermia said. Her young, kind heart, always open to receive the old, the sick, homeless families, hurt animals, reached out to him. She was ashamed because there had been a moment when his low, even, solemn voice had made her want to laugh. Oh, she was shallow and stupid! She heard her own, silly words, *how absolutely awful*, and wished she had been struck dumb before she had spoken them. She hung her head and muttered, 'I'm sorry, I wish I could help.'

'Well, you have!' He smiled at her and her heart turned over. 'Listening, for one thing, and taking me away from that party, for another. Though it isn't a party, really, more a tribal rite, like circumcision or something. And all those people, emerging from their comfortable breeding boxes to celebrate it. But I suppose we ought to go back and be polite.'

'Could we have something to eat first?' Hermia said. 'I'm so awfully hungry.'

Maggie was dancing with a man called Will Stanley. He danced like an agile bear; quite light on his feet, but plodding. He was an old friend of Elsa's and did something in electronics. He talked about a computer system he had devised for assessing the probable results of horse races. Maggie did not understand it, but it was soothing to be told something practical. Will had no children and that was soothing too. No important examinations, no feeding or emotional problems, no difficult pregnancies.

He said, 'Are you with book at the moment? What's it this time?'

She said, 'People,' and knew this was snubbing, but she felt such cringing embarrassment when asked that sort of question. Will didn't mind; he had only been thinking of something to interest her. He said, 'Scribble, scribble, Mr Gibbon,' and whirled her round, hugging her ribs and lifting her feet off the floor.

They bumped into someone.

Will said, 'Sorry.'

Hugh said, 'Maggie.'

He looked tired. His blouse – really Victorian: you could see the yellowing at the seams, the careful detail of the ruffles – was torn at the shoulder. She said, 'It's a lovely party, Hugh,' sorry for the tension round his eyes, wanting to see him smile. She was, she thought, very *fond* of Hugh; a gentle, polite, guarded boy, who thawed when he felt safe with you. Charlie loved him because he was Roy's son, but that was different . . .

He didn't smile. He said, 'Maggie, will you come a minute?'

He looked scared, She smiled at Will and followed Hugh up the stairs. In the big room, couples snuggled on sofas. Not all were young. Someone had turned the main lights out.

Hugh said, 'My mother wants you. In the bathroom.'

He sounded as if he were going to cry. He ducked his head and ran back, down the staircase.

The bathroom was down a short passage. Maggie pushed the

door open, and saw Charlie's back. He was standing over Elsa who was sitting against the wall, her legs stuck out.

Charlie turned quickly. He said, 'Lock the door.' She locked it. Charlie turned on the basin tap, and left it running, for some reason.

Elsa's eye was puffy. There was a cut underneath. A mark, anyway.

Maggie said, 'Did you fall?' Elsa was a steady, routine drinker, but she had never seen her drunk.

Elsa stared at her. The undamaged eye looked angry.

Charlie said, 'Hugh socked her one. I came up to pee . . .'

'Better get on with it, friend,' Elsa said. 'You might damage the old whats-it.'

She got up from the floor and stumbled. Maggie caught her and helped her to sit on the edge of the bath. Charlie lifted the lavatory seat.

The cut was bleeding. Pin heads of blood, like a row of garnets. Maggie said, 'D'you mean *Hugh* . . . ?'

Elsa said, 'He was wearing his nuclear disarmament ring,' and started to laugh.

Maggie wrung out a face cloth in the basin, turned off the tap. Charlie pulled the chain.

Elsa said, 'I was telling the story about me and Roy and the Hungarian.'

Charlie said, 'It's a bloody marvellous story, why shouldn't you?' His nostrils were pinching in and out.

Maggie said, 'But why on earth should Hugh . . . ?' She felt plaintive, like an off-stage Greek chorus.

Elsa said, 'I wasn't making fun of Roy.'

Charlie said, 'I know. I know, love.' He held her head against his stomach and stroked her hair. Someone tried the door. Maggie shouted, 'Just a minute.'

Elsa pushed Charlie away and stood up, leaning on the basin with one hand; with the other, she wiped the steam from the mirror. She said, 'Christ Jesus!'

Charlie said, 'What would you like us to do? Shall I tell them to go?'

'Do what you bloody like.' Elsa sat down on the bath again. 'Only for God's sake don't tell them. I know what they'll say.

Her own bloody fault, she asked for it. Well, it may be bloody true, but I don't want to hear it. Not now, not in my own bloody house. Right?'

Charlie said, 'Ought we to get a doctor?'

He looked very tired.

Maggie touched the wound. The flesh felt spongy. She said, 'It's all right, I think. The cut's very slight.' Elsa grinned at her. Maggie said, 'Do you want anyone?' What was the name of the current lover? She couldn't remember. She said, 'The bloke you were dancing with.'

Elsa shook her head. 'He'd want to beat Hugh up. He's that sort. Never hit a woman.'

'I have some sympathy with that attitude just now.' Charlie said.

Elsa said, 'Little bastard,' and began to cry.

I had not seen her cry since Roy died. We brought her home from the hospital, holding her between us in the taxi. She felt cold. She spent three frozen days with us, dumb, immobile, and then burst like a thawing pipe. I had never seen anyone cry like it. An adult, in a child's despairing rage – as if Roy were a toy that had been taken from her. She rolled on the floor, biting her knuckles; at night, in spite of sedatives, she lay shaking and sobbing. Charlie and I took Hugh into our bed because he couldn't sleep and he lay awake and said, 'What Mummy crying for?'

She kept saying, 'Oh God, why am I alive?' It was terrible because she wasn't – really wasn't – that sort of woman. Not the sort to give in and wail and scream like something elemental. She frightened me. And poor little Hugh – he was only five, and she frightened him. He ran from her, weeping, and pushed Toby off my lap. We lived in the middle of any angry storm – it wasn't grief, as Charlie said, but anger. Elsa had tried to strike some bargain with God – if you let him live, I'll be good, do this or that – and He had failed her. She was a spoiled child, venting her rage on a parent. I said this to Charlie and he said – perhaps on the father she never had! He was tender with her, respectful because she had been Roy's wife. I had no reason to be frightened, no right to be angry. I told myself I could not bear to see him taken in.

Charlie said, 'I'll go and tell them the party's over.'

Chapter Four

'She's a terrible woman,' Toby said in the car going home. 'Really. I mean, poor old Hugh's had a lot to put up with.'

Charlie cleared his throat. *That's no excuse,* was the proper, parental answer. Maggie, on Hugh's side (though she feared for the wrong reasons), waited for Charlie to give it. Instead he said, 'Well, I suppose you could say so has *she*!' He cleared his throat again (either emotion or smoking had fogged it). 'Ever since Roy died she's been very much alone.'

'She's been married again twice. And lovers on the side. Funny way of being alone,' Toby said.

Charlie said, coldly, 'None of his successors measured up, even remotely, to Roy.'

Not even you? Maggie suddenly wanted to say, but did not. Her feelings about Elsa had formed and solidified so long ago that they should have no practical application now.

She said, 'I daresay, though, it has been hard for Hugh. All those Uncles.'

A procession passed through her mind.

'He's old enough to understand, I would have thought,' Charlie said, answering her, but really speaking to Toby in the bracing tone of one generation to another. Across the impassable gulf between them. Maggie thought, *why should he be old enough, if I am not?*

Toby said, 'If he's old enough, I would have thought Elsa was, too. I mean, other people are expected to get over things.'

Maggie looked at her son, lying on the back seat of the car. A passing lamp illuminated his face. He was smiling gently.

He said, '*I'm* expected to, after all.'

'Oh, for God's sake!' Charlie said. He swung the car into their drive, braking so hard that his passengers jerked forward. Getting out, he marched across the gravel and waited for them in the lighted porch of the house. He said to his son, 'I won't have you being sorry for yourself, please understand that.' He was suddenly quivering, ridiculous with rage.

'I don't think I am,' Toby said in a surprised voice, but still smiling, as if this was a rational discussion.

Charlie opened the door, stood stiffly aside as they passed through, then slammed it shut.

He said, 'Well, if you're not, then it's not for want of encouragement. And I don't mean only your mother. I'm just as guilty. Like all my generation, pandering to our children, letting them kick us in the teeth! Laziness or cowardice, I don't know ...'

Toby looked at his mother and for a moment both were caught in astonishment. Charlie was so rarely angry. *But it's Hugh he's angry with!* Maggie thought. And then, *Oh you silly man, you're drunk!* But she was afraid to speak. Absurdly afraid. She thought, *This is only Charlie!*

Toby had stopped smiling. The hood of his burnous had fallen back. Dark, limp curls framed his face.

'That bloody ridiculous garment,' Charlie said. 'It doesn't matter in itself, you can wear a sack for all I care, but it's a symptom. Like the hair. In itself so bloody *unimportant ...*'

'I'd have cut it if you hadn't kept on,' Toby said.

'Don't be childish,' Maggie said quickly, hoping to placate Charlie, to stop this nonsense, but no one appeared to hear her. Toby was looking meek but sullen. Charlie's face was red.

'That's what gets me,' he said, spacing each word out and thumping his fists together for emphasis. 'You just don't bloody care. You go your own sweet way because you know you can, because we haven't the guts to stop you! Other people aren't so soft! D'you know what I heard tonight? One man cut his son's hair while he was asleep – shaved the whole of one side of his head!'

'Charlie!' Maggie was appalled. 'That's horrible!'

Toby was staring at his father. He was very white.

Charlie swallowed. He rubbed at one temple with the heel of his hand, pulling the eye about. 'All right,' he said. 'All right. I'm sorry.' He looked, neither at his wife nor his son, spitting the words into the space between them.

Toby turned and walked up the stairs.

'I'm sorry, Toby,' Charlie said, speaking loudly and clearly.

From the top of the stairs, Toby looked down. In the darkness above the hall, his face had a pale, moth-like glimmer.

'Good night, Toby,' Charlie said and waited. Then with a last, sad, little spurt of rage. 'Damn you, I said I was sorry!'

'Good night,' Toby said. 'I hope you both sleep well.'

He moved away, out of their sight. They heard his door close.

'I'm sorry,' Charlie said. 'Lord, I'm sorry.' He massaged his temple again and began to yawn; tears came into his eyes. 'I must be drunk,' he muttered, smiling at Maggie, shame-faced, holding out his hand.

She took it. 'We're all tired,' she said, feeling it – too tired to be angry, or really frightened, though she was afraid. Without reason, she told herself. What had happened was nothing; just a tired man losing his temper with his son. *Was* that all? Charlie had spoken as if he hated Toby, which he didn't do; was jealous, though how could he be, of his own son? But people were jealous; men of their sons, women of their daughters. She thought, *dark forces inside us all*, and shivered, suddenly.

'Cold?' Charlie said.

'A little.' She smiled into his anxious face and said, 'Come to bed. It'll be all right in the morning.'

'Of course, it was a dreadful thing to happen, but one can hardly say one was *surprised*,' Iris said on the telephone. 'At least, not surprised by the resentment, though perhaps a little by the form it took. Hugh has always been such a non-violent boy. Even when he was little and he and Hermia used to have those awful fights, he never socked her back. Of course she was younger, but all the same! I can remember her now, bashing him over the head with a spade – one of those rubber ones, not dangerous, but quite hard enough – and him just sitting there and saying, "Do stop it dear!" Angus always said he was *too* unaggressive, it made one wonder what was going on underneath. I suppose in Hugh's case one could make a quite reasonable guess! When one thinks what he had to put up with! Of course you know all about that, but living opposite we have seen it at even closer quarters! Oh, one hates to strike moral attitudes – for one thing it looks too much like sour grapes! – but joking apart, it must have really been quite awful for him. It's hard enough for an adolescent boy to cope with the ordinary competitive jealousy he's bound to feel towards his own father, but when it's one strange man after another in his mother's bed it hardly bears thinking about. What that poor boy must have suffered! Easier if he had been a girl, really, though that would have had its problems too, I suppose. What happened to him?'

'What?'

'I said, what happened to Hugh last night? Did I wake you up, Mag? I'm sorry.'

'That's all right.'

'I'm terribly sorry!'

'Iris, it doesn't matter a *bit*! No, I don't know what happened to Hugh. We stayed quite late, but he didn't show up; we think he probably went back to London with someone or other. You know, I don't think he meant to hurt Elsa – they had a bit of a row and a scuffle and she slapped his face and he – well, he happened to have a ring on his finger. Just bad luck, really . . .'

Iris laughed. 'Mag, you *are* naïve, darling . . .'

When Maggie put the telephone down, she said, 'Iris.'

In the bed beside her, Charlie groaned.

Maggie said, 'Tip-top form. All those boring years of being a faithful wife and mother vindicated by one sharp backhander.'

Charlie laughed and yawned at the same time. Then he rolled on to his back, and groaned again.

Maggie said, 'She said it would have been better if Hugh had been a girl.'

Charlie snorted and stretched out a hand. Greg was playing the recorder in the next room. They lay, fingers laced, and listened to the precise, reedy tone.

Charlie said, 'Perhaps Toby should see Angus.'

Maggie was astonished. 'I thought you didn't like him.'

'That was years ago. And I was jealous, I suppose.' Charlie squeezed her hand. 'He fancied you.'

'Don't be absurd.' Maggie was embarrassed. She said, 'Angus is a fool.'

'Don't you believe it. Iris makes him sound it, that's all. Spite, or her own silliness, I don't know.'

'Was she always so silly?'

'Umm.'

'Why didn't I see it?'

'She was very self-possessed. When you're young, that hides a lot.'

'I wasn't?'

'Paralysing jumble of doubts.'

'Still am.'

'Not really.'

'Perhaps not, then. Perhaps it's something I hide behind.'

'Could be.' Charlie laughed gently and began to stroke her stomach. She pushed his hand away fretfully and said, 'What are we going to do about Toby?'

Charlie sighed. He said in an even tone, 'I thought we'd decided. He's going to this expensive crammer and he's going to take his exams and he'll see the doctor once a month and have a brisk course of psychotherapy and take his pills . . .'

She said, accusingly. 'You think that's the wrong thing?'

'No. I'm just not sure we're being imaginative enough. I'm not sure, if someone's got off the rails on his own account, that it's the right thing to put him back on them and give an extra hard shove.'

'What's that in English, please?'

'Well. If passing his exams and going to Oxford was what he really wanted to do, then he'd have done it, wouldn't he? Kept a few rules, not smoked pot, etcetera, and stayed on at school.'

'You think it's so simple?'

'I thought I was saying it wasn't!' he said, in an honestly surprised voice.

'What you were *saying*, was that we were doing the wrong thing!'

'No, just wondering if perhaps we were.'

'How is that different?' Anger came up into her mouth like bile and she said, 'You always were good at thinking of reasons

66

for *not* doing things. It's something you're really quite marvellous at!'

'Maggie. Love.' He was still good humoured, still only comfortably tired after a late night and a bit too much champagne; forgetful of – or not prepared to remember – how angry her own fears and doubts could make her with him. He said, half-joking, 'Or you could say I start by eliminating the things it might be a bad idea to do. I grant you, it may not always be the best way of getting a quick answer...'

'It certainly isn't.'

'But the quick answer isn't always the right one. In a new situation, you have to feel your way ...'

She cut in, cold as ice, 'What do you suggest, then?'

He sighed, properly awake now, and aware...

'Well?'

He said slowly, 'What I really think, I suppose, is that we shouldn't rush into things.'

'But his exam is in six weeks' time!'

'Would it matter so very much if he didn't take it?'

'*Charlie!* He's nearly *nineteen.*'

'So?' He heaved himself up on one elbow and looked down at his wife. After a brief, hostile stare, she turned her head on the pillow. He said, to her turned cheek, 'If he takes it next year, he'll still only be nineteen. Hardly qualifying for a pension. Look – I'm not saying we *should* put it off, just that it's not inconceivable to let him off the hook for a bit!'

'What hook?'

He said, 'Darling,' and touched her chin to make her look at him; she gasped and twisted away, flinging back the bedclothes and standing up in one quick, furious movement. She slept naked; as if nakedness was indecent in these circumstances, she seized her dressing gown from the end of the bed and wrapped it round her. 'What hook?' she repeated, staring down at him coldly.

Greg's recorder had stopped. Charlie said, 'Don't shout, love.'

'*I am not shouting.* I asked you a question.'

He collapsed on the pillows. His back was aching, and the muscles in his calves. Dancing last night. Middle age. He gazed up at the ceiling, at the place where the cold water tank had overflowed last year and left a stain that looked like the map of Africa, and thought that he really must try and get regular exercise. Squash, perhaps. An hour's squash a week. He said, 'Well, the academic ladder, if you like. Exams. Qualifications. Bits of paper. I know it's always seemed the obvious thing for him, and, more important, what he seemed to want himself, but that could be just because he's never been shown anything else, couldn't it?'

'Such as?' She waited. He looked at the stain, turning it into a woman's profile: full, apple-shaped breast, flat stomach. Or a galleon in full sail. She said, 'Factory hand? Road sweeper?'

'Deep sea fisherman, if you like. It doesn't *matter*.' Irritation – not anger yet – provided enough energy to make him sit up, look squarely at her pale, indignant face. '*I* can't tell you, but because I can't doesn't mean there isn't something he can do that's different. Something he wants *for himself*, enough to get on and do it...'

'So you're giving him up?' She spoke incredulously. 'The first bit of trouble and you chuck your hand in and say, well, it's up to him now, there's nothing *we* can do any more!'

'Please don't be melodramatic. It's not the first bit of trouble as you well know. And I'm not chucking my hand in, as you put it. I was just questioning...'

'Oh, you're such a *hypocrite*!' she said, lifting a clenched fist and bringing it down hard on the brass bed rail, and then wincing with such an air of shocked surprise – as if she had really thought she could do this and not be hurt – that it checked, for the moment, Charlie's rising anger. But then she went on, nursing her painful hand with the other, 'Why didn't you say all this in the first place? Though I don't know why I bother to ask – I ought to know by now! You always have to be in the right! It's what you always do – leave me to arrange things and then say afterwards we should have done something else, or not done anything at all! Partly because you like to be right, but chiefly because you can't be bothered to think at the proper time. Not when it's your own family, that is! You can worry yourself sick over other people – if it was Hugh now! – but because it's only your own son, that's different! *He* can shift for himself, *he* doesn't matter...'

'*What are you talking about?*'

'Don't shout! You told me not to shout a minute ago!' Her smugly virtuous expression – as if all she had been trying to do with her wild talk was provoke him into the same kind of behaviour he had accused her of – maddened Charlie. He got out of bed at once and began to dress furiously, wrenching open drawers, tumbling out shirts, sweaters, while she moved behind him, picking the clothes up and folding them and putting them back, and all the time talking in a low, controlled, angry voice. 'You know quite well what I'm talking about. Look at last night! The state you were in, shouting at Toby because *Hugh* had upset you! Roy's precious son! He's so important to you, isn't he, he's dominated our *lives* – we've built our *lives* round him – that's why we bought this house, to be near, to help Elsa with him! Unless it was Elsa you wanted to be near!'

He turned on her; though he knew, in some part of his mind that stayed aloof, that she did not mean what she said when she talked like this, that it sprung from some dark, inner fear that he could not understand, only make a lumbering guess at, he was too angry now, for pity. He wanted to slap her; controlling himself, he stood rigid, red in the face, and shouted, 'You must be insane. If you want to know why Toby's in the state he is, you haven't far to look . . .' She shrank away from him, almost cringing, as if he had obeyed his first impulse and hit her, and immediately, he felt ashamed and reached out to take her in his arms. 'I'm sorry,' he said, 'I'm sorry,' stroking her hair as she leaned against him, stiffly at first and then relaxing as his hand explored the back of her head. Something felt unfamiliar: his fingers met a tangled lump, a little nest of pins. 'You left your hairpiece on last night,' he said, and gave a tug. The false curls came away, flattened and slept-on; she squealed – he must have caught a hair – and then grinned at him, shame-faced. 'I didn't mean any of that,' she muttered – she found it as hard to apologize as Lucy did, he noted, before tilting her chin and kissing her mouth.

'Your teeth are furry,' she objected, pushing him away and frowning. 'Where did Hugh go to, do you think? I hope he's all right. I suppose I ought to ring Elsa.'

'I will, if you like.' Really, he ought to go over, it was only twelve miles, but it seemed a bad moment to say so. *Ought* to go, not *wanted* – he checked this with himself half-virtuously, half-honestly, wondering if Maggie might really have some ground for complaint against him and finding none. Not now, certainly; nor, indeed, ever. What he felt for Elsa, what he had always felt, was concern and affection for an old friend who had been Roy's wife, was his godson's mother. A three-fold duty? Was that all? Well. He was *normal*, for Christ's sake! Even if Elsa's behaviour, the suggestion she kept open house, so to speak, was no more than a kind of good-humoured sexual flattery offered to all men, any man, old friend or window cleaner, it was impossible not to respond to it occasionally. But damn it all, he'd only ever kissed her in public! Well, once or twice, maybe, but no more than a kiss, usually slightly drunken. In all these years! Wanted more? Perhaps. Must he stand trial for *that*, had Maggie *never* ...? Sitting on the edge of the bed, one sock on, one dangling in his hand, he looked at her wrathfully: could *she* put her hand on her heart and *swear*...? Of course not. Ridiculous! Nor would he expect it. That kind of jealousy was ridiculous, even given reason, and in this case Maggie had none! He snorted, pulled on his sock; she turned from the window where she was standing, half-dressed now, looking inquiring, and it struck him that perhaps his restraint where Elsa was concerned might have a discreditable cause. He knew she despised men: by not accepting what appeared to be a general invitation, he set himself apart from the stallions who (by her own account) surrounded her. *He* was a decent man, loved his wife, respected his dead friend's memory! A prurient observance of convention? Or, more shameful still, was he afraid that he might not measure up to the kind of energetic athleticism she had often hinted (no, not hinted, Elsa never hinted, said outright) she liked in bed? One of her lovers had actually been a stunt man in films. She had said – remembering what she had said about the stunt man made him grunt with astonishment. He bent, feeling for his canvas shoes under the bed; whistled through his teeth as he tied the laces; stood up, shaking his head in vigorous, mock surprise (heavens, when you start rootling around, what you come up with!) and said, aloud, 'Well, what d'you know!'

'Embarrassed about something?' Buttoning the front of her dress, Maggie looked at him sharply. 'I mean, all this grunting and groaning.'

'Age.' He moved towards her, aware he was grinning foolishly; intending to touch her breast, kiss her, before she had finished buttoning, and then remembering she had objected to his teeth, or the taste of his mouth ... He rested his hand on her shoulder and said, 'You're my girl...'

She smiled, vaguely.

He said, in a put-on, cockney voice, 'You know, I never fancied Elsa, and that's the truth on't.'

She gaped at him, apparently puzzled. He thought, *why she really has forgotten*, and it disturbed him faintly, the way it always did – how she could say a thing one minute, in one of her whirlwind rages, and then drop it the next. Or appear to drop it.

He went on, doggedly grinning, 'She's too *big* for me! Makes me feel like a small boy gazing into a window full of rich, cream cakes.'

She laughed, though her eyes had lost focus a little. She said calmly – and not as if making an effort to be sensible, either – 'You know, I think you should drive over and see how she is. It seems mean, just to ring up. I know she won't admit she's upset about Hugh, but it's all an act.' And then, looking out at the garden where Greg was swinging on the gate – the creak of the hinges the only sound in the Sunday quiet – she added with rather more feeling as if this was all she had really been worrying about, 'I hope he didn't hear us.'

'Does it matter? Parents are human too!' They had often discussed this : they were both volatile, inclined to fly off the handle, shout, thump the table. Better to be natural, they had decided; better an occasional angry face than the fixed smile of false truce. 'As long as we're not always locked in mortal combat,' he said, putting his hand on the back of her neck and stroking with his thumb.

'I suppose so.' But her voice sagged and she looked tired and tragic as if she had failed at something and nothing could ever put it right. That irritated him – the 'little' voice and the sad look – seeming to stake out a claim to a kind of sensitivity he had always fought shy of, crying woe when a thing was done, and besides, was so untrue of her : whatever she might say, however she might look, Maggie was the last person to give in, give up. She was tenacious, a survivor. *A secret optimist, my wife*, he thought, and this assessment suddenly amused him. He said, feeling happy, and wanting her to be, 'What would you like to do for our wedding anniversary?'

She looked surprised, then laughed. 'When is it?'

'Women are supposed to remember these things.'

'I do remember,' she said. 'Next month.'

'The fourteenth.' He kissed her and saw her eyes go thoughtful and distant. 'What now?' he asked, stepping back.

'At least Lucy was out on her paper round,' she said.

Lucy, coming home, scooting her bicycle along the pavement, empty newspaper bag dangling from the handlebars, said to Greg, on the gate, 'You've got rust on your shirt. And your socks.'

' 'T'll wash off,' Greg said.

'Rust doesn't. It's like oil. Like *grass stains*. You ought to be more careful, that shirt's new, don't you know how much clothes cost?'

Indignation made her voice carry comically (she sounded like an overworked mother of ten, and, unseen at the window, her parents smiled at each other) but the force behind it was not maternal, but financial. Lucy had recently become conscious of money as the frailest of nets, precariously suspending them all above a pit of horror. A programme on television about a homeless family had contributed, as had articles in the papers about the cost of living and occasional groans from her mother and father when unexpected bills arrived, or a letter from the bank manager. Never one to do things by halves, she who had once regarded her parents as omnipotent millionaires, now saw them as potential paupers saved from the doss-house only by luck, She did what she could, hoarded her weekly wages from the paper shop as well as her pocket money, checked with her parents the amount they earned, how much tax they paid, how many years their house mortgage had to run. Their gently exact answers brought her no comfort: the vast sums involved only showed how terrible the fall would be, should one get ill, or die . . .

'Aunt Phoebe brought me my shirt, it was a present, so I can get it dirty if I like,' Greg said.

'She won't give you presents if you treat them like that,' Lucy answered, but thinking of Aunt Phoebe cheered her marginally. If they became poor, they could all go and live with her, in the comfortable flat full of gilt furniture and heavy mirrors where she had lived alone since her husband died. Going there to tea (triangular cress and Marmite sandwiches, cinnamon toast and small nutty cakes that crumbled to a powdery dryness on the tongue) Lucy had often thought of this possibility: sitting tidily on a spindly legged chair and watching Greg to see he did not put his sticky hands on the upholstery, she planned how they could all fit in. Two spare bedrooms, one for her parents, one for Greg and Toby; she would have to sleep on the day bed in what had been Aunt Phoebe's husband's study and was now a sort of shrine, his photograph on the desk, his gold pen in its stand, unopened law books, an airless, polished smell. Uncle Felix had died before she was old enough to remember him, but the solid luxury of his flat had established him so reverently in her mind that when Aunt Phoebe spoke of him lightly and naturally (as if he had just gone out of the room and was expected back any minute) it shocked her deeply. 'Isn't she sorry Uncle Felix died?' she had once asked her father, and he had said, 'Of course, but they were very happy, you know, although for so short a time,' which was no answer at all to her way of thinking: someone she had come to look upon as a source of safety, a lifeline, should be mourned more solemnly, spoken of in a hushed voice. Sensing something wrong, her father had tried to explain. 'They married so late, they each had an old mother to look after, and it was splendid that they even had those few years together,' but this was beyond her. 'How much money did he leave Aunt Phoebe?' was what she asked then,

73

and had been frightened by her father's shrug, his suddenly cold, 'I never asked, Lucy, it's not my business,' not because he was criticizing her (she knew children should not ask that sort of question) but because it seemed to her that he did not understand the dangers of his predicament. When he was short with his sister, did not appear to have heard something she had said, or was curt in his answer, Lucy was afraid: Aunt Phoebe did not have to pay Toby's school fees, could, if annoyed, leave her money to a cat's home as people did in books, or, which was more likely in real life, to Oxfam. Lucy did her best to make up for her parents' deficiencies. She was honestly fond of her aunt, who had provided for as long as she could remember a host of small, intense pleasures, visits to the Zoo, boxes of coloured matches, bus trips round London, marathon games of *l'Attaque*; so it was not hard for her to be extra nice and polite, though perhaps a little out of character.

At least, it had not been hard until now. Since last Sunday, Aunt Phoebe had not been to the house and had only, to Lucy's knowledge, telephoned once: Lucy had picked up the receiver and, appalled to hear her aunt's voice, had said in a foreign accent that she had the wrong number. All week, fear of her aunt, and a measure of shame, had consumed her. Useless, though she had thought of it, to write and apologize: she was not really sorry, nor could bring herself to pretend to be. It was Aunt Phoebe who should apologize, after all! When she thought of her offence, Lucy trembled. Walking to school, sitting in class, she composed long, vengeful speeches in her mind; visualized scenes in which her aunt shook, grovelled, begged Toby's pardon. He might forgive her but Lucy never could. *Never as long as I live*, she said, sometimes under her breath, sometimes aloud – once or twice startling passers-by with the ferocity of her expression. She had put away all the things her aunt had given her, the coral necklace, the books, the Parker Pen...

'Not that I'd wear any present she'd given *me*,' she said now, startling Greg, and pushing back the gate, with him on it, to wheel her bicycle through.

She had jammed him into the holly hedge. He retaliated by shoving the gate back with all his strength, so hard that the handlebar of the bicycle caught her in the chest and made her gasp.

'You shouldn't bang girls in the chest, you might give them cancer,' she said.

He opened his eyes wide, 'You only can do that if you don't sneeze into your hanky.' She sighed deeply, and he said, 'Oh, drop dead.'

'That's what I mean. I *might*.'

'I don't care.'

'I know you don't. I wouldn't care if you died, either. I'd dance on your grave, and *laugh*,' she said, hissing with rage, and then feeling it leave her as his mouth shook, turned down. Softened, she said, 'It's all right, I didn't mean it, stupid!' But tears were falling. She dropped her bike and caught his hand, half honestly sorry, half afraid she would be caught out tormenting him.

He pulled away from her, hunching one shoulder higher than the other, and sagging at the knees.

She said, 'Oh, what a baby you are, do stop it!' and then, coaxingly, 'I was just feeling cross, *you* feel cross sometimes, don't you? Look, let's go and make breakfast and surprise everyone, that would be fun, wouldn't it? We'll go in and I'll start and you can go and get Toby up and make him come down and help.'

He scowled, hiccuping, and said, 'Toby's gone away,' but in such a sulky voice that she thought he was still in a temper and saying the first thing that came into his head, to show independence.

She said, 'Don't be silly, why should he go away?', laughing at him, and he hiccuped again, rubbing his eyes with the back of his hand. Then he sighed in exactly the same gentle, almost concealed way that his father often sighed when he was growing bored with a conversation, and said, indifferently, 'I expect because they were quarrelling. I'd go away if I could, wouldn't you?'

Chapter Five

My grandson Toby arrived on my doorstep at five in the morning. He had thumbed a lorry ride and then hung about in the woods until he knew I would be sure to be up and dressed. I rise, nowadays, at four a.m. and go to bed at six in the evening; my husband sleeps from midnight to midday. This is an arrangement that suits us both, giving us the minimum time awake in each other's company. My daughter Margaret finds this situation shocking. 'It must be intolerable for you, Mother, an impossible old man, you should have left him long ago, it's not as if you owe him anything, he's never even supported you, just made your life miserable from the word go, surely now, at your age, you're entitled to a little peace ...' I tell her that shocking situations are often more distressing to the onlooker than to the people concerned in them: the things that she finds 'impossible' about her father (his obsession with the declining water table, for instance, which means I cannot take a bath and am only allowed to flush the lavatory once a day) have long ceased to worry me. Why bang your head against a brick wall when you can walk round it?

But she is too young to understand this, a girl of thirty-nine who still believes it is the exception for things to go wrong in life and that if they do you can always do something about it. I should leave my husband, my dear, lifelong enemy, and live my old age, alone! Margaret cannot believe it is ever too late; she is quite sure she can always escape. (And rescue others: she is not a selfish girl.) It might seem lucky that she has lived half her life and remained so innocent, but I think not: it is always hard, swimming against the tide.

Listening to her talk about Toby my heart bleeds for her. When he was expelled from his school, she said, 'It may be a good thing really. He's not been happy there for a long time, this is at least something decisive. A clean break, a fresh start.' 'Hope deferred maketh the heart sick,' I told her, 'you must beware of becoming like Dr Pangloss.' But she has never read *Candide*, my educated daughter: she said, 'What do you mean, mother?' and I was too tired (eight in the evening and she had woken me from the first deep sleep of the night) to explain to her. One of the things that makes me know I am old is that I cannot bring myself to explain any longer. Margaret must learn for herself that the only good that can ever come out of evil is acceptance; that there is no situation she can really change, only her attitude towards it.

You have to learn to relax like a dancer, then life will begin to flow ...

Perhaps she will never understand this. She was always a strong, impatient child who liked to get her own way and be thought well of at the same time. Getting married, for example, without a word of warning and then pretending she had only wanted to spare us the trouble and expense of a proper wedding when really she was afraid her father would be rude to her bridegroom's smart relations. Not that I can blame her for that: he behaved badly enough at his own wedding, lording it over my mother's family with his tuppenny-halfpenny pride, fresh from the war and cocky as a robin in his captain's uniform. Empty as a drum.

I didn't see it then, of course. I was proud he had chosen me, and even when I saw him at the reception, laughing with his army friends and not stirring himself to speak to my uncles and aunts as a better-behaved man would have done, I thought, this is just as it should be, he is as far above them as the stars! And I was ashamed of them, of their red, sweaty faces and stiff, new clothes as I am ashamed of myself now, remembering how I felt then, although there were excuses for me: I was young and ignorant and in love with his airs and graces and his handsome face. He was the best-looking man I had ever seen, with his neat moustache and clear skin and fine, slightly slanted eyes that were gold and clear as sherry. And he carried himself well, hard and jaunty, as if he exercised a great deal in clean, fresh air.

Margaret never saw him like that. By the time she knew him he had begun to stoop. 'Hung up his hat the moment he married you and never a day's work since,' is all she can see, not the mettlesome creature broken because he could never, after the war, find a job fit for him. 'He could have served in the shop,' Margaret says, but I would never have let him be shamed like that in front of the neighbours; it was bad enough for him as it was, living with the sour smell of greens after his father's rectory in the country with a big garden and good air and the birds singing. I had been brought up differently: though it was not what I had hoped for, perhaps, it was no real hardship to me to take over the shop when my mother died. It was a good little business and I liked being my own mistress as well as knowing that I could keep him in some sort of comfort even if the days were bleak for him, sitting in the park or the public library so that no one should know he had no job to go to.

'What frightful hypocrisy,' Margaret says, thinking of him as she knew him, bent and drooping, but he was different then, proud and suffering. It is terrible to see a man's pride taken from him, but when I tell her this, all she can say is, 'What had he to be proud about? What proper man would let his wife hump potatoes just because he had too good an opinion of himself to stoop to that kind of work?'

There is one thing: she knows now what it is like to have to defend someone!

He wasn't a bad man, only arrogant and weak. And I was no niminy-piminy miss; I had strength enough for the two of us.

The women in my family were used to weak men, chose them, perhaps, to balance their own natures. My mother was a great, strong woman with thick, freckled arms and no patience: her instinct, seeing a child, was to hit it. The shop belonged to my father but if he hadn't married my mother, he would have been bankrupt within the first year. No head for figures and no taste for work – not brought up to it, my mother said, with pride ...

My father came from a farming family that had been both prosperous and enterprising (the shop had originally been acquired as an experiment in selling their own market and dairy produce) until my grandfather, in his middle years, suffered some kind of mystical conversion. He put a bailiff in the farm and stumped the country, sleeping in ditches and begging his food and prophesying the Second Coming of Christ. The bailiff mismanaged, or was dishonest, perhaps: the only sure thing is, when my grandfather came home to die, after two years in his private wilderness, the farm had to be sold and all that was left for his widow and son was the income from the shop. My grandmother came to live above it with my father, then seventeen years old, and one servant girl. She broke all links with her own family, who had insulted her husband's memory by refusing to attend his funeral, and was too proud, or too wary, to mix much with her new neighbours. When she died my father found himself alone in the world except for the young servant whom he married quite soon after; loving her, perhaps, taking the easiest course, certainly, as it was his nature to do. My mother ran the business and left him free, which made them both happy.

He watched birds. There were a lot of birds where we lived, on the patchy, common land and the reservoirs, and though birds did not interest me, I was happy to walk there with him. I was wilful and passionate, at odds with the world, and his presence calmed me: he was a gentle, thoughtful man, not bookish, not even very clever, but percipient and kind. He never did much with his life, as they say, but he wasn't a failure because so little was expected of him: my mother who was a bully and a terror with us children (I had a brother who was killed in the First World War) was quiet and respectful with him and made us respect him too. 'You must ask your Father,' she said, whenever we wanted anything, and though he always said, 'Is that all right, Mother?' and then answered as she told him, the feeling stayed with us as we grew up that he was the master of the house without question, the one to be deferred to.

My mother was right, I see now. She would never have let me criticize my father, the way I allowed Margaret to criticize hers. I am ashamed when I think of it, not because I didn't teach her proper ways but because there was a time in my life when I wanted to hear her speak against my husband, to ease the bitterness in my heart ...

It might seem I had no reason to be bitter; that I had deliberately re-created in my own life almost the exact pattern of my mother's, but this is not really true: I started, you might say, a rung higher up the ladder than she did, being my father's daughter and not his servant, and knowing he had come down in the world made me long to rise up in it again. And I wasn't content with my father's ambition for me which was that I should be a schoolmistress, partly because I had no patience with school but chiefly because I wanted something grander than that. What, exactly, I wasn't sure: all I know is, for a short while I believed my handsome, gentlemanly husband would give it to me ...

I had no right to blame him because he could not; only my own innocence, or folly. And to be fair to myself I knew this; knew, too, that our life together wasn't all take on his part, though the things he gave me aren't things Margaret would notice because she'd had them herself all her life. He taught me about books and music – not because he cared deeply about such things himself, and in fact I was quite soon better read than he was, but because they had been part of the furniture of his life before me, natural as breathing. And I have these gifts now, for comfort in my old age, when other things would have been spent and gone long ago. He was good with the children, too, with my little boy, and with Margaret. Oh, it was her Daddy she ran to with her pains and troubles and called for in the night when she was a tiny girl, but she has forgotten that: all she can see is the shambling old man with his irritating ways and the small, foolish eccentricities that he has cultivated, over the years, to cover up his weakness and his failure ...

And this is my fault ... Until my son died, I had behaved as my mother had done, made Margaret obey her father and encouraged her affection for him, but when this terrible thing happened my nature seemed to change entirely: it was as if I had become a different woman overnight. Not cowed or broken but hurt and savage. Although he was ill a long time, I couldn't believe he would be taken from me; and when he was I was like a caged wild animal in my fury, twisting and turning and biting all who tried to touch me. My husband, my daughter (in the worst of my rage I hated her for living when he had died), even my poor old father. He said, 'At least you had him with you for eight years, that is something to be grateful for,' and I turned on him and shouted that he was a sanctimonious fool and if that was all he could find to say, he could take his preaching tongue and get out of my sight. It was my son who was dead, MY SON! I screeched at him like a peacock. Margaret was in the room and I saw her put her little hands over her ears, but I felt no shame. My husband took her away, but my father stayed, sitting by the fire and saying nothing until the heat went out of my anger and I knelt beside him and wept.

I was the age Margaret is now.

My father stroked my hair and said, 'My poor child.'

He was dying himself then, thought I didn't know it: he kept it from me until the end, simply saying one morning when I took up his tea, 'I think I'm going, Sara, you'll find everything in order in that top drawer.' Although he lived some hours after that, it was the last thing he said. He died as privately and undemandingly as he had lived; when he was gone, I saw how little I had ever really known about him, and yet I had a sense of terror and confusion, as if I had lost some guiding force. It seemed he had been not only the still centre of my life but also a kind of rudder: without him, I lashed about. There was nothing extraordinary about him except that he lived without striving, was content to be himself.

Toby is a little like him. When he was a baby, I thought I saw my dead son in him; now he is almost full grown, I see my father. There is the same gentleness, the quiet, the feeling of some inner stillness you should tiptoe round. Sitting in the kitchen that morning, half-asleep, poor child, holding a mug of tea between his hands to warm them while the fire got going, he watched the flames crackle yellow and blue over the sticks, sitting a long time without moving, as my father used to do, when my mother lit the fire ...

After a little, his grandmother sat back on her heels, sighed, brushed her coaly hands on her apron and said, in the grumbling, old woman's voice she used to disguise any temporary lapse into tenderness, 'It's no good, you know, you'll have to telephone them.'

He yawned, then smiled, teasing her, 'Six in the morning, Gran?'

'You think they'll be asleep?' His smile, his pale face, had softened her more than she cared for. She said, with a little puff of adventitious indignation, 'You should know your mother by now. She'll be half out of her mind!'

'They were asleep when I left last night. They won't wake up much before ten o'clock.'

He yawned again, involuntarily, rubbing his eyes and blinking.

She thought, *dead tired, poor child*, but said, sharply, 'You'll be out for the count yourself by then, if looks are anything to go by. What you mean is, you want me to ring up, do your dirty work!'

Margaret would want explanations, answers. Was entitled to them. She would be hurt because Toby had left home without telling her and come to his grandmother. Why had he? *She* had never fussed over him, spoiled him – it was his parents who had done that, discussing him endlessly with anxious pride as if he were some rare, delicate creature they were privileged to look after! Making a rod for their own backs – she had often told them, and now it seemed she was proved right! Thinking like this, Sara felt a certain angry satisfaction and then, immediately, a sudden misery so deep she could have wept. Poor Margaret...

She said, 'She'll want to know when you're going back. Not that you can't stay here for a bit if you want, though I don't know what your grandfather will say. You know what he is!' For a moment she thought of her husband gratefully; a shield, a wall, something to hide behind. 'He's old you know and old people haven't the patience. They've been through it all before. Oh – your mother led us a dance if the truth were told! Wanting this, wanting that, staying on at school, going on to college – as if money grew on trees instead of having to work and slave for every penny! Not that she didn't work hard herself, I'll give her that, she was always a worker...'

'I'm not staying, Gran.' His voice broke into what she saw, immediately and self-protectively, as an old woman's aimless garrulity. (Once, she would have admitted spite or jealousy; but she was kinder to herself now, gave herself more often the benefit of the doubt.) And yet a certain shame broke through. Her daughter! Sometimes she saw herself as a ship leaving shore, casting off lines and sailing for deep, quiet waters. She longed for the peace of the empty ocean, no ties left. But this one still held her, this one, turbulent link; and through it, through her daughter, this one grandchild, this difficult boy ...

'Of course you can stay as long as you like,' she said. 'Don't pay any attention to me.'

He smiled at her, but something had gone from his eyes. Some light.

'I just came to see you,' he said. 'Not to stay. Or only one night, perhaps. Then I'm going to my friend Hugh, in London. I can't go home. I can't do what they want or be what they want.'

'They don't want anything except your good. Both your mother and father. They'd do anything for you.'

But she felt a faint, sly triumph. *Now she'll learn something.*

'They've done too much already,' he said. 'I don't want any more. I don't want to go to university. All they can teach you is about the world as it used to be, and things are changing so fast there's no time for that. I've got to think things out for myself.'

'Thinking things out often means brooding and idleness in my experience. What will you live on? Or do you expect them to support you?'

'No, Gran, there's no *problem*. I mean, you can get a job on a building site at fifty pounds a week! The important thing is how you live, not what you do!'

'That'll be a fine thing! That'll please your mother! After your good education, a jobbing labourer on a building site!'

But in fact, the way he had spoken, quiet and decided and remote, had impressed her. This was the way a young man should be, standing on his own feet, not humped on his parents' backs. She said, 'As long as you find out what you want to do in the long run, that's the main thing, I suppose.'

He sighed a little. 'I don't really know anything, Gran, I was just talking.' He lay back in the chair and said, so softly she could hardly hear him, 'How can anyone know what they want to do, or even who they are? I don't. There's no form to anything. Just this – this chaos in my head . . .'

She said, uneasily, 'Stuff and nonsense. A boy your age!'

He said, 'By the time you get to know anything important, you're old.'

'Too late then,' Sara said. She felt, suddenly, both impatient and tired. He wanted her to tell him something, *give* him something – she had felt this all along and put it from her. She was so tired. Tired in her spirit – though growing a little stout, her body was so strong and supple still that she felt, sometimes, it let her down: no restful illness for her, no chimney corner . . . She got up from her knees, grunting a little but only for show, acting age and stiffness as if to ward off any demands that might be made on her, and looked down at her grandson. He looked up at her and she knew what he saw: a big woman with plump, fiery cheeks, energetic and powerful. But a ruined fortress, only the strong walls standing . . .

She said, despairingly, 'Well, what am I to say to your mother?'

'That's ridiculous, Margaret, and I've heard some ridiculous things in my time. Saying he must be ill just because he doesn't want to go to Oxford! If you really believe that, then it's you need a doctor, not him! Can't you get it into your head that he just doesn't want what *you* want? Maybe you want it for him because it's what you wanted for yourself at his age, but that's no reason why he should. He has a right to make up his own mind as you did then! I didn't stand in your way, you may remember, and I was right not to, though I didn't see it at the time anymore than you're seeing it now; money was tight and I had your father on my back. Not that *I* ever suffered from workhouse fever . . .'

. . . 'I don't see that its different, I'm afraid I don't see that at all. The boy's not a blank page for you to write on . . .'

... 'Plenty of time, plenty of time – my dear girl, how can you be certain he'll have plenty of time to do what he wants after he's taken his degree? *How do you know how much time he's got . . . ?*'

... 'I am not being morbid, Margaret. It's just that I am old enough to know that the best-laid plans . . . Do you think I didn't make plans for my poor boy? Oh, you've been lucky so far, your life has gone as you wanted it, and no one is more pleased about that than your mother, but don't let it make you inelastic. If you can't give a little over this small setback, what will you do if something really terrible happens, sudden death or cancer; you're not immune, you know . . .'

... 'No, I don't see virtue in misfortune. And we're not discussing my character; I daresay I have my faults but they are not the issue at this moment. We're discussing your son whom you say is sick because he wants to get out into the world and find his own way . . .'

... 'Well, you can only speak as you find and he seemed perfectly sensible to me. I must say sometimes you paint such an alarming picture that I'm astonished when he actually turns up to see him looking so comparatively normal! It's not easy for someone of my generation to accept this raggle-taggle look, we had a bit more self-respect and I can tell you I wouldn't have put up with it in *my* son, and I'm rather surprised, not at *you*, but at Charlie, allowing it, but we won't start *that* argument now! The only advice I can give you is to let him go his own way for a bit and stop concentrating on him. There are other people who could do with a bit of your time and attention, Lucy and Greg and poor Charlie . . .'

... 'Why poor Charlie? Oh, I don't know, dear, it just slipped out. I suppose he just seems to work so hard and sometimes I think you don't quite know how lucky you are to have a good man like that, a good husband and father, no thought for himself; try not to take him for granted, he's just as important as Toby, when all's said and done . . .'

... 'No, of course I didn't mean you neglected them! Why are you so edgy, Margaret? I know you've got your work and that must worry you – I mean, some people would say bringing up a family was a full-time job in itself! – and you've been worrying about Toby and you have cause to, though not as much as you make out, boys have been turned out of school for not keeping the rules before, he's not the first and I daresay he won't be the last! So don't turn it into some great tragedy, or you'll end up by making him feel he's been hardly done by. And that *would* be a tragedy: hard work and discipline is what that boy needs in my humble opinion . . .'

. . . 'Yes of course I'll tell him to ring as soon as he wakes up. He wanted to ring earlier but I told him you'd be worn out after gallivanting all hours of the night – where you get the energy, I don't know! He's sound asleep now, a good breakfast inside him and he was ready for bed, I can tell you, though if I'd had my way he'd have had a bath before he got between my clean sheets, but you know your father . . .'

Toby came out of the lavatory and met his grandfather on the landing, a skinny, wrathful figure in striped pyjamas.

'Pulling the plug!' he said. 'D'you know how many gallons of water that uses?'

'I'm sorry, I forgot,' Toby said, untruthfully: he had, through the bathroom window, observed his grandfather looking at his rabbits in the garden, and thought there was time for the clank of the plumbing to die down before he returned to the house.

'I'm thinking of your future,' his grandfather said. 'Water is the country's life blood. Sixty gallons per person, per day, flushed into the sewers. Wasted. And that's a low estimate.'

Toby nodded, held by his grandfather's eyes; topaz brown and glittering like live jewels in his lined, yellow, sapless face.

'The ground water-level in the metropolitan area has sunk to two hundred and fifty feet below mean sea-level. These are facts I'm giving you. Between 1900 and 1950 there was an observed drop of one hundred and fifty feet. In London now, flowing artesian wells no longer exist. And people like you pull the plug without thinking! Bath without thinking!'

'I don't bath all that much,' Toby said, but his grandfather, unused to dialogue, continued as if he had not spoken.

'Prodigal waste. And quite unnecessary.' Enraged, he wagged

one finger, brittle as a dried twig, an inch from Toby's face. 'I'm clean. My body is clean. Do I smell? Answer me, do I smell?'

'No sir,' Toby said.

The respectful address calmed the old man down. He straightened his back, hitched his pyjama trousers, and looked pleased. 'There you are, then. And do you know how I keep clean? I wash my body all over every day; do you know how much water I use? One pint of warm water, no more. Quite sufficient for one's daily needs. Not that I would ask that of everyone. Rome wasn't built in a day and you can't expect people to change their habits overnight. But there is one very simple step that could be taken. Are you listening to me?'

'Yes sir,' Toby said.

His grandfather looked at him tight-lipped for a minute, then gave a brief, satisfied nod. 'Showers. The shower uses less water and is more cleanly. Wallowing in your own filth is not only repulsive, but sitting in warm water relaxes the sphincter muscles and is a common cause of piles. If I had my way, no new houses would be built with a bath and I would encourage the removal of baths in existing houses, either by law, or some kind of tax inducement. I have given a lot of thought to the matter and I consider this would solve our water problem within five years. A tax on baths, say one hundred pounds a year. One might have to bring in some kind of state grant for the installation of showers, but in the end that would be a small price to pay. I'm not talking out of the top of my head, I've worked it all out in my report.'

'Is it finished yet?' Toby asked.

'Another month and we should be round the bend and into the straight. There's a lot to do, you know, a lot to do. But I don't complain, it's my life's work, you might say. What are you going to do with yours?'

The sudden question, put with no change of tone, took Toby by surprise. He blushed and said nothing.

His grandfather grinned. It made him look sly, but sane.

'School's washed its hands of you. Maybe that's no bad thing. Organized education is only suitable for mediocre people. You don't want other people's ideas stuffed into you. You're like me, got enough of your own up here!' He tapped his temple with his forefinger. 'Best education I ever had was in the trenches. That's where I was at your age. Under fire. Not in trouble with girls, are you?'

Toby shook his head.

'You can tell me, you know. I've seen a bit of the world, I can give you two bits of advice; if you catch anything go to a reputable doctor and if you get a girl pregnant don't marry her. Just as well hang chains on your hands and feet. Your grandmother impeded me at every turn, every idea I had she put paid to, one way and another. Scraping and saving, penny here, penny there, trapping my mind with the things of this world when it should have been free to soar like a bird. Women are incapable of abstract thought. They are at the mercy of their emotions. It is the fault of their biological function. I suppose you know all about that?'

Toby smiled.

'Well, then,' his grandfather said, 'don't expect sense from any of them. If you want help, you can always come to me. No questions asked, and anything you tell me will be absolutely confidential. Is that understood?'

'Yes, Grandfather,' Toby said.

Chapter Six

When she came home from hospital, my mother seemed different. Quieter and gentler. The shop was closed downstairs, so it was like Sunday all week, and she lay in bed most of the day with the baby in a cot beside her. She let me hold him; he was little, but heavy, and my arms got tired. My mother said he was the biggest baby in the hospital. 'My enormous son,' she said, and smiled at nothing in particular. She asked me how it felt to have a baby brother. I said I didn't know yet, I hadn't had him long enough, and she smiled again, but at me this time, and put him back in the cot. She often smiled at things I said that I hadn't meant to be funny. I told her about my friend at school who had been going to have a brother too, but he died before he was born. I said, 'I don't suppose his mother watered him properly,' and my mother laughed and then took me in her arms and kissed me and said, 'I'm not laughing at you, darling!' I knew she was, but I didn't mind because we were so warm and friendly together, the gas fire popping and my father coming in from the cold with frost on his moustache and a bunch of tight, red roses in his hand.

'What must they have cost!' my mother said. Her eyes had gone dark and she lay back on the pillows as if she suddenly felt tired. My father picked the roses off the bed without a word and took them into the kitchen and stuck them in a vase on the table, but it was too hot for them there, and by the time my mother was up, out of bed, they were drooping on the ends of their stalks.

Once she was up and the shop was open, she was different again. She changed quickly. One minute happy, joking with the customers and singing round the flat; the next she was quiet, and I could tell from the splintered look in her eyes that it was best to keep out of the way. My father knew it, too: he seemed to be watching her most of the time and listening carefully, not to what she said, but to the tone of her voice. She was tired, he said, one day when she was cross with me. It was tiring, looking after a shop and my brother, too. 'And you and me,' he said, 'though I'm the real liability. I'm the millstone round her neck.'

He worked at the library all day until it was time to meet me from school. We would go and have an ice-cream and then walk on the common. Often we didn't get home until the shop was closed; we would feel our way through the sweet-smelling, musty dark, and my father would strike a match to light us up the stairs. We could hear my mother singing to the baby, but when we opened the door, she always stopped. She would be nursing him and smiling, and when we came in she would look up and smile at us, but differently, as if she were making a special effort, and I knew that she really wished we hadn't come just then and that she could be left alone, at peace with her baby.

It made me feel lonely and sad. I was sad for her, too, because she was so tired. She sighed a lot and everything she picked up seemed so heavy. I tried to think of funny things to make her laugh. I said one day that it must feel peculiar, feeding a baby, all that milk squirting out like a water pistol. But she didn't even smile; she just looked at me with splintered eyes and said, 'He drains me. If you're not a good girl and don't help a bit more, he might drain mummy to death.'

I sat quite still. I felt hot and cold together. Then she did laugh, but it was a queer, high laugh and her cheeks had turned red. She said, in quite a different voice, soft and coaxing, 'Have you thought what you'd like for your birthday?' My birthday was a long way off; I was going to be six years old. I couldn't think what to say. I said, 'A bike.' My mother said, 'Trust you!' and pulled a face. Then she laughed through her nose and said, 'Well, we'll see. But money doesn't grow on trees. Nor bikes, for that matter,' and I laughed because she had meant me to, but I still felt frightened, inside . . .

I tried to be good and help. I dusted the sitting-room and polished the gramophone records with black boot polish. It was the wrong thing to do. They were ruined, she said. I had ruined them. She sat in the chair feeding the baby and cried, tears and milk spilling out of her and I was so afraid she would die. I said, 'Please don't drain to death,' and she stopped crying at once and looked at me, frowning and still. She said, 'What do you mean, silly child?' and I knew she had forgotten. Then she put the baby down and came to me and picked me up and sat me on her lap and rocked me. She said, 'My poor lamb, my poor lamb, I'm so tired, I'm so sorry.' I said, 'What can I do?' and she laughed then and said, 'Just be a good girl and work hard at school and make a success of your life. I know it's an awful old muddle just now, but I'll be strong again soon, get everything straightened out. Shipshape and organized . . .

'She was always an organizing woman,' Maggie said. 'Wasted in greengrocery. Now she's got nothing else to organize, she's started on the past, ticketing, docketing ... And my character! She says the trouble with me is, I've got workhouse fever!'

She laughed, too merrily, as if, by making a joke of it, this inhibiting characteristic would vanish.

Charlie wanted to say, *must we talk about your mother?* He was tired of trampling over this old battle-ground. Tired anyway; Friday evening, the end of the week ...

He was suddenly afraid he might say it. It was one of his private fears that one day when he was tired and off guard he would accidentally say something unforgiveable. Not what he rationally thought, not a considered opinion, but some idle, cruel remark that had simply drifted into his mind. Like saying to his new secretary, a pleasant, shy girl fresh from Cambridge, *Why don't you do something about that cavalry moustache?* Or to his wife, *Must we talk about your mother?*

To quieten this fear, he stood up energetically, picked up the whisky bottle, held it up to the light, squinted thoughtfully at the level and re-filled his wife's glass. He said, 'Ice? I can get it, no trouble,' and then, smiling at her, 'She criticizes where she loves, you know that.'

But of course she couldn't believe it. Maggie was thirsty for praise, though she'd never admit it. Too insecure, too proud. He smiled at her again, with special tenderness, and then turned to stand on the edge of the terrace, looking across the lengthening shadows of the cropped lawn to where Lucy and Greg were playing some complicated game involving a number of empty cardboard boxes. Some game. Some secret game. He had no idea what it could be. His own childhood was so far away; he had passed through it like a traveller through a flat land, remembered nothing. No peaks, no valleys ...

Maggie said, 'She's never forgiven me because one of my sons didn't die.'

He said, shocked, 'Oh balls!' And then, ashamed, 'It really is such nonsense! What you mean is, *you* felt guilty when your brother died. Or something like that.'

But he felt helpless. How could he know? He had no point of reference. When his father had died, he had felt nothing. He had gone home for the funeral and then straight back to school, feeling nothing but pride in the importance the event had given him. He had hoped strangers in the carriage would notice his black tie and realize its significance; when one woman had done so and offered him a bar of chocolate, he had refused it, sadly shaking his head and gazing, for the rest of the journey, pointedly out of the window. Back at school, he had sought Roy out at once and told him. 'My father is dead.' That was all it had meant: a bribe to an older boy, to make him notice him.

He felt as he often did, when he thought about himself, somewhat disenchanted.

Maggie said, 'No, I don't mean like that. I mean what I said. You can say it's not true, if you like. That's a different matter.'

She was smiling up at him with patient irony, squinting against the low-slanting sun. He moved to shade her. 'I don't think it is true,' he said.

'Charitable Charlie!' she said, and pulled a face. 'I'm sorry! I didn't mean to be spiteful. It's thinking about Toby makes me lash out.'

He sighed, hooked a chair near to her with his foot, and sat down. He took her hand and held it on his knee.

She said, 'I see him surrounded by – oh, *immense* dangers. Lost in some dark forest.'

She laughed at herself, but her eyes watched him. She was exaggerating her fear, so he could more easily reassure her.

She said, hopefully, 'Maybe I've had one whisky too many.'

He pressed her hand. 'You mustn't *worry*. Not just because there's no point, because there's no need . . .'

He went on, stroking her hand, talking to comfort them both. Toby had been gone a little over two weeks, that was all. All right, he hadn't written, or telephoned, but they had agreed, hadn't they, that it was best to let him be for a while? And it wasn't as if they didn't know where he was. He was staying with Hugh, for God's sake, in Elsa's London house! Not roaming the streets!

He listened to his calm, reasonable voice saying these things.

Maggie said, 'I don't like the idea of Elsa . . . I mean, when *we* can do nothing.' And blushed, ashamed to admit this.

'Elsa's not doing anything for him, you know she hardly uses the house in the summer. I'm not sure if she's even seen him. I suppose she would have said if she had. She was on my train this morning.'

As soon as he had spoken, he wished he had not told her this.

'Didn't you *ask* her?'

'Well, I suppose I didn't want to sound too fussy!' The astonishment in her eyes made him aware how ridiculous this was. He said, defensively, 'You know what Elsa's like! Besides, I could hardly ask her about Toby – at least not keep on – without mentioning Hugh, and I suspect that's still a sore point. Certainly, it seemed a tactless subject to harp on in a crowded railway carriage – when did you last see my son, your son, etcetera – if she didn't want to discuss it, and it struck me she didn't. Though she did say she'd been to the house once or twice . . .' He smiled at Maggie's suddenly eager look. '"I pop in occasionally to empty the ash trays" was what she said, *exactly* . . .'

He stopped, remembering something. The way she had looked when she said this! The narrowed, blue gaze, the fleeting, conspirator's smile. Oh, it was nothing, almost certainly; just one of Elsa's meaning looks! But recalling it menaced him suddenly.

'I don't trust Elsa,' Maggie said. She crossed her arms across her chest and shivered.

'You'll catch cold if we sit here much longer,' Charlie said, seizing on this.

It was, in fact, growing chilly. The sun had gone from the garden and the western sky was marbled with small puffed clouds. The children had abandoned their game and were coming towards the house, each dragging a cardboard box.

Charlie watched them, with love, as he stood up, stretching himself. 'You trust Hugh, though, don't you? Isn't he your blue-eyed boy?'

Hugh said, 'He's all right, Uncle Charlie. No trouble, honestly. He can stay as long as he likes.'

Must you call me Uncle? Charlie wanted to say. Hugh was taller than he was : walking into the restaurant, he had been conscious of the boy's angular height, the respectful – but surely exaggerated? – inclination of his head, and resisted the temptation to straighten up, tauten his muscles, run youthfully up the stairs. He had observed too many of his friends caught in this trap; threatened by the presence of younger men, pulling in their bellies, tweaking at thinning strands of hair.

Charlie did not feel threatened. Since he had never been handsome, he was spared these middle-aged conceits. Now he slumped deliberately in his chair, yawned cavernously, rotated his little finger in his ear. 'As long as you can put up with him, then. And Elsa doesn't mind.'

Hugh sipped at his Campari like a girl. 'Why should Mummy mind? I pay rent for the basement.'

Mummy! But the diminutive was not really ridiculous : used so unselfconsciously, in that lordly, gentle drawl, it simply put Elsa in her place.

'Have you spoken to your mother since the party?' Charlie spoke sternly, performing his godfatherly duty, although he had decided, finally, that Hugh was hardly to blame. Or Maggie had convinced him. Elsa invited trouble : she could provoke a saint.

'I wrote to her,' Hugh said. 'And apologized handsomely.'

He smiled. *Graceful*, Charlie thought, and added, *cold*. A cold, graceful boy . . .

He was ashamed of his hostility. There was no basis for it. Hugh's ease of manner was not affectation but a natural, effortless assurance. Charlie was only irritated by it because it deflated him; made his sudden, sweating concern for Toby seem absurd.

As of course it was. Fear was catching; he had caught fear from Maggie. Sitting opposite Hugh, he felt old and foolish.

He said, 'How's the job?'

Hugh was clever. Coming down from Oxford with a first in history, he had landed a traineeship at the B.B.C. Ten places and an entry of over four thousand.

Neatly spooning avocado pear, Hugh frowned carefully. Well, it was quite interesting, of course. But more limiting than one had hoped for. Not that one expected power immediately, one knew one had to learn, but the standard of the people above one was so mediocre, they might have been appointed expressly to frustrate original talent. The trouble was the B.B.C. was such a paternal organization, it kept people on long after their usefulness was past. For so many of the top men, what passed for constructive thought was merely admitting complexities without investigating them ...

Listening to him made Charlie, who had left half his soup, start on his steak and kidney pie with an increase of appetite. Perhaps, after all, young men had not changed so much.

He said, 'I tried for a job at the B.B.C. twenty years ago. They turned me down. Its a comfort to hear the ones who got in are such an inferior bunch.'

He spoke easily. Past failures did not irk him, he was not an ambitious man, or, rather, had long ago settled for what he could comfortably get, knowing both his steady value as an editor and his limitations, which were laziness and a sort of melancholy kindness: he tended to give jobs to people who needed them and to take, occasionally, pieces that were not quite as good as they should have been, from old contributors down on their luck.

'That's why you didn't get in, of course.' Hugh spoke solemnly, without condescension, and Charlie sighed a little: he had only meant to amuse, mildly, and could wish the reply had not come so pat. He thought that he preferred clumsy people, on the whole, and then, that beside this model of cool expertise, Toby must seem so unfinished. What was the attraction for Hugh? On Toby's side, it was obvious enough. Hugh had always been his hero. Charlie smiled, suddenly remembering a little boy calling, *Hugh, Hugh, wait for me* ...

'I'm not sure I wouldn't have been wiser to go into journalism, really,' Hugh said. 'Not just because there's more scope, in a smaller world, but because I'm a words man, basically. Frightfully out of date I know, but I simply can't see myself as a disciple of McLuhan. My old-fashioned education, I suppose. That's why it is such a *good* thing Toby isn't going to a university. He has such a marvellous, visual imagination, it would be *destroyed* by the academic grind. And since he wants to go into films, the younger he starts, the better. I have this great friend who is a marvellous director and he has promised to see Toby some time. I shall try to get him to clean himself up a bit before he does. One has to make certain concessions.'

Charlie looked at Hugh, but his fair, narrow face showed no more than a remote, adult concern. Was this what he felt, then – an impersonal kindness? Or something more? Charlie wanted to say, *Do you love Toby?* but was afraid to seem prying and prurient, Had Roy, at this age, loved *him*?

Charlie said, 'I didn't know Toby was interested in this sort of thing.'

Hugh smiled patiently. He had finished his main course. Now he shook his head as the waiter came round. Charlie ordered coffee and brandy for himself. Hugh refused both; after the Campari, he had drunk only water. He looked at his watch.

Charlie felt nervous; the palms of his hands were clammy. He said. 'Toby's very young, you know.'

Hugh continued to smile. His voice was gentle and reassuring : its tone seemed, to Charlie, to underline his own impotence. 'He has a very plastic personality still. He needs time to mature. Frankly, Uncle Charlie, I think he can do that best alone. Not at home, certainly. He feels he has let you down so terribly badly, the guilt would be too much for him, create too many intolerable tensions.' He paused, then added, delicately, 'I don't mean you are to blame, of course.'

'No.' Charlie looked at his hands, flat on the tablecloth. His little finger, the one with the signet ring on it, was trembling slightly. He felt they were discussing Toby as if he were some kind of invalid, or criminal. He said, in a hearty voice, 'Well. His mother worries, naturally. Whether he's looking after himself properly. Eating regular meals.'

He cleared his throat and grinned, dissociating himself from this trivial anxiety.

'Maggie needn't worry. Hermia comes and cooks sometimes. Hermia Tate. You know. She's a rotten cook, but it's better than doing it oneself. And Toby likes her. She's really good for him, very supportive. He needs someone to show off to, and I'm not much good for that.'

'No, I wouldn't think so.' Charlie said.

'I mean, I'm not around enough. He likes to be alone but it's not terribly good for him. He needs some sort of framework to function in.'

This made sense, Charlie acknowledged, though grudgingly; he resented being told what was good for his son by this diplomatic, elderly boy . . .

Hugh said, 'I'm not sure Hermia would want her mother to know. I mean, not that she comes, but that she comes so often. She's supposed to be busy at this frightful secretarial school – shorthand in the morning, crash culture course in the afternoon. Tailored for the dim daughters of the suburban middle-class. A racket, really, it ought to be stopped by *law*,' he finished, with a sudden access of youthful indignation that Charlie was comforted to hear.

He smiled and said. 'I don't see why her mother need know, do you?'

For the first time, Hugh looked uncertain, even a little shy : a very faint colour rose in his cheeks.

'Well. I'm not likely to tell her,' Charlie said.

Maggie said, 'Iris says she'll ask Hermia. Oh, it's all right. I was very circumspect. I just said, Hugh had told you he thought Hermia had seen Toby once or twice, and as *he* hadn't been very forthcoming, I wondered if Iris would mind asking. Casually, of course.'

She looked cheerful : the prospect of even third-hand news had invigorated her. It angered Charlie – why should she be subjected to this? Why should *he*?

He said, 'Ludicrous! Two intelligent adults – well, in their right mind, anyway – reduced to begging for nuggets of information. Terrified to ring up their own son.'

She shook her head. 'It's what we might be drawn into if we did. We can't help feeling we know what's best for him.'

'Maybe we even do!'

'Charlie!' She laughed at him with a prim little air of superior knowledge. 'You *know* we decided! And I think we're right. What *we* want, what *we* think – he's had too much of that. He's not just a blank piece of paper for us to write on!'

Charlie thought he could recognize a direct quotation when he heard one. Whose? Iris's? It saddened him that Maggie should be so lost, her confidence so shaken, that she allowed Iris to put words into her mouth.

He said, 'Has Iris asked Angus what he thinks?'

Following his train of thought, she looked at him coldly. 'Even if he said anything sensible, she'd make it sound silly. That's what you said.'

'Did I?' He supposed he might have done.

She said, frowning, 'At least Iris always knows what *she* thinks! In my present state, I find that an enviable achievement.'

'If her mind is ordered, it's only because it contains so little.'

'Iris isn't stupid!'

'Oh, I daresay she spring-cleans occasionally. Throws out the old ideas and re-furnishes with new ones.'

He grinned: the image pleased him. Maggie looked reticent; there was an edge to her voice. 'She's sympathetic, though. And *helpful*. Which is more than can be said for some. Elsa, for example – *she* sees no problem. I'm to stop fussing and let the little bastard get on with it! Or my mother. Or your *sister*! I rang her today and she says she thinks we're just irresponsible, letting him leave home!'

Her eyes – before she turned away to hide them – were brilliant with pain, and Charlie caught his breath. So this was how she spent her day, was it? Telephoning people who were likely to punish her! Though he believed it was not self-indulgent, the extent of her guilt repelled him a little and frightened him more: he was not qualified to deal with it.

He said, 'For God's sake, why talk about it?'

She said, 'What else have I got to do?' in a voice so soft and hopeless that it made him want to hurt her.

He said, 'Get on with something. Your book – well, if you can't do that, I see that might be difficult – something *physical*. Clear out the attic. Paint the kitchen. Get drunk. Take a lover. *Anything*. Only just don't sit here, waiting ... Christ alive, what are you waiting *for*?'

'I don't know,' she said. 'Charlie, don't bully me, I don't know...'

They pull the blinds down when people die: His room was at the front because he liked to watch the cars go by at night, lights in a lacy pattern across the ceiling, swirling and swelling like an anaesthetic at the dentist's. I thought, perhaps dying would be like that, swirling lights, and a noise in your head, booming up to a point, and then nothing. Every day when I came home from school, I got off the bus and turned the corner and walked along our street, looking down at my feet moving, at my skirt bunching between my knees, feeling sick and counting. Twenty-five, thirty, thirty-five ... if I get to the grocer's before I count to ninety, then I can look up and the blinds will be ... Which would be worse, up or down, I didn't know, nor what I was hoping for. All I remember is the waiting, and that it seemed to be for something worse than his dying, which was understandable and ordinary; all people die.

He was so thin, I didn't like to touch him, I was afraid he would break. And the room smelled; he was too tired to go to the bathroom, so there was a commode put in the corner that had carved wooden arms and a round seat to cover the pot, and my mother burned heather stalks when he had used it. I hated the smell, I said it was disgusting, and my mother said, 'I'll disgust you, you you niminy-piminy girl ...'

She was waiting, too. She stood outside his room, listening, and there was a look on her face which I knew about because it was like the fear inside me; shapeless and dark, nothing to do with his dying ...

When he did die, I wasn't there. My grandfather took me to the pictures in the afternoon to see an old film with Charlie Chaplin in it. It was a very funny film; I wore my yellow dress and we had tea, afterwards, in the restaurant above the cinema. There was a pretty waitress with a lilac apron and a lilac bow in her hair and we had chicken and chips and peach sundae ice. When we came out the air twinkled with sun and smelt cold and salt, like the sea. We got on the bus and my grandfather started to tell me something but I wouldn't listen, I was so full of the film (or perhaps I knew what it was and didn't want to hear) and when we got off, and turned the corner, I looked at my feet and my yellow skirt, and counted, but only for fun; I didn't look up at the blinds. We went in, through the shop, and my mother was coming down the stairs; I didn't look at her face, just her legs coming down. She said, 'It's over', and I thought she meant the film (or pretended I thought that) and I was going to tell her about it and say, what a pity she'd missed it, but then my grandfather pushed forward, in front of me, and said, 'God bless you, Sara, my poor child.'

I could hear my father crying upstairs. My mother put her arms round me and pulled my head down on her shoulder in an uncomfortable way: at thirteen, I was already as tall as she was. She said, 'Darling, something terrible has happened,' and for a moment, the ground seemed to rock under me and I felt the terrible thing coming; dark wings round my head. She said, 'Your little brother is dead,' and pressed my head closer in that uncomfortable way; her voice throbbed like a gong and I felt, suddenly, a dreadful embarrassment because it seemed as if she was acting, and then relief, like a cool breeze ... This wasn't, after all, the terrible thing I had been expecting, the formless thing; it was just what we had known, all along, was going to happen ... I said, 'Is that all, then?' I felt her go stiff, but she said, quite gently, 'What do you mean, darling?' and waited for me to tell her. But it was no use; I couldn't explain to her what I meant, though I could, to myself, later. It was something like, now we knew what was there, now we could see it, we could face it and begin to bear it; we weren't helpless as we had been before, when we didn't know what was going to happen, or even what we were afraid might happen; when we were just waiting, not knowing, and afraid ...

Iris said, 'Darling Mag. I have to tell you something frightful. I got it out of Hermia last night, well, not *got* it out, she was glad to get it off her chest, poor lamb, it's been awful for her, living with this and not knowing what she should do. Not that I do either, really, it's a terrible thing to have to tell anyone, but there's no point in beating about the bush. Mag, Hermia says he's on heroin. She says you know all about it, that he's been a heroin addict since he was *sixteen*, but I know that can't be true, because you would have told me. Maggie. *Mag* – are you there?'

'Yes,' Maggie said.

'Oh good, I was afraid we'd been cut off, we're having the most appalling trouble with our telephone. Mag, I'm so sorry – I've agonized over this, whether to tell you or not, I lay awake all last night...'

'I'm so sorry,' Maggie said.

'You know I didn't mean it like that, I may be a stupid bitch, but I'm not so ... What I meant was, I couldn't believe it. I said to Hermia, *I don't believe it*. Angus says he doesn't, either, it's some game he's playing, but we talked it over and he thought I should tell you all the same, because even if it's not true, it's still bad he should find he has to pretend ...'

'Did Angus actually say, *I don't believe it*?'

'Well, not exactly, how could he, he's not seen Toby? What he said was, it wasn't necessarily true, just because Toby says it is, even if Hermia's seen him ...'

'Seen him what?' The telephone receiver was slippery under her hand. She took a handkerchief from her trouser pocket and wiped it carefully.

Iris did not answer. Maggie waited. Iris said, 'Inject himself.'

'Where?'

'In ... in his arm, I suppose. I didn't ask. Oh God, it makes me feel sick. The idea. Mag, don't ... don't torment yourself.'

'Do people pretend about that?'

'I think so. Angus says they do. He says, the whole thing is so complicated. Drugs are attractive, not just in themselves, but to put the wind up the grown-ups. *Pour épater les mamans!* Or to get attention – no, that's too trivial – a sort of cry for help! And, of course, it gives them a sort of status among their own group ...'

Maggie said, 'But Toby's always had a host of friends. At school, and ...' This was absurd! She swallowed; there seemed some sort of obstruction in her throat. She said, 'Of course, one cannot altogether discount the possibility that what he has told Hermia is true. Or partially true. Not that he has been an addict since he was sixteen, nor that we know, but that he is now.'

She could hear deep breathing at the other end of the telephone. Iris said in a choking voice. 'Mag, this tears my heart out ... my poor love, you should *cry* ...'

Maggie said, in a light, almost humourous voice, 'It would not appear a very useful occupation in the circumstances. Does Angus say what we should do? Oh, I'm not asking for his professional opinion, second-hand over the telephone, but if he did suggest anything – what we should do immediately – I would be most grateful to know.'

Iris said faintly, 'Look in his room for – well, syringes, that sort of thing. But if you find anything, don't assume – I mean, before you get it analysed – after all, it may be nothing, just a prop, like cold tea on the stage. Oh Mag, I simply cannot believe we're having this conversation! Get him out of Hugh's flat . . .'

'Does Hugh know?' This was – incredibly – a moment of pure surprise. She thought *But Charlie saw him, only the other day . . .*

Iris said, 'I asked Hermia that. She said Toby makes an awful mess in the flat. Filthy clothes, stinking saucepans . . . One day when it was especially bad, she said to Hugh, I don't know how you put up with it, and he said, Oh it's all right, he's a very amiable junkie.'

'I can't believe that,' Maggie said, and then thought *Why not? Why not hit rock bottom while we're about it?* She shifted the telephone to her other hand, wiped it again with the handkerchief, and thought, *You think you've reached the ground floor but there's always the basement*, and this idea amused her, so that when she spoke next, her voice tinkled coldly with laughter. 'And what's Hugh on? Opium? Goodness, we seem to have missed something, don't we? When I *think* of our innocent girlhood! Smoking behind the tool shed – do you remember those stale cigars of your father's, the ones we had to lick down the sides before they would stay alight? And the cooking sherry, and our *sex life* – ringing up boys, not speaking when they answered and then putting the phone down and giggling . . .'

Iris said, gently and quietly, 'I really am so very sorry, Mag.'

'It's all right. I'm not hysterical.' She felt, suddenly, a deep, shamed affection for Iris. She said, 'I'm sorry too, It's a dreadful thing to have to tell anyone, and I do thank you. Since I had to hear it from someone, I'm glad it was you.'

She meant that; at least, for the moment, she meant it.

'Thank you,' Iris said. 'And please, if there's anything I can do, or Angus, we're both here. Just ask. That's all. Except . . .' Her voice, which had been steady, began to shake a little, 'except one thing. I do admire you, Mag, taking it like this. I was so afraid you would loathe me. I think you're wonderful.'

'Oh I am not, at all,' Maggie said. 'It's just that it's always simpler if it is one's nature to expect the worst. And it is mine. I have the feeling that I have been waiting for something like this for quite a long time.'

As she put the telephone down, this seemed to be true. She felt a curious excitement, almost elation, as if her whole life had been a preparation for this moment, and now it had come, there was nothing left to fear. Not the way she measured fear, anyway; what there was had form and substance, she could come to grips with it.

She said softly, as if whispering to an enemy, 'Pride, that's your trouble, my girl,' put out a hand to steady herself on the hall table and looked at her face in the mirror above it. *Much the same*, she thought, *no change*. And then, *What did you expect, you posturing fool?*

The face in the mirror puckered hideously. She watched the tears come, then straightened her shaking mouth and said, more loudly this time, 'I hate you, Iris Tate. How I hate you!'

When she stopped speaking, the house was so quiet and empty. Although hot still, it was a drab day; the heavy air, trapped between damp earth and woolly sky, seemed thick and mouldering. *Like the inside of a cabbage*, she thought, and then, *Charlie* . . . She touched the telephone and stopped. It was not yet two o'clock; Charlie had a lunch, he had said so at breakfast, She could call her mother. Or Elsa . . .

She shook her head violently. What for? What use were other people? She had wasted enough time, these last weeks. Lifting the telephone – it was like an alcoholic, reaching out for the bottle!

She made for the stairs. Climbing them seemed an effort. Lucy's door stood open, and Greg's; Toby's was closed. She thought. *How symbolic*, and laughed aloud as she opened it.

The air smelt stale. His bed was humped with folded blankets; his school box, still roped, waited in the middle of the floor; his books on shelves, on the cluttered desk, in ragged piles against the walls. Everything he had was here, except the clothes he had left in. She had told Charlie to ask Hugh if he wanted anything, clean shirts, clean socks, and Charlie had forgotten ...

She stood nervously, rubbing one hand against her thigh, looking round her as if this room could tell her something. What? A bookish, untidy boy. She tried to think of him, to visualize, but any picture she could summon up, Toby winning a race at school, going up for a prize (oh, his proud, gleaming face) fled at once like a shadow. She began to cry again, for this failure; said, through tears, through clenched teeth, 'You think this is bad, do you, well you just wait till it sinks in!' then sat down on the lumpy bed and moaned quite loudly, rocking backwards and forwards, arms hugged across her chest, thinking, *Thank God I am alone so I can do this*, although she felt, in fact, not that she was acting, exactly, but that she had suddenly found herself upon some public stage, spotlighted, lines unlearned. Perhaps it was this sense of theatre (life presenting no blueprint for this scene) that made her cry out, on a rising, almost petulant tone, 'Why doesn't someone come?'; or perhaps it was simply that she had already heard the car, some inner prompting feeding her the cue before she was properly conscious of wheels on gravel. Certainly she flew up and was at the window before the car had completely halted, which it did violently, the chassis rocking slightly as the handbrake grated. It was a low-slung, scarlet convertible, a young man's car; looking down on it, Maggie saw its unlikely owner emerge – saw, precisely, the top of one of her sister-in-law's remarkable hats, a toque made of purple satin, pearl-encrusted. As always, she was carrying something: today's offering was napkin-covered, in a basket. *Her entrance fee*, Maggie thought, with no more than everyday exasperation, and then, appalled, *Why, Phoebe is the last person*. But she ran down the stairs.

Phoebe said, 'I suppose I shall know what I'm looking for when I find it.'

Lifting her head from a pile of old clothes, she regarded Maggie bleakly. Maggie, emptying the cupboard of the dusty hoard of years (everything kept, even his woolly animals, his plastic cars) sighed and sat back on her heels. Phoebe was in full regalia, hat, suit, pearls, diamond pin – the sort of royal garden party uniform Felix had liked to see her in: he had been dead nine years and she still dressed to please him. Looking at her now, and relating her appearance to the nature of their search, Maggie felt laughter tighten inside her like a pain. *It's not funny*, she told herself, *not funny at all*, but the prim injunction was useless, or came too late; she began to laugh, hoot rather, swaying the upper part of her body, clapping her hand over her mouth.

That tragic, military face, under that hat!

Phoebe watched her, flushed, tight-lipped; the expression she had borne consistently since Maggie had told her what had happened – blurted it out, through tears and bursts of involuntay, excited laughter. Phoebe had said nothing; her only comment was to make Maggie sit down and drink a glass of gin. (Though Maggie hated gin and knew that Phoebe knew it, she felt, obscurely, that Phoebe's instinct was right: something she found nasty was more suitable in the circumstances, more medicinal.)

Phoebe said, 'Maggie, I think we should wait until Charlie gets home. It's not right you should have to do this alone.'

'You're here,' Maggie said.

'That's not the same.'

Maggie said, patiently, 'We have to do it. Charlie can't get home till after four. And the children will be back by then.'

'This is a terrible thing, in a house with young children.'

'Yes.'

'What did Charlie say?'

'Once more unto the breach, dear friends.'

Phoebe sighed. 'How that poor boy can be expected to keep his mind on his job!'

'It's not my fault,' Maggie said. This seemed petty. She went on, quickly, 'Perhaps there's no point, really. I mean, if Angus is right, if it's a sort of exhibitionism, he'd leave the evidence where we could easily find it. Like the letters,' she added. An afterthought.

'Letters?'

Maggie thought, *You silly cow, why can't you keep your mouth shut?* She said, 'Well, he used – I mean he doesn't so often now – he used to leave half-finished letters lying about. Like, Dear Aunt Phoebe, thank you for such and such, and then, well, just a spate of nonsense, really. *Complaint*. How can I live in this terrible house, the noise, the lawn mower, the demands made on me. Meant for *us*, do you see?'

She remembered one sentence: *I used to love my mother but that is over now.*

'How very odd,' Phoebe said. 'I must say,' – Maggie knew, by the deep breathing, the tightening of the jaw, the nervous fingering of the diamond pin, that something unpleasant was coming and was, mysteriously, glad of it – 'I must say that if it is nothing but showing off, then it's worse than if it were true.' The beaky nose lifted triumphantly. 'It shows that the boy has no feeling for others at all!'

She was only making a point; she hadn't thought it through. But Maggie felt a fearful joy.

She said, 'You'd prefer that? You really mean you think it would be better for him to die?'

How unfair, she thought, *how cruel*! Thought, but did not feel: it was a relief to have someone to shoot at, some target for hate...

Phoebe sat down on the bed. Her tight skirt rode up, revealing gaunt thighs. Her knees were pressed tightly together, as if to suppress their trembling, and Maggie was moved – more moved, in some strange way, by those veined, bony old legs than by the sad, raddled face above them.

She said, 'Of course you don't think that. I'm sorry.'

Phoebe said, 'I am glad Felix is not alive to see this day.'

The desolation in this absurd remark was immense. Maggie sat very still.

Phoebe said, 'I was only thinking of you and Charlie.'

'Toby is more important.'

'To you, of course.' She said, piteously, 'You are both so unselfish. I was being selfish for you.'

Maggie said, 'Don't be sorry for us. I daresay it's all our fault, really.' She thought, with contempt, that she would only say this to someone who was sure to deny it.

'Nonsense.' Phoebe's chin was shaking; her mouth moved like an old, soft purse, opening and closing. 'I don't mean I'm not fond of the child, he has delicacy, charm – he can charm the birds off the trees, as they say, let alone his old aunt, but . . .'

'Who can?' Lucy said.

She stood in the doorway, glowering beneath her school boater.

She said, 'Christ alive!'

'Don't say that,' her mother said.

'Toby's *things*,' Lucy said. 'What are you doing?'

'You're home early,' her mother said.

'There was this rotten *match*. I didn't want to go, so I made my nose bleed. What are you . . .'

'How did you make your nose bleed?' her aunt said.

'Oh, I just – it's *easy* – shall I show you?'

'No thank you,' her aunt said.

'Well, I just poured with blood, all over my tie and my maths books, so Miss Sainsbury said I could go home. Toby will be *mad*.'

She looked round the room. Her mother and her aunt sat still. When Lucy had finished inspecting the mess on the floor, she looked at their faces. Her mother had been crying.

Her aunt said, 'We were looking for something Toby wanted. Some papers . . .'

'His passport,' her mother said, quickly, and smiling. 'He thought it might have run out. He doesn't want it at the moment, but you never know.'

Since her mother was looking straight at her, she accepted this. She felt uneasy, but she accepted it.

'I know where that is. With his . . .' *With his poems*, she had been going to say, but remembered in time that they were private. 'Under the bed,' she said, dropping her satchel and crossing the room and kneeling down. 'You didn't have to make such a muddle, this room looks like a disaster area,' she said, quoting her form mistress. She pulled the suitcase out and threw back the lid. There were some socks and a few old gloves covering the private notebooks, she tossed them out to get at the passport – there was so much rubbish on the floor it hardly mattered – closed the suitcase smartly and pushed it back.

'There's no need to add to the mess, it's quite bad enough as it is,' her aunt said. She picked up a sock or two and one of the gloves, pinching the fingers. She made a small sound, a squeaky intake of breath.

'Phoebe!'

Lucy couldn't see her mother's face – she had got to her feet and was standing with her back to the light – but she sounded frightened.

Aunt Phoebe said, 'Just a pin, or something. Sorry.' She smiled, but her face and neck had turned crimson.

Lucy gave her a quick, shy look. The blush had reminded her of what she had forgotten when she first came in. Had her aunt remembered too? The thought embarrassed her terribly. She turned to her mother and said, in a loud, rude voice, 'I'm hungry, isn't tea ready, my stomach's *flapping*.'

Chapter Seven

Aunt Phoebe had said that before. I can remember when she said it, exactly; we were riding on camels round that oasis in Tunisia, and she was angry because Toby had got up late and kept the rest of the coach tour waiting. I said, 'Nobody minds, everyone likes Toby,' and she said, 'Oh, I dare say. He can charm the birds off the trees, but that's no excuse for bad manners!' I thought of birds roosting on trees, beady-eyed, feathers fluffed against the cold, and then, that Aunt Phoebe looked a bit like a bird herself at that moment, perched on her camel with her legs drawn up, beaky-nosed and ruffled and refusing to be charmed. She was angry because everyone else liked Toby so much more than she did, though except for odd times like this when she showed her true feelings, she acted as if she liked him, calling him 'Toby dear' and buying him presents like that gorgeous burnous. She is quite different from my grandmother who is often sharp with Toby, even rude, sometimes, but loves him really: you can tell by the way she watches him and smiles when he smiles.

Life can be confusing: people not saying what they mean and not meaning what they say. Aunt Phoebe pretended to be glad, in Tunisia, that everyone was so fond of Toby that they didn't mind waiting for him when the coach stopped at old, ruined towns that no one else was much interested to see, but I could tell by the way she sighed and stretched her jaw that she thought they were all very foolish to be so taken in. When he got back to the bus, long after the rest of us were in our seats and fanning ourselves because it was so hot when the bus was still, she would say things like 'You're not the only pebble on the beach, you know!' and give one of those laughs that are meant to take the sting out of unkind remarks but really make them worse because you don't know how to reply to them. Certainly Toby didn't; he always looked bewildered and a bit frightened, even when someone said – and someone always did – that it didn't matter, they didn't mind ...

Everyone was nice to him, on our coach. There was one especially nice old lady who was interested in ruins, too. She and Toby scrambled round together, peering at maps and squinting up at the sun. She was by herself, and I think she would have liked to be friends with Aunt Phoebe and me as well as with Toby, but I had to stop that after I had heard Toby say to her, once when he didn't know I was near, 'My parents couldn't come because my father's in hospital with cancer and going to die.' Of course I was terrified, then, that she would say something to Aunt Phoebe like, 'I'm so sorry about your brother,' so I kept them apart, thinking of questions to ask Aunt Phoebe whenever the old lady was near, and making sure we sat at a table with only three places in the dining-room. She was very easy to put off, this old lady, because she was timid and humble, but since I didn't know who else Toby had been telling lies to, I had to make sure that nobody had a chance to get friendly, and that was quite hard work. I stayed close to Aunt Phoebe and talked all the time and when people smiled at us I looked straight through them. Aunt Phoebe said, 'Are you shy, dear? What a surprise you are, I would never have thought you were a shy little girl!' I said, 'I'm not, either, it's just that I like being on holiday with you, I don't want to bother with these other people,' which sounded so false I was sure she would suspect something, but she didn't seem to: she looked surprised, perhaps, but pleased all the same ...

It's queer, really. Toby doesn't tell lies to me. Perhaps he's shy, and grown-ups frighten him, so he has to think of things to say to interest them. Or make him seem interesting, I'm not sure ...

I think he likes children better than old people; I mean, really likes them, not just to look down on and tease. The children in Tunisia were lovely; little and thin with great, dark, sad eyes. When the coach stopped, there was always a crowd of them, watching from a distance. Some of the people on the bus tried to coax them with money and sweets, but they were nervous as birds, fluttering away when anyone went near. Aunt Phoebe said there had been very few tourists in this part of the desert and we were as strange to them as visitors from Mars would be to us.

But they didn't seem to find Toby strange. Perhaps because he didn't smile at them too much, or say 'How sweet,' or try to take their picture. He just stood still and after a while the children would come and stand round, and touch him, and smile. Wherever we went, this happened: he would stay quiet till they were used to him, and then, when he moved, they followed him, like gulls after a plough. Once, we stopped in a village so that people could take photographs of some baby camels by the road, and Toby disappeared; when the coach was ready to go on, there was still no sign of him. It was too hot to wait in the bus and we stood in a patch of dusty shade by one of the houses, while the driver blew his horn. Aunt Phoebe was looking disgusted under her big straw hat. Then someone said, 'Here comes our Pied Piper,' and there was Toby, coming through a white archway with a crowd of children beside and behind him, hanging on to his hands, his clothes, and I felt so happy, suddenly, that I wanted to cry, because the name was so beautiful and so right. I laughed at the man who had given it and he blinked, as if he was surprised, and said, 'I think this calls for a picture,' and lifted his camera as Toby came towards us, crinkling his eyes up and smiling.

We got back in the coach and even when we were moving it was dreadfully hot, air like dragon's breath and sand blowing in the windows, but I was happy, thinking what Toby and I would do when we were older; how we would travel through the world, Toby the Piper, and me the Piper's Assistant, carrying his books and buying the tickets, and whenever we came to a hot, poor village like that one, we would stop and wait till the little, thin children came running and then we would wipe the flies from their eyes and put ointment on them, and give them food and tell them stories . . .

After we got home, the man sent me a copy of the picture he had taken – I don't know why he sent it to me instead of to Toby, but he did – and I showed it to my mother and told her about the plan I had made. I wanted her to be proud of Toby and not worried all the time about his future. But she laughed in a cold and angry way and said, 'Oh that boy!' Then she looked at me and her eyes seemed to shiver like cracked glass. She said, 'It's all right, Lucy, I'm not cross with you, only with Toby and his childish fancies!' My father said, gently, warningly, 'Maggie . . .' and she looked at him with those cracked eyes and said, 'Charlie, do me a favour, don't encourage the child in her romantic delusions about her brother!'

I said, 'It wasn't Toby's idea, it was mine, and it was a good idea, I'm not a half-wit loon, we can get the money from Oxfam, they'd want to help people doing a job like that! And I'm not romantic, either. Toby doesn't want to work in a stuffy office like a stupid grown-up. I think you're horrible and mean and I'll never tell you anything again as long as I live!'

I ran into the kitchen and stuck my head into the roller towel, banging myself against the back door and howling with rage. After a while she came after me and said, 'You're right, Lucy, I was mean and horrible and I'm sorry, you're a sweet, loyal child.' I knew that wasn't a compliment, just a way of saying I was too young to have much sense about anything, so though I stopped crying and took my head out of the towel, I didn't look at her.

She touched my cheek with one finger and made me turn my head. She said, 'You love Toby, don't you – not asking, or sneering, just making a statement.

I said, 'I don't see what's peculiar about that.'

'Nothing peculiar,' she said. 'I'm just glad you do.'

I felt full; my throat felt full. I said, 'He's the nicest person in this family. He's the nicest in the world.'

She hugged me and said, 'Well, you may be right, at that. Come on chicken, I've said I'm sorry, give us a kiss.'

I did kiss her, though I still felt angry. People shouldn't change so quickly.

Crossing the landing on the way to the bathroom, Lucy heard her mother weeping. She said, 'Charlie, Charlie ...' Her bedroom door was open and Lucy could see her through the hinge; crouched on the bed, the telephone in her hand.

Lucy stood rigid. An hour ago, at bedtime, her mother had sung nonsense songs; played, with each of them in turn, a game of Scissors, Paper, Stone. She had laughed and been happy ...

Now, suddenly, she was laughing again; the kind of laugh that has tears in it, painfully and wonderfully happy at the same time and Lucy knew that nothing terrible had happened after all, but something joyful and unexpected. Her legs, which had been like stone pillars beneath her, felt weak and rubbery with relief.

Her mother said, 'Darling, this is almost too good to be true ... I suppose it's quite *certain*? I mean, there's no possibility that the lab could have made a mistake?'

Lucy held her breath. Not understanding the question, she was transfixed by it; felt her mother's tension; waited, with her mother, for the answer.

'Thank God,' her mother said. 'Oh, I do thank God,' in a voice so solemn and happy that it struck Lucy's heart with awe. She thought, *As if someone cried out on a mountain.*

Her mother said, speaking more quickly and naturally now, though the happiness was still there, running like a bright thread through her words, 'Oh, I know that, I know we're not out of the wood, I do understand that. But it's like – oh, a great weight lifting. Charlie, I know something now – the truth about all those corny old phrases. Faint with relief, drunk with gratitude, I feel it all – it seems so absurd one ever bothered to think of new ways of putting things, all that sweat and labour and one could simply write in clichés all the time and get so much nearer to the truth . . .'

Silence. A long one this time. Then her mother laughed again and said, more gravely, 'Yes, I'm sure it was the right thing to ask Angus. I can't think why we didn't before, he was the obvious person, really. Thank God for some of one's friends, anyway, if not for others – that *bloody* Hugh, I could chop him in pieces and serve him up for dinner! . . . Oh, yes. Yes, I *know*, but I can't help . . . Yes . . . Yes . . . I love you, too . . .'

Lucy moved with speed before the telephone was set down. She waited in the bathroom longer than was necessary before she flushed the pan; then emerged, yawning and rubbing her eyes.

Her mother called, 'Lucy?' and came, smiling, from her room.

Lucy yawned extravagantly.

'What made you wake up?' her mother said, but didn't wait for an answer. 'Something nice has happened,' she said, following Lucy as she trailed, yawning, into the bedroom and climbed into bed. Her mother looked at her, looked round the room, picked up a necklace of glass beads from the dressing-table, ran it through her fingers, sighed, put it down, looked at Lucy again. Her face was shining; her mouth twitched as if she longed to tell a secret.

'What?' Lucy said, abandoning her sleepy act and sitting up in bed.

'Toby is coming home.'

Though this was not quite the momentous announcement her mother's excitement had suggested, Lucy smiled and hugged her knees.

'He's not going abroad, then?'

Her mother looked questioning.

'He wanted his *passport*.'

'Oh. Yes.' Her mother sucked her lower lip. 'Yes,' she said

again, 'well,' and smiled shyly at her daughter. 'The thing is,' she began, and stopped.

Lucy sighed. 'Oh, I'm *sorry*,' her mother said, and sat on the bed. But in spite of her apology, she seemed unwilling – or found it difficult – to go on.

Lucy prompted her. 'When is Toby coming?'

'Tonight, perhaps. At least, I hope tonight.'

'Don't you know?'

'Well. Daddy's gone to fetch him.'

'Have you made his bed?' Lucy asked, but her mother was gazing slantwise at the window in a kind of trance. When Lucy repeated her question and she turned to her, her eyes were full of such happiness it confused Lucy and frightened her a little. There seemed something piteous in it.

'Oh, yes, I'd better make his bed, hadn't I?' her mother said, and smiled. Then she took a piece of the cotton bed-cover, pleated it between her fingers and spread the edge out like a fan. Looking at her handiwork, she said, 'Toby's not well. I thought I'd better tell you before he comes, so you understand. He will need a lot of rest and quiet and we shall all have to help him a great deal and be very patient.'

She seemed to be talking to herself more than to Lucy.

Lucy said, 'Has he got appendicitis?'

Her mother looked startled. 'No, of course not.'

'What has he got then?'

Her mother said impatiently, 'He hasn't *got* anything. It's not like that.'

Lucy's irritation rose to answer her mother's; it was as if some spark ran between them, triggering off an identical reaction. 'I'm not two years old for Christ's sake!' she said, and glared.

But her mother did not glare back. Instead she said, 'I'm sorry,' and then, sensibly but quickly, as though to get something disagreeable over, 'We don't know yet exactly what is wrong. Apparently he can't, or won't, get out of bed, or eat anything, or even talk very much. We think it must be some kind of nervous breakdown.'

Lucy said, 'A girl at school, Leonie Parker. Her father had that. She said he just sat all day and cried and Leonie said it was fantastically funny, but when I went to tea he wasn't crying, just sitting and doing nothing. He didn't look ill to me. Or funny really.'

'I should hope not,' her mother said, with indignant energy, but her eyes had glassed over : she was not interested in Mr Parker.

Lucy said, 'Is Toby crying?'

'I don't know.' Her mother looked helpless. 'I haven't seen him.'

'How do you know, then?'

'Hugh told us. Or rather he told Elsa, and she rang Daddy.'

Lucy was bewildered. So much had gone on behind her back. That telephone conversation alone, with its burden of grief and what seemed almost unbearable joy; beside it, nothing she had been told seemed to carry any weight . . .

She blurted out, 'Why were you angry with Hugh?' remembering, too late, that this gave her away, but after one sharp, questioning look, her mother simply smiled and answered straightforwardly, 'Toby has been doing something he shouldn't and Hugh should have told us.'

'How could he, that would be sneaky,' Lucy said.

'Don't be silly, Hugh's not a *child*.' But her mother frowned, as if perhaps there was something in this answer. Then her brow cleared, as if she had been thinking, and had now made up her mind. She said, 'Toby has been smoking – not ordinary cigarettes, that's bad enough, they give you cancer, as I hope you know – but marijuana. A kind of drug.'

'Hash,' Lucy said.

Her mother stared.

Lucy said kindly, 'We had a lecture at school. At least not our form, the Upper School, and Rosalind, that's the Senior at our lunch table, told us. There's hash and other things that are much worse. You must always say no, like to strange men in cars.'

'I see,' her mother said. 'Why didn't you tell us?'

'I thought you probably knew.'

'Well. Yes.'

'There you are then. You always know things I tell you.'

'I'm sorry.' Her mother spoke quite humbly and sincerely,

but her eyes were shining and abstracted as if she were really thinking about something else altogether. It was just what she had been doing all along, Lucy realized; saying one thing and feeling another. It made no sense: Toby was ill, she said, and yet this happiness shone out of her!

Lucy said, 'Mr Parker had been working too hard,' and her mother looked surprised.

'Well, that's not Toby's problem!' Having laughed as she said this, her expression changed; became doubtful, then solemn. She bent over Lucy, settling her back on the pillows, tucking the sheet round her neck. She said, 'Now, you're not to worry, chicken. Or I'll be sorry I've told you! Perhaps I shouldn't have done, anyway, only I was so glad he was coming home. He'll be all right, once he's safely back, and we're all here to look after him, so you can just go to sleep, don't worry and go to sleep...'

The room was dusky and quiet; her mother's voice purry and gentle. Drowning must be like this, Lucy thought; being in warm water and holding on to a rope and not wanting, really, to let go, but the water so warm round you, and feeling so tired...'

Her mother kissed her on the cheek; the springs creaked as she stood up.

Lucy said, 'What is wrong with Toby?'

Her mother laughed. Lightly and softly, like snow drifting. She said, 'Stop worrying, darling. Go to sleep, didn't I tell you?'

Mr Parker sat in an armchair by the window while we had tea at the table. He had bright eyes with clear whites and darting, brown centres. When I first sat down he looked at me and laughed, a high laugh, like a horse neighing; but then he seemed to forget me and just stared out of the window. Mrs Parker gave him a plate of little sandwiches and he went on looking out of the window while he ate them, cramming them into his mouth with the palm of his hand, his fingers spread out and covering his nose. After a bit he stopped eating and began to pick up the rest of the sandwiches (very slowly, one by one) and drop them on the carpet. Although Mrs Parker could see what he was doing, she took no notice, just went on pouring tea and offering things to eat and asking questions about school.

When the telephone rang, she went to answer it, and called from the hall, 'Leonie, dear, it's for you,' and Leonie got up and went out, but Mrs Parker didn't come back. Mr Parker got up from his chair and went over to the television and turned it on. He looked at me while he did this. The sound came on, very loud, so that Leonie had to come and shut the door. I was shut in with Mr Parker. I went on eating, cutting my cake into little squares to make it last, but in the end I had to look up, and he was standing on the other side of the table and smiling like a wolf, with long, white teeth. I said, 'Do you want some cake, Mr Parker?' and he smiled and said, in a voice that was meant to be like mine, 'Do you want some cake?' I felt something shoot down inside me, down my throat into my stomach, like a thin sword of ice. He said, 'Cake, cake, cake, Mr Parker,' and picked it up in his hand (the whole cake, only three slices cut out of it) and began to crumble it up very slowly, his thick, pale fingers sinking into it. For a minute I was afraid, as if his hands had closed on the back of my neck, and then he said, 'What did I do that for?' and looked so surprised, like Greg when he had done something he didn't know was naughty, that I wanted to laugh. I even felt pleased and excited because I could see, quite suddenly, that it was something I would like to do, pick up a whole cake and mash it up with my fingers and watch someone's face while I did it. Then he said in an ordinary voice, 'I have to be careful, you know, they're trying to poison me, my leech of a wife and my bitch of a daughter,' and I was frightened again, not because he believed this but because I knew he believed it. I thought, 'I know how he feels, crumbling cakes and poisoning. I can see into his world,' and it made me so afraid that my hands began to shake.

I said, 'Please Mr Parker, do sit down and be good,' and then Leonie came in and said, 'Oh Dad, for God's sake!' and went up to him and took him back to his chair by the window. She gave him a push in the chest and he sat down, stiff arms and legs sticking out like a teddy bear's and she sighed and winked at me and began to pick the lumps of cake off the carpet. Mrs Parker came to the door and looked in and made a tchk, tchk noise and went away and came back again, this time with a dustpan and brush, and laughed silkily, and said, 'Well, Leonie, my chickadee, if Lucy has finished her tea . . .'

We went out at once and ran upstairs to Leonie's room. I put my hand over my mouth to stop the laughter spilling out, but once we had shut the door we fell on her bed, and I giggled and giggled and said, 'Oh Leonie, your father . . .'

'Crazy,' she said, 'Crazy as a bloody coot,' throwing herself about the bed and laughing and laughing. But I saw her eyes, still and watching above her laughing mouth, and I knew what she was thinking. 'What will she say to the others tomorrow, at school?'

I said, 'Oh, I think he's funny, he's fantastic,' and then, 'You ought to see my grandfather, I've never told anyone, it's a dead secret, but he's mad too, mad as a bloody hatter, he won't let you pull the chain when you've been to the toilet,' and she shrieked and wrapped her arms round me and hugged me and we rolled backwards and forwards together. I said, 'Even if what you've done is serious, you just have to leave it there, floating ...'

She screamed out then, as if this was the funniest thing in the world, and we both went on for a long time in this way, quietening down now and then to moaning and hiccuping, then one of us would remember something, Leonie about her Dad or me about my grandfather, such as, 'He walks about in his pyjamas with his Thing hanging out,' and we would both start off again, sometimes a real, new, bubbling-up of laughter, sometimes half-pretence, until our stomachs felt sore. And in the end, saving us – saving me anyway, because it was becoming more and more of an effort to laugh louder than Leonie – her mother came to the door and rapped sharply and said, 'Now, that's enough, girls,' rolling the r in girls in such a fantastic way that we roared out louder than ever. Then she flung the door open and said, out of a red face swollen up and tight as a balloon, 'Leonie, you are behaving outrageously, what dreadful behaviour for a Sunday afternoon!' She went out and Leonie pulled faces at the closed door, rolling her eyes and wobbling her head and hanging her tongue out of one side of her mouth. I said, 'You're mad too, loony, loony, lunatic,' and I rolled on my stomach, kicking my legs and stuffing a pillow in my mouth, but only to show her I was still laughing ...

Toby wasn't mad. In fact, he had hardly changed at all, or only a little, in small ways. He still stayed in bed late, but now he got up at once when his mother called him and came downstairs and sat in a chair, not doing anything, not even reading, just smiling quickly and brightly when anyone spoke to him. He didn't seem bored; it was more as if he were waiting, all the time, for someone to tell him what to do, and once she was used to this it seemed to Lucy that he was much the same as he had always been.

She thought her parents had changed more. They were very quiet when Toby was in the room, speaking not much louder than whispers and opening and closing doors very gently, as if noise might worry him. Her father came home early almost every day and as soon as he got in he would look at her mother as if, without saying anything, he was asking a question. Then he would pour drinks and play chess with Toby, both of them sitting very still and quiet on either side of the low table, and sometimes her mother would come from the kitchen where she was getting supper, and stand behind Toby and look at the game and then at her father, as if, in her turn, she was asking a question, and he would look up at her and give a small, tight smile, in answer.

Her father always won the chess games, though it seemed to Lucy that quite a lot of the time he was trying very hard not to. This surprised her, because her father liked to win, even if it was only Snakes and Ladders: he saw no point, he often said, in being a good loser. But he was being a bad winner now, Lucy thought: when he had won he said things like, 'That was a sneaky move of mine I'm afraid, old man,' speaking regretfully, not pleased and smiling; and then, one evening, he said, 'You know I'm not feeling up to chess, too much mental strain after a hard day, what about draughts instead?' and sent Lucy upstairs to look for the pieces in the toy box.

He won at draughts, too. Toby didn't mind (had never minded about games, this wasn't new) but her father minded for him. He sat, pleating his lower lip between his thumb and forefinger and watching Toby as if he were willing him to make the right move. He said several times, 'No, no Toby, think again,' and the last time he said it, Toby sighed and said, 'It's no good Dad, I can't,' and sat back in his chair and closed his eyes. Her father waited, watching him; then he said, 'Well, it's a hot night...' He smiled, though with a sigh behind the smile, collected the pieces and closed the board. When her mother came in, he said, 'Supper ready?' and she shook her head, looking first at him, then at the closed draught board, then at Toby.

Toby said, not very loudly, but with a sudden, crisp distinctiveness, 'It's like a shutter coming down. Or a guillotine,' and Lucy saw her mother's eyes widen and shine suddenly, with a curious, dry brightness. She took a step towards Toby and half-lifted her hand as if to touch him, his hair, or his shoulder. For a minute her hand hovered, trembling a little like a bird on a current of air; then it fell to her side, curling into a tight, closed fist: Lucy, watching, saw the knuckles whiten.

Her father said, 'What about another drink in that case?' and her mother laughed, apparently merrily, and said, 'Well, why not, while we're waiting?'

A lot of the time it seemed to Lucy that her parents were waiting, like Toby, for someone to tell them what to do. After supper they sat on the terrace with Toby between them, watching the bats swerve and slip in the darkening air, waiting for someone to say something. But when one did speak, the other would often say, 'I'm sorry, I didn't quite catch...' and lean forward with polite attentiveness, like a shy guest at a dinner party.

When they were alone, they talked more. Mumble, mumble in the kitchen, or in their bedroom late at night: lying awake on the other side of the wall, Lucy could hear their voices droning on like summer bees. And in the daytime, her mother talked on the telephone, to her own mother, to Aunt Phoebe, but mostly to her friend, Iris, who had a new, solemn way of asking for her if Lucy answered when she rang, saying, 'Can I speak to Mrs Flower, please?' – as if she had forgotten Lucy's name, or even her existence! It made Lucy feel very odd, but more lonely than resentful. She would have liked to listen in to these conversations, but her mother was always careful to say, 'Put the phone down,' when she took the call on the bedroom extension. Sometimes she said, 'Lucy,' or 'dear', but not very often.

Even Elsa, who had always been so friendly and jolly, behaved in the same dismissing way. She turned up one morning at the beginning of the school holidays (wearing a full, orange skirt and a white, gipsy blouse with a rent on one shoulder) and when Lucy opened the door she said, simply, 'Is Maggie in?' and came on, past Lucy, not even smiling at her, and went straight to the kitchen where her mother was peeling potatoes. She said, 'My poor darling, I had to come,' and closed the door, shutting Lucy out. Lucy listened for a minute, but their voices were too soft to hear. She went on to the terrace where Greg was sitting, finishing a jigsaw puzzle for Toby who had gone to sleep in a deck-chair. Lucy watched him, carefully sorting out the difficult pieces of blue sky; then she kicked the table leg in a mixture of pain and rage and said, 'Am I *invisible*, a ghost, or something?'

Greg looked up and regarded her steadily through his thick, fair lashes for a full minute before he sighed and said, 'If you were a ghost, you couldn't have jogged my puzzle. Why don't you go away?'

A man came. *He* remembered Lucy. He said, 'Hallo, you're Lucy, aren't you, do you remember me?' He was a tall man, handsome as an actor, with a heavy forehead like a white cliff hanging over pale, tea-coloured eyes that were large and clear as mirrors. Like a cat's eyes: Lucy, looking into them and trying to trace a stir of memory (herself smaller, a flash of gold in a cave) thought of a cat, crouching still with folded paws and great, glassy eyes, reflecting every moving leaf, every bird ...

She said, 'You're Uncle Angus, Hermia's Daddy,' and he smiled, opening a full-lipped, red mouth to show gold-capped teeth and said, 'Smart girl!'

Her mother said, 'You're quite memorable, Angus.' She spoke sedately, as if this was not altogether a compliment, but her eyes flickered and smiled at him and Lucy thought she looked prettier than usual: she had made up her eyes and was wearing her new, green dress. She smiled at Lucy and said, 'Darling, would you like to take Greg down to the shop and buy ice-cream for supper?'

'Can't Toby go, it's his turn to do something?' Lucy said, remembering more about Uncle Angus: a hot afternoon like this one, and, while the other grown-ups had talked and laughed, he had fixed up the sprinkler so that she and Greg could keep cool. They had taken off their clothes and run in and out of the sweet, sparkling water, and then he had picked up the hose and chased them with it: jets of ice and Greg squealing, and her hair, cold and tickling down her back ...

She said, 'I had long hair then,' and felt excited, talking to this big, handsome man who had chased her with a hose when she was a naked little girl. She half-feared, half-hoped, he would remember. 'Of course that was a long time ago when I was young,' she said, and when he nodded and looked at her gravely and directly, so that she could see herself in the pale, brown glass of his eyes, she felt the blood rise in her cheeks and tossed her head and laughed, to distract attention from it.

'I'm afraid Toby can't go because Angus has come especially to see him. So run along, there's a good child, and don't argue.'

Her mother spoke cheerfully and carelessly, but it was clear to Lucy that she had deliberately intended to humiliate and reduce her in front of Angus; to drive her away, so she could keep him to herself.

She said, 'Come to see Toby, I *bet*!' and then, a quick glance suggesting more damaging criticism, 'You've got lipstick on your teeth, it looks quite repulsive if you really want to know!'

She turned on her heel, shouted, 'Greg, come *on*,' and marched away. Foolishly trying to make amends, her mother called, 'Good-bye, darlings,' but Lucy neither answered, nor turned her head. Neither did Greg, which was surprising: even when injured (and he had not been!) he was usually a most punctilious child. He said nothing until they reached the main road. Then, when they paused at the crossing, he put his small, rough hand in hers and said, suddenly and clearly, 'You and I are quite probably adopted, don't you think?'

Lucy shouted with amusement, partly at the absurdity of the idea, partly at the old-fashioned way of talking (the pedantic, baby scholar) which was peculiarly his. But he did not seem to mind her laughter, or even being told he was 'a funny little boy.' When she asked him how he ever thought of such a thing – 'such a *wicked* thing,' she added, with abrupt and fearful emphasis – he simply shrugged his shoulders and even gently smiled, as if what she said was irrelevant and unimportant: she was entitled to her opinion, but he knew what he knew, had spoken as he always spoke, out of a calm, inner certainty that Lucy respected because she knew she lacked it. Once they had crossed the main road and he was running ahead of her, skipping and humming, she felt an uneasy chill, as if the sun had clouded over . . .

Lingering in the High Street, gazing at her ghostly reflection in shop windows, and later on at supper, watching Toby across the table, she drew up a line of argument. She and Greg were fair and Toby, dark. He was not like them at all and he was marked, not they: he had Aunt Phoebe's nose. And it was him they loved: everything that had happened and was happening now – her mother saying sharply, 'Lucy, do eat up, we don't want to sit here all night,' when Toby's food lay untouched upon his plate – so underlined this simple fact that she was amazed she had not seen it before. Or perhaps she had seen, and concealed it, from shame?

She felt ashamed. How could she have expected anything, how *dared* she, even? They who owed her nothing, rightly had nothing for her: it was apparent in their every word, their every look! It was Toby who wanted nothing from them, who sat like a dead tree in his chair, who got everything, unasked: their smiles, their concern, their love. His birthright . . .

He went early to bed. Both his parents – *his* not hers! – went to say good night to him. Greg went to sleep unkissed. Lucy undressed, deliberately not cleaning her teeth. When her mother finally came, the last light had almost gone; a tree at the window dark against an only slightly paler sky. Her mother was a shadow bending over her, tucking her up perfunctorily; her voice sounded tired and hoarse. (Across the landing Lucy could hear her father's, still talking to Toby.) Her mother said that Aunt Phoebe was taking her out for the day tomorrow, wasn't that nice? Lucy did not stoop to answer this, and after a pause, her mother continued, hesitantly; she was sorry if Lucy would rather not go and that it had been arranged without asking her, but 'poor Toby' was to go into hospital tomorrow and it would, really, be easier if Lucy and Greg . . . At this point, Lucy sighed loudly; her mother retaliated, 'Don't sulk, *please*,' and when this, too, produced no response, went on more gently, if a little wearily, to say that it was nothing to worry about, Toby wasn't seriously ill, they just wanted him in hospital for a day or so to make a few tests. Lucy was not – really not – to worry.

Lucy said, through gritted teeth, 'I'm not worried. Haven't you just said there's nothing to worry *about*?'

'Fuss, fuss, fuss, just because Toby's probably got to have his appendix out,' she said to Aunt Phoebe in the Natural History Museum. This was not an entertainment she cared for, nor did the prospect of the Science Museum (so that Greg could press buttons) cheer her more. She had hoped for a film, but, 'We can't waste this lovely day in a frowsty old cinema, can we?' had been Aung Phoebe's cry. The day was, in Lucy's opinion, more wasted on dead, stuffed birds, but she did not make this point: uneasiness blunted her tongue.

Aunt Phoebe gave her a sharp look. 'Is that what your mother told you? I thought...' She stopped and frowned.

What she did not say, Lucy's guilt supplied: *I thought you loved your brother!* She said, 'But what else could it be?' and looked away.

'*Oh*,' Greg cried, 'a kittiwake!' and turned with glowing face.

'Goodness,' Aunt Phoebe said. 'You look just like your father when you screw your eyes up like that!' She touched his head lightly, with love, and smiled at Lucy. 'Doesn't he just!' She spoke with determined gaiety, as if willing Lucy's recognition, her answering smile.

Lucy nodded and felt an uncomfortable thrill. Of course this was the truth! She was the only outcast! Greg had known it too (the resemblance to his father had been remarked upon before, Lucy remembered) but true to his nature, had included himself out of kindness. Certainly he did not dispute his Aunt's statement now; merely smiled, very sweetly, before giving a complete and accurate account of the mating and nesting habits of the kittiwake.

'My, you *do* know a lot!' Aunt Phoebe said, again smiling brightly at Lucy who could only reply, heavily, 'But you know he knows about birds!'

As of course her Aunt did know; hadn't she arranged the day purely for her nephew's pleasure? Lucy recognized this with resignation, not resentment: in the circumstances, it was natural she should favour her proper, blood relation, give him everything he liked. The Museums, the picnic in the park, the boat on the Serpentine, the drive back with the car roof down (alone with Lucy, Aunt Phoebe would have kept it up, to spare her fluttering, draped hat), the special supper with his favourite foods: cold salmon, strawberries, thick, yellow cream ...

He ate and ate. Replete, *stuffed*, he sat back on a small, gilt-legged sofa, belched delicately and beamed his thanks. 'This has been the best day of my life, Aunt Phoebe. I wish I could stay with you!'

Aunt Phoebe gazed fondly. 'Well, perhaps ... oh, look, mucky child, you've got cream on your shirt. Lucy,' – this without a look – 'could you get my handkerchief out of my bag? On the hall table.'

Sickened, Lucy was glad to escape. The crocodile bag stood open on a polished, consul table beneath an Italian gilt mirror. She looked at herself: framed in carved gilt, her sullen, un-loved face ... In the handbag, the clean lawn handkerchief, the gold compact, the lipstick holder studded with mock rubies, the skin wallet, neatly lined with new, pound notes. Lucy took one, scowling, but without guilt – she was owed *something*, after all – folded it, and put it in the pocket of her dress.

In the sitting-room, Aunt Phoebe sat beside her nephew and wiped his shirt. She said, 'You know, pet, if you'd like to stay for a bit, you can. You can have the little bed in the study, and Lucy ...' – she turned, smiling – 'I mean, both of you must stay, of course!'

'I don't want to,' Lucy said.

'But dear ...'

'Thank you very much, all the same,' Lucy went on hardily, watching her Aunt's expression and discovering, with pleasure, that politeness could be used as a weapon. 'But I'm sure Greg can, if he wants to.'

'I do want to.' On the little sofa, Greg snuggled closer to his Aunt. 'Are *you* going to adopt me now?' he said.

'I don't mind being alone,' Lucy said, though in fact she listened for noises, was aware of the ticking of clocks. Still, her parents were always home before it was quite dark; the evening visiting hour at the hospital was seven to eight and they were usually back by nine. They suggested she ask a friend to stay. 'I have no friends,' Lucy said, glorying in this martyred lie, even when it evoked no response.

Not that her parents were uncaring; indeed, they were often especially kind, but in a gentle, impersonal way as if she were not their daughter, but a shy child who had come to live with them. They were different with each other, too; considerate and careful, no banging doors, no sudden storms. In this unfamiliar climate Lucy felt disorientated: it was as if they had all sailed from some safe, if choppy harbour, and were drifting in a flat, tired calm in some quite foreign sea.

She was not actively unhappy, not even bored. Her parents were afraid she might be. Her father said, 'Why don't you go to the cinema, you can always take someone with you,' and offered extra pocket-money. 'I don't need money,' Lucy said, which was true: what she wanted, she took – from her mother's bag, the cleaning woman's purse, her father's change, scattered on his dressing-chest. She had stolen casually before (odd pennies, the occasional chocolate bar) but now her activities were more methodical and wider-ranging. She did not want the things she took: lipsticks and toilet-water she did not use, Woolworth jewellery she did not wear – what she enjoyed was the strategy. Dedicated and addicted as an old-time general planning an ambush, she haunted the supermarkets, noting the lie of the land, the safest times, though safety was only a factor in so far as it reflected her skill: not to be caught, was merely a matter of pride...

She felt no guilt. Her parents had never told her not to steal. She knew it would never occur to them that she might do so, and felt a certain tender respect for their innocence. Only Toby, who knew what she was capable of, might guess what she was up to.

She tried not to think about Toby. It shamed her that she did not know what was happening to him. She ought to know, she was old enough, and it seemed that her parents thought she did know, because they talked about him in front of her and yet she still did not understand. They talked of 'tests' and 'treatment'. Odd words recurred, some like 'Dr Maud,' and 'schizoid' spoken with a kind of fear, and others, 'insulin', 'therapy' and 'E.C.T.' – like D.D.T., she supposed, a kind of antiseptic – more easily and straightforwardly.

'We'll take you to see him when he's a bit better,' her mother said. 'The treatment he's having makes him rather tired but he'll be better soon. He sent you his love.'

She nodded. This evening, she was lying on the sofa, reading. She fixed her eyes on her book, wriggled into a more comfortable position, turned a page.

'You do understand,' her father said, quite sharply. 'You do understand what's wrong with him?'

This direct question was an affront. She said, without raising her eyes, 'Of course I do, I'm not a child.'

But her heart began to beat hard in her chest. She was afraid he was going to tell her, and she was afraid, because whatever it was, frightened *him*. Her *father* was afraid! She had known this all along, she thought now : perhaps it was why she had not listened properly when they talked, why she had never asked, straight out . . .

Her father said, 'Well, then . . .'

Her mother said, 'Charlie!'

He said, 'She might at least look *up* . . .'

Lucy unfolded her legs, slid off the sofa, and walked from the room without looking at either of them, her open book pressed hard against her chest. She walked to the back door, which stood open to the night. It was very still, no wind, the the trees at the end of the garden and on the far side of the river seemed especially hard and black and distinct. She heard crickets, and her parents' voices through the open window; her father's angry, her mother's softer, tireder. She moved closer, along the terrace.

Her father was saying, '. . . he's her *brother*. You've always said she's so fond of him! That's why it was important she should stay, you said, so she shouldn't feel shut out! But she's not once even *asked*!'

'She's a child,' her mother said. 'Charlie, can't you remember?'

Hearing her mother plead for her, made Lucy cry. Sobs came from deep in her chest and seemed to tear their way through her throat until they burst from her mouth, like bubbles. She stumbled to the other end of the terrace and jumped off, to hide behind the coal-house. She crouched there, fighting those painful sobs, her knees drawn up to her chin. It was not fair! She could never be like Greg and do and say the right thing! She loved as much as he did, felt as much – more, even – and yet it was as if something malign worked in her, twisting and distorting the true feelings of her heart and making her clumsy and graceless so that everyone despised her! 'I hate myself,' she said aloud, and at once, the expression of this quite genuine emotion enfeebled it and made it falsely dramatic. 'I wish I was dead,' she whined, and collapsed sideways, her head against the coal bunker, and hoped that someone would come and find her in this despairing position.

Her father did. He gathered her up in his arms and carried her – heaved, rather; she was too big to lift easily – back on to the terrace. He sat on the edge and held her, uncomfortably. He said, mouth against her ear, bristles pricking her cheek, 'Sweetheart, you're having a rotten time. I know it's unavoidable, but I'm sorry. Perhaps you shouldn't be so much on your own. Wouldn't you, really, rather be with Greg and Phoebe?'

She shook her head and pulled away, to look at him. His eyes were dark pools of jelly.

'Well, would you like Phoebe to bring Greg home and stay *here*?'

She shook her head more violently.

'A friend, then? There must be someone. Jennifer?' When they were smaller, she had been their baby-sitter; a thin girl, with catarrh.

'Christ, no!'

'Well,' he said, sighing. 'Well, I don't know.' He held her elbows and looked at her. Enough light came from the house to show his face which seemed cracked with hundreds of small lines, like a very old piece of china. 'What about Gran? I don't know if she could come, but she might. Just for a bit, till we're out of the wood.'

She thought of a wood, dark and menacing; trees snapping above her. Once, a long time ago, she had been lost in the wood round her grandmother's house, and Gran had come to find her . . .

'*Would* you like that?' His voice was thin, on the edge of something; exhaustion or despair. She knew he had nothing else to offer her and nodded, dumbly.

Chapter Eight

'Why didn't you ask me before?' Sara said. 'If I'd known you were leaving that poor child alone, day after day! Oh I know you think Lucy's so sensible, so old for her age, but it suits you to think that, doesn't it? That's your way, other people have to fit in with your idea of them, be as you want them to be...'

She has always been the same, seen people as objects to be manipulated; her husband, her family, all grist to her mill in one way or another. That first book – oh, we were all disguised up to a point, she took the trouble to change our names, but it was a shameful thing, all those wicked lies set down for all to see! That young woman, having an affair with her husband's best friend, all that hopping in and out of bed and no one knowing which child belonged to whom! And these were supposed to be good people, let me say, not cheats and liars! 'All I can say is,' I said to her, 'I hope your children never read this book.' She thought I meant the sex and laughed, and I was too ashamed to explain what had really shocked me, which wasn't that – now I am old, I enjoy in books what I don't get in bed – but the cruel mock she had made of her father and me!

The heroine had been damaged by her upbringing. The sins of the fathers – that was the moral! The capricious, domineering mother, domineering because she was frigid – what a thing for a girl to set down about her own mother! – and her weak, clever husband, trapped by her jealousy of his intellect, tethered, like a young horse in poor pasture, wasting his life and his energy on affairs with other women that she allowed him to have because they did not threaten her, take him out of her sphere as another kind of success might have done. She drove his gentle, scholarly friends away, sneered at his ambitions, and only let him off the leash from time to time to keep him quiet, the way you might loose a dog to run to a bitch in the park.

That was the point, of course: his little girl had been deprived of a real father with a proper pride in his manhood!

Oh, he had women; a cinema usherette, a plain little school-mistress he met at the library. It amused him to see me jealous of such poor little creatures; it was the only way he could hurt me. And I was jealous. He was a marvellous lover. Even when we were quite old, I could hardly bear him to touch me in public: his hand burned me ...

That book was so unjust! Even making the mother a rich woman – as if she could not bring herself to admit her own poor beginnings! I daresay what I did was nothing to write home about, but it put food in her belly and shoes on her feet! And it was all I could do, what lay to hand: I had no training, only my two hands and my strong back and my hope of a better life for her.

She would deny this of course, would say I was jealous of her chances; that from my prison I envied her freedom. 'You were glad when Toby was born because I was trapped, too,' she said once, but that was a lie, a lie! Of course I was glad and proud – my first grandchild! – but I was sorry she had been caught so soon; caged, before she had time to test her young wings, free in the wide air. But if I had said so, she would have denied that as well; claimed that it was my ambition that was thwarted, not hers, that all she had ever wanted was a husband and a baby and a ram-shackle old house she couldn't keep clean ...

I said, 'You could have left school at fifteen if all you wanted was babies,' and she said, 'I wouldn't have met Charlie if I had, would I?' and gave me a triumphant look as if this was a real argument, instead of being simply frivolous and silly, to suggest that all those years of hard work and sacrifice were justified be-cause she had met Charlie at Oxford! She said, 'Education isn't wasted, mother, because you don't immediately turn it into pounds, shillings and pence,' – implying that this was how I, with my narrow, bourgeois mind would naturally look at it!

Of course she knew she was trapped, but she put the words into my mouth because she couldn't bear to say them herself. Too proud and too obstinate. I said, 'We had no choice in my day, we had to accept the babies as they came along and make the best of it, but I thought things were different now,' and she looked at me blankly as if she really didn't know what I was talking about. Almost everything I said at that time was received with the same blank, incredulous stare as if to say, 'What do you know about the way people like us run our lives, what do you know about anything?'

I knew one thing. She said, 'First Phoebe, now you! She thinks Charlie is too young to be a father. As if I had sprung it on him! So ridiculous, when anyone can see he's like a dog with two tails!

Ever since Hugh was born, he's longed for a son of his own!' She laughed, but I was sorry for her because I could see the truth she didn't see. There's no harm in wanting to follow the people you admire, no harm in Charlie wanting a boy because his best friend had one, I suppose, but it made my blood boil to think my poor girl had been used in this way. She thought she knew so much, but she was so innocent, really, not only of other people's motives, but of her own. She was a clever girl but uncertain of herself: it had been a long climb up from our greengrocer's shop and she was still dazzled by what she had found on the heights. I was sure she loved Charlie, but I was equally sure she had been impressed by his nice accent, his confident manners, and felt it was an easy way to better herself. Oh, I know it is a common mistake to see the present in terms of the past, but at the time the baby was born I hardly knew Charlie – there had been a coolness between Margaret and me because of the hasty marriage – and so it was natural for me to remember that I had been taken in by my husband in just that way.

People pretend nowadays that class isn't important, but my generation recognize barriers still. The first time I met Charlie was after he wrote to ask if we would come to London to visit them because Margaret was pregnant and the doctor did not want her to travel. (Not one word from her!) When we arrived, his friends the Honeys were there, invited, presumably, to oil the wheels of this meeting. ('Roy and Elsa have just dropped in,' Margaret said – as if she thought I'd been born yesterday!) Charlie and Roy could not have been more charming, attentive to me and listening to everything my husband said with polite, if slightly bewildered expressions, but the tone of their voices and their graceful ease of manner placed them, as if they had worn a badge. Beside them, Margaret seemed timid and circumspect, like a shy little girl anxious to do the right thing. I thought, 'Why, she has made the same mistake that I made,' and my heart ached for her.

Not that Mrs Honey was out of the top drawer, exactly. Loud and common was how I set her down. Margaret told me later that she was very rich, but that didn't alter my opinion. I knew the type – preening herself, showing off, quite sure every man in the room was mad with lust for her. She even flirted with my poor old husband, closing her fingers on his arm as she spoke to him and encouraging him to make a fool of himself – eyes gleaming and ropy old hands longing to touch her. Miss Cock Tease we would have called her when I was young (and no harm, really: why shouldn't women try to get the fun they want out of men, it's the other way round often enough?) but she made my girl look prim and dull and I resented that. It was unfair, too, because although she was handsome in a blowsy way, she was such a slut, with holes in her stockings and grubby straps showing. And her poor, pale little boy looked as if he could do with a good wash, even though he had a Nanny. 'I hope you're not going to follow that Elsa's example and hand your baby over to another woman to look after,' I said to Margaret, because I could see she thought everything Charlie's friends did was wonderful. She said, 'I wouldn't dream of it; Charlie and I think it's quite wrong to abandon a young child to a stranger, it can do untold harm,' and then added, flaring up – whatever you say about Margaret, she was always a loyal child –

'Why do you say "thåt Elsa"? Didn't you like her?'

'Oh, I've nothing against her personally,' I said, which was true. I wouldn't have trusted her further than I could throw her – it was Number One for her, first middle and last; anyone could see that with their eyes closed – but I rather enjoyed her swashbuckling, actress's manner, as if she was always on stage and the rest of the world her audience. As far as I was concerned, the only thing I disliked about her was the way she treated me as if I was an old, old friend and we had been intimate all our lives long.

Elsa pressed her face against Sara's, first on one side, then the other. 'Dear Mrs Evans, how long *is* it? You don't look a day older.'

'Unfortunately I feel it,' Sara said. 'Are you keeping well?'

She had walked from the station to save Margaret the trouble of fetching her and now, finding her sitting with Mrs Honey, idle on the sunny lawn, this thoughtfulness seemed absurd. She disengaged herself from Elsa, kissed her daughter's colder cheek and said, 'Where's Lucy?'

'Shopping. It's all she seems to want to do at the moment. Very useful for me, of course, but she seems to enjoy it, too. Really!' Margaret spoke the last word with laughing emphasis, looking at her mother's face.

'Oh, when you don't have to do it!' Sara said. 'That's always the way!'

The younger women sprawled on the grass in their summer dresses; Sara sat in a deck-chair in her best suit and felt heavy and rumpled and old. She looked at Elsa – creamy skin, tawny hair, green eyes like glass in the sun – and thought, *Why she must be older now than I was when I first met her.*

Margaret said, 'Why didn't you ring from the station? Lugging that heavy case!'

'I still have the use of my legs. And I thought you might be working.'

'I have been. Not writing – I can't at the moment. But cleaning out Toby's room. Elsa's been helping me.'

A mattress and several blankets were spread about the lawn, airing in the sun.

'Unusually energetic for you,' Sara said.

Margaret lifted herself on one elbow and plucked at the grass. Selecting a blade, she put it between her lips and said, 'Well, don't be shocked now, but you might as well know. Toby's had lice.' She spat out the sucked grass and gave a little, excited crow.

'Is that funny?' Sara asked, shocked only by the laugh.

'In the circumstances.' Margaret sat up, hugging her knees, shaking back her hair. She spoke quickly with occasional small laughs, grimaces, glances at her mother. 'I rang the hospital yesterday to say I'd be a bit late, and the nurse who answered said Toby wasn't allowed to come to the 'phone, he had to stay in bed. Naturally I asked her why and she said she couldn't tell me, I would have to speak to the doctors when I came. The gloomiest voice, *sepulchral!* You can imagine how I felt! I got in the car and drove there like a bat out of hell and there he *was*, sitting up in bed, playing Monopoly with a nurse! Quite cheerful. *Smiling.* "I've got lice, Mum!" I sat down and burst out laughing, of course. The nurse looked so astonished!'

'I daresay she was,' Sara said.

'Well,' Margaret said. 'After what I'd been expecting.'

'And what was that?' Sara wanted to ask, but Elsa's presence inhibited her. She was lying on her side, stretched out like a cat in the sun. Silky hair in her armpits, cracked varnish on her toenails, one sandal mended with string...

Margaret said, 'They think they must have been lurking in an old pair of jeans or something. He's been up and dressed these last few days. But the Sister said I should ask the local authorities to fumigate his bedding at home, just in case. Then I happened to speak to Elsa ...'

'Came to the right place *there*,' Elsa said, rolling on to her back and blinking up at the sky. 'You name it, I've had it. Lice, anyway. Hugh brought the little buggers home from a fruit-picking camp, a couple of years ago. So of course, innocent boob that I am, I ring the Public Health Department. "Good morning," I say politely, "I want to be de-loused." "I *beg* your pardon, Madam?" "I've got lice," I say, "I'm not complaining really, but you get tired of uninvited guests after a while, you know how it is." Deathly hush at the other end. "You deal with this sort of thing, don't you?" I say. "Lice, bedbugs." "Oh, I'm afraid not, Madam, we don't have the facilities in this district." "What do people do then?" say I. *Long pause ... !*' Elsa paused herself, stood up, brushing her skirt, and smiled directly at Sara. 'Do you know what he said then? "*We don't have that class of person round here.*"'

'How very extraordinary,' Sara said. She would have liked to show amusement, as she was clearly expected to, but her daughter's burst of laughter, loud and simulated, froze something in her. She said, with a polite, baffled smile, 'But why didn't you just get some D.D.T. from the chemist?'

It was Elsa's turn to laugh. She stood there, hands on hips, eyes full of light, and laughing ...

'It's a relief to have something to laugh about,' Margaret said later, standing in the doorway of the guest-room while her mother unpinned her hat in front of the glass. She spoke reproachfully, as if it was dull-witted of her mother not to appreciate this simple, human impulse. Sara, watching her face in the mirror, thought she looked thinner and older, but the stir of pity she felt then was overlaid by embarrassment and a kind of shame that her daughter should meet this crisis in her life so childishly. *Giggling*, she thought, *like a silly girl*, and carefully replaced the long pins in her hat before setting it down on the dressing-table and turning round, her face stiff and unsmiling.

'I can see that,' she said. 'Though if Toby were my son, I'd not want this story spread around. For his sake, if not for my own. And your friend Elsa is not the sort to keep it to herself, I hope you realize.'

'Oh, for heaven's sake, it's not *important*!' An impatient movement, a little sigh. 'Though as it happens, it was Charlie who told her. He thought she would help me to cope. Not that I couldn't manage, really, but I've been a bit tired. I'm afraid the house is in rather a muddle . . .'

'Well, you've had a lot on your plate,' Sara conceded. But her own room was clean, the furniture polished, a bowl of roses on the bedside table. She said in a grumbling voice, 'You know I could have made my own bed, no need to roll out the red carpet for me.'

'Don't be silly, mother,' Margaret said, half-frantically, and Sara bowed her head, acknowledging her stupidity, and worse, her helplessness. *Why have I come?* she thought, *What use am I?* She found herself searching for something to say as if this was a social occasion and felt, suddenly, tired and heavy, as if her limbs were made of lead. 'However did he pick up lice?' was all she could think to say, finally.

Margaret shrugged her shoulders. 'Apparently it's quite common in the mentally ill. They're incapable of taking normal care of themselves, you know that.'

'I'm afraid I don't,' Sara said. She felt so deeply tired, she wished she could lie down on the bed and close her eyes. Perhaps it had been foolish to walk from the station, in this heat. She said, bracing herself, 'Margaret, I'm sorry, but you haven't really told me. What is wrong with Toby?'

She was not, she realized later, much wiser. Lying awake in the hot, summer night – no blanket, only a sheet above her – words and phrases flashed before her eyes; luridly, illuminating nothing about them, like advertisement signs in the darkness. Schizophrenic. Not schizophrenic. Schizophrenoform. *Is he mad then, are you telling me Toby's mad?* No, mother! (Oh, those incredulous, raised eyebrows!) Dr Maud diagnosed schizophrenia, but Angus disagrees. A temporary, psychotic state, induced by drugs . . .

It was as if they were speaking in a foreign language; the odd words she knew leapt out and she seized on them gratefully, but was aware she had not gathered their full import. They were trying to explain to her, but it was like being shown some dark, strange place with only a candle for guidance. She was humbly afraid of demanding more light, of asking too many questions, not from shame at her ignorance but from fear of causing pain.

What drugs? Oh, Pot. L.S.D. Nothing else, thankfully, though we did have a heroin scare. And the hallucigens are not addictive, only produce a psychological dependence. There's no reason why he shouldn't recover completely, and in a way it may be a good thing we've had this shake-up! Angus says . . .

Margaret's face! Shining with hope and energy one minute – *always a brave child*, Sara thought – closed with fear the next. Speaking so confusedly; staccato sentences, painful little jokes. *Hysteria of course* – but it chilled Sara's sympathy to watch her, waving her hands like a foreigner, giving short, breathless trills of laughter. As if she were falling apart.

Charlie, too, chilled her. Watching Margaret, he was quiet, almost immobile, none of his usual face-pulling – but there was something wrong in his stillness. As if he were on guard, at bay . . . *Against Margaret*, Sara realized, and this was a shock. She could accept her own judgement of her daughter (hysterical, disintegrating), but that Charlie might judge her too, as harshly, frightened her.

He had said, in a steady, reserved voice, 'Angus is very anxious to comfort you. You must watch out for that. We can't know for some time how much permanent damage has been done.'

And Margaret turning on him, 'Charlie, you're impossible. Any normal man would be glad Angus is so hopeful!'

'I am glad, if it's true. If he can be brought through this, I shall be happier than I've ever been in my life. But I won't subscribe to phoney optimism. There are too many things we haven't had an answer to yet, and false hope is worse than no hope at all, can't you see that?'

'God give me patience,' Margaret said, rolling her eyes upwards.

They had quarrelled in front of Sara before, but harmlessly, half in fun. She had thought, *like quarrelling puppies.* Now, helplessly watching, listening, she sensed something new : vindictiveness, like a naked sword between them. Of course, she thought, they're bound to blame themselves, hit out at each other.

She had said, anxious only to help them, spare them, not at that moment thinking of Toby at all, or no more than she would have thought of any sad young life, wasted and suffering, 'If Toby has been taking these drugs and making himself ill, then it's not your fault, that's some comfort!'

And Margaret had turned on her. 'What comfort? He's made his own bed? Do you think we're so shallow we'd cheer ourselves like that? Even if it were true, and if course it isn't! The drugs are irrelevant, really – why did he *take* them, that's the point! We must have failed him terribly...'

'My dear girl, what are you talking about? The things that boy has had from you! Expensive schools, books, holidays – everything he could possibly want he's been given. Too much, I sometimes thought, I don't mind telling you now!'

Honestly bewildered, Sara had felt that on this point at least she was entitled to speak – and had been first startled, then shrivelled, by the contempt in her daughter's eyes.

'Those aren't the important things! Surely even you can see that! Children need more from their parents than shoes on their feet. Iris says ...'

'Oh, that Iris!' Sara had said, rallying, and was encouraged by an answering gleam in Charlie's eye. 'Talk, talk – talk the hind leg off a donkey, that one, give her half a chance and she'll make you think black's white.'

'*All right.*' Long, hissing, exasperated sigh. 'Leave Iris out of it. But please try to understand, mother. Toby must have felt rejected in some way and I daresay we knew it, subconsciously, otherwise we wouldn't have loaded him with what you choose to see as all these *rich gifts* ...'

'There's no need to use that tone to me,' Sara would have said then, though mildly, but was forestalled by Charlie getting up and saying – growling, rather – on his way to the door, 'I'm sorry but I can't stand this, it's so bloody *pointless.*' He went out, the front door slammed; afrer a brief pause they heard the car start up, gears grind, the engine cough, stagger, splutter into a roar . . .

'Well,' Margaret said. 'Well!' She lifted her shoulders in a theatrical gesture and grinned at her mother.

Seeing this smile, half-shamed, half-angry, Sara wanted to say, 'Don't be hurt. He's only gone because he couldn't see what to say or do. It's always harder for a man because he can't wail and cry and ease himself that way. So don't be angry or hurt, don't waste your strength, keep it for what's coming, because you'll need every ounce you've got and more besides, more than you've ever dreamed of needing. Ther'll come a point when you'll think, *I can't stand any more*, but you'll have to, because you won't have any choice, so don't wear yourself out now, fighting with Charlie, it's only yourself you're fighting, after all . . .'

But then Margaret had said, 'Damn Charlie. I'm sorry, mother. I must apologize for him!' And hearing her speak in this no more than irritated voice, as if all that mattered were Charlie's clumsy social behaviour, and seeing her get up and pour herself another whisky when she had already had enough this evening, in Sara's opinion, what she actually said was, 'I can't say I blame him, the way you were going on! Thrashing about, attacking everyone in sight! Oh, I know you're upset, and with reason, but Charlie's not your whipping-boy. He thinks the world of Toby, you know that, but he can't keep things up at your pitch when he's tired after a long day's work. You can work when it suits you, but he can't and his job's your bread and butter, you should remember that and study him a bit more. A man can only take so much . . .'

'Spare me the platitudes, please,' Margaret had said.

Lying awake, hearing that bitter, dry, hurt voice speak again in her mind, Sara groaned softly in the darkness. She had meant to help, wanted to help – or had she? Surely if all she had wanted was to console her daughter, then instinct would have told her what to do, what to say? Was there something else, then, some contrary, spiteful demon working within her and distorting her intention? Oh, it was all so confused! Easy comfort – *poor Margaret, dry your eyes, have another whisky, I don't know how Charlie could treat you so* – was no use. No kindness, anyway. When you saw a child playing with fire, you snatched it away and slapped it! Watching Margaret with Charlie, hearing the fury in her voice and the cold withdrawal in his, she had been so afraid! Trouble can bring people together, but it can also drive them apart . . .

She had wanted to comfort Margaret; she had also wanted to warn her, gently and sensibly. She was her mother, surely she could do that? But there was such a distance between them and everything she could think to say seemed to separate them further; each time she spoke, Margaret's replying voice was a little harder and drier. In the end, Sara had pretended tiredness, yawned, said, well, it had been a long day and she had always been an early-bedder . . .

But Margaret had not followed her. After midnight now, and she was still moving about downstairs. Sara shifted in the bed, seeking cooler comfort for her aching legs, staring into the darkness. Why wasn't Charlie home? *An accident?*

The telephone rang. She lay still, listening to that peremptory sound, terrifying in the silent night; to Margaret's voice answering, speaking briefly. She heard her laugh and thought, *Thank God!* Then the *ting* as the phone went down; The click of sandals, coming up the stairs.

Should she call out? What more natural? *Who was that, dear, Charlie?* But she felt a curious reticence. As if *she* were the child lying here, afraid her mother would be angry to find her still awake . . .

Her door stood a little ajar. Sara coughed and turned in the bed, creaking the bedsprings.

Margaret pushed the door open, flinging a shaft of light across the room.

'Was that Charlie?' Sara said.

'No. Elsa. Apparently Charlie landed up there and had a bit too much to drink. Too much to drive home. Elsa's tucked him up for the night.'

Margaret's voice was brightly conversational. This was a stranger, talking.

Sara said, 'That's a relief, I suppose. I must say, I was a bit worried.'

'Well, you can go to sleep now,' Margaret said.

'You too.' Sara hesitated. 'Sleep well, dear.'

'I'll try,' Margaret said, and laughed.

Sara thought, *what can I say*? 'Well, maybe it's a good thing he had that little flare-up. It often clears the air.'

'Who's being Dr Pangloss now?' Margaret said, and softly closed the door.

The hospital was in a part of London Sara knew. Shabby streets, a belching power-station; the mean backside of the city.

'It's a very good hospital,' Margaret said. 'We're very lucky. Of course Angus pulled strings.'

'What a place!' Sara said. The grimy façade made her heart thump. It was turreted like a castle, or a prison.

In the entrance hall, a thin boy with a straggly, red beard was arguing with the porter; a big man, planting his impassive, benevolent bulk between him and the door. The boy began to cry, weakly.

'Trying to get out for a fix,' Margaret said in a breezy undertone, drawing Sara past, down the corridor. 'No locked wards here, but it's an intensive care unit, so there's plenty of staff.'

She smiled at her mother, looking young, Sara thought, and incongruously festive in a red linen dress with an armoury of clinking gold chains round her neck. Since Toby had been ill, she had bought a lot of new clothes. It passed the time, she had explained as they drove to the hospital – occupying the whole journey, it seemed, with an exact and careful description of each purchase. Sara had been bewildered: she did not know this girl, talking with the absorbed attention of some young city typist about a grey, worsted dress with buttoned sleeves, a black and silver trouser suit. Not one word about Toby.

Now, stopping outside a closed door, she said abruptly, 'You may find him a bit odd and forgetful because of the E.C.T. but that's *all*. Not mad. Not pretending to be Napoleon!'

She giggled, sharply.

Sara said, 'E.C.T.?'

'Electro-Convulsive Therapy. It often causes a temporary loss of memory.'

'Will he know us?' Sara asked in a hushed voice.

'Of course!' Again that sharp, feverish giggle, like an excited, green girl at a party. 'Don't worry, mother, there's nothing to worry *about*. Just behave naturally!'

She pushed open the door and marched through it, into a large, square ward, full of dusty sunlight. Sara, following, tried not to think *this is a mental hospital*, and walked deliberately, eyes carefully averted from the beds.

Margaret said, 'Here we are, darling,' in a carrying, clearly enunciated voice, as if she were making a public announcement. As they approached the bed, a blonde girl stood up, rather awkwardly. She wore a wide, enveloping cloak and completely screened Toby.

'You remember Iris, Mother?' Margaret said. 'This is her daughter, Hermia.'

'There's certainly a likeness,' Sara said, not quite thinking it. She looked with pleasure at the young, open, generous face.

'I'm fatter, though,' Hermia said, as if this was something she felt compelled to draw attention to.

'Personally, I like to see a girl with a bit of flesh on her bones,' Sara said.

Hermia blushed. She said, 'Well. I was just going.'

Margaret said brightly, 'Thank you for visiting this dreadful boy!'

'Oh, it's no trouble.' Hermia smiled round, vaguely. She met Sara's eyes and for a moment looked straight into them before smiling properly, very sweetly and fully. She said, 'Toby's talked about you,' and blushed again. She said, 'Well, 'Bye all.'

When she was half-way across the ward, Toby said, 'Bye Hermia,' but too softly for her to hear. Sara brought herself too look at him and was surprised to find him unchanged. Paler, perhaps – though he had never had much colour – certainly thinner, beakier. She thought, *Phoebe's nose*! She touched his hand and said, 'Well, this is a fine thing!'

Margaret perched on the end of the bed, legs tucked girlishly beneath her. She said, 'Well, what's been happening, darling? Tell us the local scandal!' Her eyes darted round the ward.

The bed next to Toby's was occupied by a fat man who lay, fully dressed, on his side; his visitor, a small, grey-faced woman in glasses, sat on a chair beside him. The man did not once look at her, seeming to stare, resentfully and moodily at nothing, but her eyes, enlarged and swimming behind the lenses of her spectacles, never left his face. She had a dry, pale mouth that wrinkled rhythmically, as if drawn by a thread.

Leaning forward, Margaret whispered, 'He never speaks to her! She just sits there, all the time, poor soul, and he doesn't even look at her.'

Sara frowned: although there was some distance between the beds, the whisper seemed too loud.

Margaret said, to Toby, 'Does he *ever* talk? Did he go to the party?'

'Party?' Sara said, wonderingly.

Margaret laughed, as if firing a gun. 'Oh, didn't you know, they have an endless round of jollity here! Never a dull moment. Parties, pretty nurses – isn't that true, darling? Was it fun, last night?'

Sara felt disgusted by her daughter's cheerful, social manner. She felt her hands begin to tremble and folded them in her lap.

Toby said, 'Coffee and team games, Gran. A sort of nuts social.'

'Ssh! Darling!' Eyes sparkling in mock alarm, Margaret put her finger to her lips.

Toby gave a gentle, exhausted smile, and lay back on the pillows, watching his mother.

'I expect it was quite an experience, though,' she said. 'In its *way*, I mean!' She laughed with nervous vigour; then composed her face into almost frowning solemnity and went on in a lower, urgent tone, 'Not one you might have chosen, maybe, but that's no reason for not making use of it! In fact, what you *ought* to do, is to keep a notebook, jot down things as they strike you! Descriptions of people, what they say, the backgrounds they come from. It's an opportunity, really, all these people, all different, but all at some crisis in their lives so it's easier to see beneath the surface. The bearded boy, for example, the one you were playing cards with the other night. What makes *him* tick?'

'Heroin makes him tick,' Toby said.

'Well. Perhaps that's not so ...' She looked vaguely about her. 'That nice looking African, then. The one writing away near the door.'

'He's a nut,' Toby said. 'A roaring nut. He thinks he's Tolstoy. I don't see what's so interesting about a roaring nut.'

'Perhaps you don't *now*! That's why the notebook! Even something that doesn't seem important at the moment may come in one day.'

'I'm not likely to be a writer, Mum,' Toby said. He sounded amused and tender. Like a kindly but resigned old man, Sara thought.

'Darling, how can you possibly know?' Margaret cried with a bright and rippling smile, and suddenly it seemed to Sara that her daughter's face was more pathetic in its eager hopefulness than any of the sadder faces in the beds around them. Listening to her she felt, on one level, moved and pitying – this was the music of grief – and on another, deeply and critically uncomfortable: really, Margaret's voice was much too loud, all these other people listening!

When she had gone to speak to the Sister, she said to Toby, 'I must say, your mother does run on, doesn't she?'

For a moment, it seemed to Sara that his face was a mask through which his eyes looked, trapped and pleading in a way that frightened her: they seemed to be asking something from her that she did not know how to give. Then he smiled, a crooked, shy, willing smile that reminded Sara of her dead father, and said, 'It's all right, Gran. No one listens to anyone else here.'

On the way home, stopping at a traffic light, Margaret said, 'Did you see the burn marks on his forehead?' and began to cry, suddenly, as if a dam had broken; a cascade, a bursting waterfall. The light changed to green and she slammed the car into gear and started off jerkily, swerving out of her lane. A horn sounded behind them.

Sara said, 'Stop in a lay-by. You can't drive like this.'

'Oh, it's all right, d'you think I usually sing all the way home?' Margaret said, her words bubbling absurdly through her tearful mouth but with such a bitter force behind them that Sara was confused and frightened. There seemed no natural way to behave. Her instinct was to take her daughter in her arms, but she was driving. And anything she said was likely to be taken amiss. She sat with folded hands and said nothing.

After a little, the car slowed down. Margaret sniffed noisily, like a child, and said, 'I know you think I ought to grin and bear it, but I can't. I know I've got to, but I can't. Not yet, anyway.'

Her voice, though still belligerent, was calmer. She glanced sideways at her mother with a damp, apologetic smile. Sara smiled back, but felt unable to speak.

'The thing is,' Margaret went on after a minute, 'there are so many possibilities to face. And nothing we can do can alter any of them. There is *nothing* we can do, in fact, and that's one of the hardest things to bear. Oh, it's a kind of selfishness, I suppose, or pride, but it just about beats everything for pain. To know whatever is going to happen to him is already decided, quite probably, and all we can do is wait and try to be ready for what it's going to *be*.'

She sounded emotionless now, almost cold; not as if she were beyond feeling but had for the moment dispensed with it, the better to see what lay in front of her.

She said, 'Several things. One is, of course, that he'll get quite better, quite soon, and be able to do whatever he wants to do and even be, in a way, better and stronger because he will have learned something from this experience. This *is* a possibility and there's no point in discounting it just because it seems too good to hope for. Or that he'll get almost well again, maybe even completely in the end, but it'll be very slow, take years even, and he'll be very crushed for a long time. I suppose it would be more realistic to assume that. You can't expect any-one to rise up at once and push over mountains after some-thing like this ... I thought he was better today. I mean once or twice *he* was there, *Toby*, not some stranger lying in that bed! I can't tell you how marvellous that is!'

She smiled with a kind of shy exultation and Sara wanted to reach out and touch her hand but held still deliberately: it seemed a moment for stillness, for waiting and listening.

Margaret's voice changed, became a fraction lighter and

harder; it was as if she erected a barricade of glass, offering protection against wind and weather but concealing nothing. 'And of course, to go further down the scale, it is possible that he will never build up again, that his personality has been so denuded, so *thinned down*, that there is nothing to build *on*. In that case, at best, he will be able to do something, earn his living, even if in some humbler way than we'd hoped for, and at worst he won't, he'll never be able to support himself, or only in a protective environment. At home, or some kind of institution . . .'

Sara saw iron gates; a high wall topped with broken glass. 'Oh no . . .' she could not help saying.

'Well . . . You see, Angus may be over hopeful. Charlie's afraid of that. Toby may be a schizophrenic. It's the last imaginable thing, but we have to try and imagine it because we may have to face it and learn to survive it, and we may as well start learning now. People do survive things, worse things than this, though *that's* no comfort to know you can come to bear anything . . .' She stopped and cleared her throat, but when she spoke again her voice was hoarse. 'In fact I'm beginning to see that I am going to be able to bear it, *whatever* it is, and that frightens me . . . Because when I've got to that stage, it will be a kind of healing, I suppose, but a kind of death, too, the end of something. No more live, growing flesh, just scar tissue. Numb. If he doesn't recover and I come to accept that and find I can live with it without kicking and screaming like a stuck pig, then it won't be anything to be proud of, not a lesson learned but something *forgotten*, the beginning of death. As if he were dead inside me . . .'

Her voice faltered. She gave a short, sad laugh and said, 'I suppose you think that sounds stupid.'

'No,' Sara said. In fact, she had listened with a growing respect and pride. Her daughter was not falling apart, disintegrating; if she had appeared to be, it was only the kind of convulsion that precedes growth. She wanted to help her, to cry out, *But don't you see? It's death we have to learn to live with, it is something to be proud of, to have learned that* . . . But she was shy of saying this, in case it seemed banal. She said, 'Of course it's not stupid. It's never stupid, to say what you feel . . .'

Margaret was frowning. They were stopped in a traffic jam now, and she had begun to fidget, craning her neck to see beyond the solid line of waiting cars. She said, 'If it is what I feel, not just what I think I ought to! However honest you try to be, once you start putting something like this into words, it becomes less real at once because you've changed it, if only a little, re-arranged it in some more acceptable form, *used* it in some way...'

Sara was surprised: it had seemed to her that her daughter had been speaking of what she genuinely thought and felt and she had honoured her for it. She said, 'Well that's true of most people, but I expect you feel it a bit more, being a writer; I daresay you'll put it all into a book some day,' not meaning a criticism by this, intending, indeed a measure of comfort, but Margaret reddened as if she had accused her of something.

'That's the damnable *thing*,' she said almost savagely, putting the car into gear and edging forward. 'I find myself standing back and watching, and thinking how I could use this – oh, not often, only for a minute or two, now and again, but it still makes me sick with myself...'

'I don't see why. People have to write about what they know,' Sara said, finding within herself no echo of past resentment, merely a mild astonishment that she had not more clearly understood this before.

'Because it wouldn't be the truth, for one thing. Couldn't be. I don't know anything, I don't know what I really feel, let alone what Toby feels, or Charlie ... That's bad enough, but what really makes me sick is that the idea of writing about it should even cross my mind! For God's sake, this is something *real* that's happening, not some rotten play I've been given a ringside seat to...'

She fumbled in her handbag that lay open on the seat between them and blew her nose loudly. Sara wondered if she should say, 'Well, at least you could ask Charlie what *he* feels, instead of battling with the poor man all the time,' seizing on this practical point as being the only one on which she might have something useful to offer; but the traffic jam had cleared, making this a bad moment, and then she thought that it would probably be the wrong thing to do anyway: if she spoke up for

Charlie it would sound as if she blamed her daughter. Which she did *not*, she suddenly realized. She was fond of Charlie and sorry he was getting a rough ride just now, but it was Margaret whose side she was on; blood was thicker than water. *She needs me*, she thought, delighted and amazed that this should be so, remembering how old and unwanted and useless she had felt for so long; Margaret always acting in front of her, never presenting her true face, never seeming to want anything from her ... Oh, she had been so bitterly resentful, seeing her own sorrows rejected, her painfully earned understanding, but now, in this last half hour, it was as if something had been cleared away, some cluttered rubble of old, irrelevant emotions, leaving a clean purity of feeling that flowed into, and filled, every corner of her being. *I must help her*, she cried inwardly, and then, *but how?* Words were no use: they were hollow and empty, old envelopes for other people to stuff their own interpretations in. If she said, *Don't worry, dear, I'm sure Toby is not as ill as you fear*, Margaret would be scornful and would be right to be, because she would not be speaking from knowledge but out of this sudden, transforming feeling of lightness and hope which had nothing to do with Toby at all. No. Only practical things were open to her ...

As they drove off the motorway and turned into the winding, dusty-hedged road to the river, she said, 'Margaret dear, would you like me to make pancackes for supper? The rest of that chicken we had last night, and mushrooms and herbs. And I thought that tomorrow I might make one of my cassoulets. Easy and cheap, and Charlie likes it ...'

Chapter Nine

Mushrooms like cushions, cushiony smooth, a bit sticky, but stickier on their black undersides; smelling different on top from below, and, mixed with the special mushroom smell, warm and strawy. Horse manure, Toby said, mushrooms grew best in fields with horses ... This was a long time ago, on holiday in a farmhouse where there was a goose behind the gate, hissing and curving its wicked neck, and Lucy was afraid that one day the gate would be open and Toby wouldn't be there ... She was so small that she still wet the bed, dreaming of water, and waking in the warm, damp dark to strangeness, a strange room with a grey square of window, and her mother coming and lifting her and saying. 'Ssh Lucy, ssh Darling.' She had been Lucy then, so it must have been after she was adopted, but it was the earliest thing she could remember. However hard she tried, she couldn't remember anything before that ...

Watching her grandmother slice mushrooms (shop ones: pink underneath and not so big and flat) Lucy said, 'What was I like, when I was a baby?'

Her grandmother chopped, one strong, spotted hand flat on the back of the knife blade; green parsley and pink and white mushrooms. She said, 'A cartload of monkeys. Into everything, chatter, chatter all day long.'

'Not when I was a girl, I didn't mean. When I was a baby, in my pram.'

'Much like any other baby, I expect.'

'How much did I weigh, when I was born?'

'Goodness me, I can't remember. Ask your mother.'

'She doesn't remember. She only remembers how much Toby weighed. Not me, or Greg.'

'Well, he was the first, you know, that's always the way. You take things easier as you get older, less fuss and tarra-diddle. Your mother treated Toby as if he were as fragile as an egg, and your father wasn't much better.'

Lucy said, 'Did you ever know anyone who was adopted, Gran?'

Toby said, 'Dad.'

'Yes?' Charlie leaned forward. They had been sitting in silence for half an hour.

'Oh. Nothing.' Toby's throat moved as he swallowed.

'You can tell me,' Charlie said.

The boy looked at him – shyly or slyly? 'Hermia's having a baby.'

Charlie sat still. For a moment he could not encompass this. Then, as it sank into his mind – oozed, he thought, like a stone through mud – slow ripples spread. How long has he known this? Is it true? Or something else to frighten us? Oh, not deliberately, not unkindly, but from some deep need to involve us, to keep us close to his side. He thought wearily, *But I'm here, we both always have been, doesn't he know that?* He remembered something he had read somewhere, *A schizophrenic can never have enough love*, and fear pierced him like a sword. But Angus was sure this wasn't true; he had to trust Angus. This was only an interlude, it would not recur. Toby was basically sane. He had to hang on to that . . .

He said, clearing his throat, frowning, pleating his upper lip between thumb and forefinger. 'Is she sure?'

'Yes.'

'Is it yours?' Speaking carefully, calmly, to hide embarrassment.

Toby smiled flickeringly. Pride, shyness, terror? Charlie could not determine. Perhaps all three.

He looked at his son. Last Christmas Eve, after they had dressed the tree and wrapped the presents, he had visited his sleeping children, wearing his red dressing-gown, cotton-wool stuck on his chin. Maggie giggling behind him as the landing creaked, hissing, 'No, that's Greg's stocking, you fool, the one with the trumpet . . .'

Lucy's room, Greg's, then Toby's door. Maggie giggling again, 'Ssh, don't wake him!' And Charlie, stumbling over his dressing-gown cord . . . Looking back at that playful scene, he felt deeply humiliated, as if it had been acted in public. What a ridiculous, shameful charade! The full-grown young man in the bed, and fond papa, creeping in with elaborate, traditional care to hang, by a string loop to the end of his bed, an old ski-ing sock containing three monogrammed handkerchiefs and a bottle of after-shave lotion. Contraceptives would have been more to the point he thought, and said sharply, 'Do her parents know?'

Toby shook his head. His lower lip trembled.

'You must have been out of your mind!' Charlie said – and caught his breath.

'Oh *Dad*,' Toby said, and began to cry, tears spurting sideways from his slitted eyes.

'Oh God,' Charlie said.

'I don't know what to do,' Toby said.

He rolled on his side and hid his face in the pillow. Charlie was conscious of eyes on his back. Though they had been talking softly, whispering almost, this was a public ward. He refrained from looking round, feeling first helpless, then bitterly resentful. *All these bloody loonies*, he thought, *what is my son doing here* – and then pushed out everything except his weeping child. Sitting on the edge of the high, hard bed, he heaved at Toby until he had his hands beneath his shoulders, was embracing him, the drooping head pressed awkwardly against his arm. Holding him like this, he thought how thin he was, even though he had put on weight since he had been in hospital. He had always been thin, of course; he had often come home to find Maggie in tears because he wouldn't eat, pushing a spoon at him as he sat in his high chair, turning away his closed, determined mouth ... A determined, solemn little boy, rather solitary, perhaps, but he had grown out of that when he went to school as Charlie had known he would; grew, in fact, into the kind of son any man would have been proud of, sensitive and gentle, but ambitious and bright and quick ... *A royal child*, Charlie thought, *these filthy drugs*, feeling the weight of anger and love as a burden that was almost too heavy to bear. He eased one hand free and stroked the wet, bristly cheek of his grown son. He said, 'Darling, don't cry.'

Toby gave a convulsive hiccup that made him leap like a salmon in his father's arms. Charlie released him and he rolled on to his back, blinking, eyelashes spangled with tears, like dew. Charlie took the clean handkerchief from his shirt wrist and wiped his eyes. Toby sniffed noisily and said, 'Hermia's not frightened, or anything.'

'That's something, I suppose.' Charlie did not want to consider Hermia. He said, 'Does she want to get married?' and was surprised to hear his voice sounding ironic and dry, like a lawyer's.

Toby shook his head. 'I'm hardly much of a prospect. But it's not that. She has some kind of romantic idea...' He smiled shyly. 'I think she's been reading a novel about an unmarried mother.'

'Has she, indeed!' Charlie said.

Toby said, 'I don't know what I can say to Angus. I find it hard to talk to him anyway.'

Charlie said grimly, 'Well, you have a gripping topic now.' It seemed unfortunate timing; or an unfortunate combination of circumstances. The seducer in the hospital bed and the wronged father ... Perhaps Angus would be spurred on, now he had a vested interest in Toby's recovery. Charlie thought. *I must not laugh about this.* He pressed his hands palms together between his knees and frowned impressively. 'Angus is hardly likely to set about one of his own patients. So don't worry about that. I'll talk to him. Or your mother will.'

Toby said, 'She hasn't told her parents yet.'

Charlie thought. *I shall be a grandfather.* He squeezed his hands between his knees and looked down a precipice.

He said, 'Well, she'll have to, won't she? How pregnant is she?' He thought of a silly joke – *Oh, only a little bit pregnant* – and grimaced nervously.

'Six weeks and five days,' Toby said. 'She's been sick.'

'I see.' Charlie released his hands, sighed, scratched the side of his nose. 'Well, I suppose we can't do anything till she's told them.' And what could they do then? Oh God, this was a farcical situation. He wanted to pick his son up and rush from the hospital, running through dark streets, holding him ... He said, 'Look, I haven't quite hoisted this in. Nor have you, I expect. You're in no condition. But don't let it press you down too much. The heavens won't fall, I promise you. The important thing is to get well, you concentrate on that . . .'

He spoke encouragingly, firmly, but was aware of hollowness, of papering over cracks. And Toby's eyes had gone beyond him . . .

Elsa was standing at the end of the bed. Hair loose and flowing, arms full of flowers and fruit, she looked like a goddess of plenty. 'Well, me old son of a gun,' she said.

Lucy's grandmother said, 'I only ever knew one woman who adopted a baby and that was one of my neighbours. She kept it a dead secret, pretended it was hers, fattened herself out with a pillow, and then went off to her mother's and came home with the baby. He was the spitting image of her and I daresay she'd have got away with it if his real mother hadn't asked for him back. They can do that, up to three months. Well, I'd no idea, she'd taken *me* in – but one day I was going past her house and I saw the blinds were down. So I knocked and went in and there she was, weeping and wailing, and it all came out. She said, "I don't know what I shall do! Except for my husband, everyone thought he was mine! Even my mother – when I went to her, I pretended I'd come straight from hospital!" I was shocked, I can tell you, such silly lies and deception, but then I thought that was unkind : some people can't help setting store by trivial things. So I made her a cup of tea and said, "Well, what you can do is say he's ill and gone to hospital, and a bit later on you can say he has died!" And do you know, that comforted her; she dried her eyes and drank her tea and said, "I can't thank you enough, Mrs Evans, I was at my wit's end." So that's what she did – put it about that the baby had some rare stomach complaint and trotted off every afternoon, regular as clockwork, just as if she was off to visit him! She kept this up quite some time; weeks, I think – I remember wondering if perhaps she couldn't bear to announce he had died, even though he had gone from her life and so was dead to her, in a way. Then one evening she came in and said the adoption society had offered her another baby, and what was she to do? She couldn't pretend this one was hers, not so soon. Oh, she was in such a state! Happy and scared at the same time – it was hard to tell which was first in her mind, the baby or the neighbours! I lost my patience with her. I said, "Are you really sure you want this baby?" and she stepped back as if I had hit her and said, "I ache for him, Mrs Evans, but I love him too much to want him set down as different." And I was ashamed then – it seemed it was me, not her, who was shallow and silly. I said, "What's the new baby like?" and she said, "A bigger baby than poor little Tom, and different colouring. I think he's going to be more of a copper nob." I said, "Well, that's a pity, but never mind; as long as he's bigger, that's the main thing. You bring him home and brazen it out and tell everyone this is your Tom, back from hospital." "Do you really think it'll work?" she said, but she was beginning to smile and her eyes were shining ... And it did work, you know; she wheeled out this great, fat baby with a mop of red hair, and all people said when they looked in the pram was, "Goodness, hasn't he grown!" The funny thing was, this one was a bit like her husband. Something about the eyes. I remarked on the likeness one day and she said, "Yes, I see what you mean, but the red hair comes from my side; my father was ginger, you know." I laughed, but she looked at me very straight and cold and after that she hardly spoke to me again. She'd nod and say good-morning if we met in the street but that was all; she even stopped coming into the shop. They moved away some months later, to be nearer her husband's job she said, but he worked at the power station and that was only a short bus ride away from where she lived now! She wanted to get away from me, that was the truth of it! Not that I'd have given her away by one word or one look, but I can see she would never have been comfortable with me next door, knowing he was another woman's boy. I know some people would say it doesn't matter, there's no difference as long as you love the child, but not to my mind, there's no substitute for your own flesh and blood ...'

'Did you really think he seemed better?' Charlie asked, sitting in Elsa's car.

'Can't you see it?' She smiled, as if with some secret amuse-ment and switched on the radio; syrupy music enveloped them.

'We're so close to him. Other people can judge better.' Charlie raised his voice a little. He ached for reassurance. 'It's nice of you to visit him. I didn't know you had been.'

'Oh, I do good by stealth. Only a couple of times, in fact, just to take sweeties and fags. Where can I drop you? I'm driving out later, but I want to go to Chelsea first.'

'Anywhere,' Charlie said. He had been going back to the office. He didn't want to go back to the office. He didn't want to go home. He couldn't explain this. He didn't want to have to explain anything.

Elsa's eyebrows were raised. He wondered why she was going to her house in Chelsea. An assignation? He yawned, cracking his jaw. 'Any tube station.'

'Don't be stupid,' Elsa said crisply.

Charlie felt as if he were groping through fog. Aching-eyed and so tired. He wished he could crawl into a hole and sleep. Nothing seemed to be of any importance.'

'Where do you want to *go*?' Elsa said. She sounded as if she were laughing.

'I don't really know,' Charlie said.

There had been a tart who lived in their block of flats, on the same floor. She had a lined, pretty face; plump, short body, thin legs. The boy, Charlie, travelling up in the lift with her, grew faint with her scent; was riveted by the wiry black hairs, flattened by her stockings against the backs of her calves. He had fantasies of climbing the fire escape to peer through her window and catching her, not naked, but in her underclothes. Sometimes he lingered outside the door, hoping she would come out, half-dressed, take in the milk or the papers. He wrote a poem, 'To My Mistress with the Withered Thighs'. Once he went to her flat to take some mail that had been delivered to their flat by mistake and she had invited him in. She was wearing a pale blue satin gown that had fallen apart at the neck, showing her crêpey cleavage and the top halves of large, pale breasts, bulging over her tight brassière. When she moved, he saw the red mark where its edge had dug into her. He had thought that when she released them her breasts would burst out and swell up, slowly and monstrously, like very soft, down cushions when pressure is removed. He had never seen a woman's nipples: he imagined them dark and puckered, like the end of a balloon. And lower down, dark, crinkly hair would conceal a hole like a cavern.

... She asked him if he would like a coke and a biscuit and he followed her through the living-room to the kitchen. The flat smelt of dust and unemptied ash trays, of cats, and of her scent, which was spicy and sharp; the curtains were closed and in the greenish, filtered light, the animal sleaziness, both of her and her surrounding lair, was more powerfully evocative of sex than anything he had ever encountered. Or was ever to encounter again. It was as if an offer had been made, that Saturday morning when he was thirteen years old; a promise of something mysterious and feral that had never been fulfilled ...

Elsa said, 'Draw the curtains if you don't want to be had up for indecent exposure.'

He tugged, disturbing dust. He coughed and said, 'Time you spring-cleaned.'

She said, 'How domestic!' Lying on her back, ankles crossed, breasts flattened out; head turned on the pillow, laughing.

He said, 'You'll catch cold.'

Her legs were long and tapering, a bit loose at the top of the thighs. A tawny tuft, a white, scarred belly, a navel like a secret eye. He picked up the eiderdown and covered her.

She said, 'I think I'll probably sell this house, anyway.'

'I never understood why you kept it on.'

'Tax relief for entertaining foreigners. Roy's house is too far out to qualify. Rates, ground rent, cleaning.'

'Cleaning?'

'So my accountant says. Really, I suppose I kept it on for Hugh. A nice little pad in London.'

Charlie thought of Hugh, who had paid rent for the basement. Did the accountant know that? He began to put on his clothes, trying not to appear in a hurry, and caught sight of himself in the wardrobe mirror. A stocky man, in baggy underpants. He pulled on his trousers, dragged his shirt over his head, bursting off a button. He grovelled on the floor to find it. There was fluff on the carpet. He sneezed and said, 'What time does Hugh get in, usually?'

She laughed, shaking the bed. 'Poor old Charlie! Didn't you know? Hugh's in Turkey.'

'No. I didn't know that. You might have told me.' He thought, *Poor old Charlie, good for a laugh*. Standing in front of the mirror, he frowned hideously at his reflection as he tied his tie. 'He's not been at the B.B.C. long enough for a holiday, surely?'

'Oh, he packed that in. They didn't make him Director-General immediately.'

'So what's he going to do?'

'Come into the firm, I think. Heir Apparent is about the only role that would really suit him. But it'll be on my terms, not his!'

'I believe you,' Charlie said. But wondered who would win.

'He doesn't yet. He's gone off to Turkey to think it over.'

'When's he coming back?'

'When he's thought it over, I suppose.'

'I see.'

Charlie combed his hair with his fingers; licked his thumb and smoothed down an eyebrow that stuck out like a prawn's whisker. He felt empty, gutted. He thought, *How soon can I decently go home?*

He said, 'I hope he's sensible. Doesn't try to pick up any drugs, I mean. I'm told that in Istanbul every third peddler is a copper's nark.'

Elsa said, in a tone of pure amazement, 'Hugh doesn't take drugs.' She laughed. Charlie could see her in the mirror, laughing at him. 'You thought – just because Toby did!'

Charlie thought, *I must take this in*. Hugh didn't take drugs. Presumably one believed Elsa. Hugh didn't take drugs, but he had stood by and watched Toby . . .

He said, very slowly, 'It seemed a reasonable assumption. Or an excuse, perhaps . . .'

Elsa said, 'He wasn't Toby's nursemaid!' She pushed the eiderdown aside and stood up, stretching her arms above her head, smiling at him.

She said, 'Oh, come *off* it, Charlie! What should he have done? What should *I*, for that matter? Said naughty, naughty, and run to his Mummy and Daddy? It wouldn't have stopped him, only worried you.'

Charlie said, 'Did Hugh start him off?'

Elsa stared at him; then sat down on the bed to put on her

tights. She was rather slow and careful about this. She said, 'Are you looking for someone to blame?'

'No. I don't know. Perhaps.'

'Then you've come to the wrong place. Hugh wouldn't start anyone on anything, or stop them, either. He wouldn't *bother*. He's like me. I don't expect people to tell me how to run my life. I don't tell *them*.'

'How righteous,' Charlie said.

Elsa's face stiffened. She said, 'Just now, I didn't say, what about Maggie, did I?'

'No,' Charlie said. He felt cold, tired, rather sick. He had had nothing to eat except a beer and a sandwich at lunchtime.

'I think people should go their own way,' Elsa said, and snapped her mouth shut.

'Oh, it's fun to look on,' Charlie said. Anger tightened his forehead. Elsa hadn't wanted him, or no more than the next man. She had simply watched him make a fool of himself. And he hadn't known what he wanted, either; he had been experimenting, like Toby. A silly young fool and a silly old fool. There was some connection there.

There was no connection. Only some spell was broken. He had loved Roy. But Roy had died long ago. He didn't give a damn for his randy widow, his cold son...

Elsa said, 'Charlie, if he'd been on the hard stuff, I would have told you. I didn't know pot or L.S.D. could make anyone ill.'

He said, 'Of course not, why should you?' and smiled at her easily. He felt tired, but free.

Waking in the dark, Maggie thought she heard Lucy crying, but when she got up and went to her the child was asleep and breathing deeply and naturally. The moon was shining on her face and Maggie went to the window to close the curtains. It was a still, solemn, beautiful night, the trees in the garden solid and pale as carved stone, and, as she stood looking out, she felt calm, almost happy. It was almost as if she didn't care any longer, she thought, feeling no guilt because she did care. *I am out of pain*, she thought, *nothing has changed, but I am out of pain*.

Nothing had changed. Only her mother had changed towards her in a way that went deeper than could be shown or acknowledged. She had insisted on cooking supper, clearing it away, making a hot whisky toddy at bedtime, but behind these ordinary, bustling kindnesses, Maggie had been aware of some new, emotional spring, as if her mother had suddenly let down a barrier, opened her heart, and had felt almost ashamed to say no more than 'thank you' in answer. But there seemed nothing else she could say. Apart from anything else, she had felt guilty – as if she had tricked her mother into being sorry for her by weeping in the car – but now, looking down at the grey and silver garden, she was simply grateful, if a little shy: over the years she and her mother had fallen into such a fixed pattern of behaviour towards each other that to alter it now might prove difficult, even embarrassing. Perhaps they couldn't alter it, she thought; perhaps after a brief truce they would go on in the old way, she scoring points, justifying herself, her mother fighting back, tartly lining up faults in her character. It was often easier to build up a new relationship than to change an old one. But she meant to try. How, she didn't know: leaning her forehead against the glass of the window, all she could think was, *I must see she doesn't do too much* ... When she had gone into the kitchen after kissing Lucy good night, her mother had been cleaning the floor, hands and knees and pail and scrubbing brush. She had said, 'Really, Mum, this time of night!' feeling an amused pride in her mother's energy and strength, but when Sara stood up, saying predictably, 'Any time you feel like it is the right time,' she had been startled to see the throbbing colour in her cheeks, the dark blue-ish tint of her mouth ...

Oh, it was nothing. Or it was the light in the kitchen. Her mother was all right; solid as a mountain. Sitting with her whisky and milk at the kitchen table a few minutes after, she had looked energetic and spry as a woman twenty years younger. She had repeated her intention of making a cassoulet for Charlie. She had said, 'I must ring your father sometime tomorrow.' Then, 'I think I might wash your bedroom curtains, it's a pity to waste this good drying weather.' And when Maggie protested that this would be too much for her, 'Rubbish, a bit of hard work never hurt anyone, if you don't work you never get anywhere, you know that as well as I do . . .'

Remembering this now, Maggie felt a sudden ache of sorrow. Her mother had worked all her life and got nowhere; her intelligence given no chance, her energy wasted on making ends meet, keeping heads above water. Any personal ambition abandoned so early on that Maggie had never known, she realized now, if she had ever wanted anything for herself, or what it could have been . . .

But it was presumptuous to be sorry for her mother. Pity was patronizing. Though what she felt was larger than pity, a swelling, generalized sadness that seemed to lift her and sweep her forward, like music. She felt a sudden, curious excitement as if she was beginning to understand something she couldn't put into words. She thought, *lazy fool, words are your job.* It was something to do with the way one changed and grew. There were the unendurable things; death and madness. No point in being finicky, in arguing the toss. You broke up, or you learned to endure; you died or survived. Your own personal evolution . . .

She wanted to laugh. It was like being drunk, she thought, or drugged, or in a fever. Those moments of illumination when you hold the turning world in your head. Real, or an illusion – a trick, to make you go on living? She thought, *How will I feel tomorrow, sober, in the morning light?*

A car turned into the lane and stopped; beyond the hedge she saw its low black roof. The moonlight silvered it. A door slammed. She waited. The car moved off and she saw Charlie come in through the gate and approach his own house like a burglar, walking on the grass to make no noise.

Chapter Ten

Maggie said, 'But this is absolutely marvellous, darling.'

'I don't understand you,' Charlie said. His voice sounded thin to him, as if he were hearing it from a distance. Sitting at the kitchen table, watching Maggie heat milk on the stove, he felt as if his mind were removed from this scene, bobbing about somewhere near the ceiling, looking down. But his body felt heavy and stiff as if it never wanted to move again. He said, 'Have you heard a word I've been saying?'

She said, with quick, smiling impatience, 'Oh, I heard you.' The milk rose in the saucepan; she blew on it, poured it into two blue cups, placed one in front of him and sat down holding the other. She was wearing his old red dressing-gown with the sleeves rolled up. She said, 'I'm sorry about the milk, you'll have to fish off the skin ... Of course I heard you, but it's Toby I'm thinking of. All these weeks, lying there like a vegetable, not saying anything beyond yes or no, and not always that. Don't you remember what it's been like? Now, if what you say is *true*, if you haven't made it all *up*, then it sounds as if he's come back to life!'

Her eyes were bright and excited. She looked so happy. Charlie stared at her.

She said, 'Don't you *see*? You said he was crying – don't you see how marvellous that is? He's capable of feeling something, feeling it enough to *cry*. That's terribly important, Angus has said so since the beginning. What one is frightened of in this sort of illness, what one has to look out *for*, is the shallow emotional response.'

Charlie said, 'Angus is going to be pleased.'

She didn't appear to have heard him. She said, 'This is a breakthrough!' She had put her cup down and was waving her hands about. Charlie watched her, amazed.

He said, 'Have you been drinking?'

Hurt wrinkled her face, but when it passed, she was smiling. 'I had a hot toddy, but my mother made it so you can guess how much whisky ... Oh, lord above, what does it *matter*? If I were tight as a *tick*? Charlie,' – she flung her hands wide, imploring him – 'girls have had babies before, that's not new. The important thing is, Toby's told you, it *means* something to him ...'

Charlie coughed. 'If it's true.'

'*Charlie!*' Her voice went up high. 'Would he lie about this?'

'I'm afraid I don't think he did. I say afraid, not because I don't take your point, but because it just seems to my pedestrian mind that it would be a deal simpler all round if it wasn't true.'

She snapped back in the same sarcastic tone, 'Oh, I grant you, it's a difficult social situation.'

They looked at each other with glazed, angry eyes. Then, at the same moment, both their mouths twitched. They smiled, a little sheepishly.

Maggie put her hands palms downwards on the table and looked at them. She said, speaking slowly and deliberately as if she were trying to unwind some taut, inner spring of excitement, 'I'm sorry, but I was just so glad! It was the way you told me, as if he had talked about this, reacted to it, in a perfectly normal way. So normal and natural, in fact, that you hadn't even noticed it! *Toby says*, you kept saying – well, it's a long time, isn't it, since Toby has really said *anything*? That's what made me so happy and I'm afraid it still does. If he is going to get better, then nothing else – well, I won't say it doesn't matter, but it falls into place. One's son going mad, or getting a girl pregnant – which would you choose?'

It crossed Charlie's mind that these were not really clear-cut alternatives, but he could not bring himself to say this.

He said, 'It's not our daughter.'

She nodded gravely. But suddenly her eyes shone.

Charlie laughed. 'D'you think it'll pay Iris out?'

She said indignantly, 'Of course not.' Then she sighed. 'I don't know. There are so many levels. One – the proper one, if you like, the one I hope I shall act on, is that I'm terribly sorry for everyone concerned. Honestly shocked and distressed. But

161

there is another one on which I can't help feeling – well, Iris has always been so smug, dropping hints that everyone who doesn't devote every waking minute to her children can't be doing a proper job. All those hours I sit at my typewriter, etcetera! And then telling me Toby was on heroin! Even if it had been *true*, there's a perfectly good psychological reason why the bringers of bad tidings got their heads lopped off. I *did* want to get my own back! I even had a sort of fantasy – I can tell you because it's so silly – that I might go to bed with Angus. Not because I wanted to or because he asked me, as a matter of fact it was you put it into my head saying that he – well, you remember! Anyway, I played over this ludicrous scene in which I offered myself, so to speak, and Angus thought it was gratitude because he'd taken Toby on, and *he* said, if it was all the same to me, he'd rather have a case of whisky . . .'

She laughed, crouching forward over the table, hands round her cup. There were dark hollows under her eyes that made her seem beautiful to Charlie. He was touched by this foolish story, but too tired to laugh with her.

He said, yawning, 'I must say, you have a riveting inner life.'

She said, 'I don't know why I'm talking so much. I suppose it's the relief, something concrete happening, something you can talk *about* . . . So you rattle on, any old trivial nonsense. As I said, there are all these levels. But there's another one that isn't so trivial, on which I really do feel that this isn't altogether a catastrophe, that it might, just conceivably, be a good thing for Toby. To have something else to think about, someone to care for . . .'

'Dear God,' Charlie said. He was really shocked. He thought, *I really am shocked.* He stood up and began to walk about the kitchen. 'Someone else is involved in this! You can't say, oh it might be a good thing for Toby – as if Hermia was a piece of occupational therapy like clay modelling or basket-work. She's not an *object*.' He thumped his clenched fist on the draining-board, making the cups rattle in the rack. He thought, *how hypocritical.*

Maggie said, 'Does he love her?'

'I don't know. I didn't like to ask.'

She said, 'I will think of her. I mean, I will *soon*. I was just saying how I felt now, about *him*. That this might give him the jolt he needed. Something to live for. Oh, it sounds so corny.' She smiled, rather helplessly.

He said, 'This is just hypothesis. We don't know what it'll do to him. In fact it might . . .' She was looking so frightened that he stopped. 'Of course I don't know. How can anyone? We can hardly ask Angus.'

He thought, before Toby was born, I was so pleased. He had telephoned Roy the morning the rabbit test came through and said, 'Hang on to your hat, we're having a son.' And Roy had said, 'Congratulations, you have a fifty-fifty chance.' He had put off telling Phoebe.

He said, 'He's so young.'

'People always say that. Your sister, for example.'

'I was twenty-one. And I had a degree. He's not nineteen yet. Have you *thought*? Marriage, jobs, mortgages . . .'

Her mouth trembled. 'You said once, since he'd gone off the rails, it was the wrong thing to push him back on them. I didn't think you were right, but perhaps you were. We should have changed direction, offered him a different scene. What I was trying to do was acting like some old-fashioned Nanny with a feeding problem – if you don't eat up your rice pudding, Master Toby, then it'll be served up every meal until you do!' She began to cry. 'I was so happy, earlier this evening. I don't know why . . .'

Charlie thought, *earlier this evening I was with Elsa*. It was now half-past two in the morning. There was an electric clock on the wall. He watched the second hand moving.

Maggie sniffed, blew her nose. 'Do her parents know?'

'Not yet, apparently.' Suddenly laughter began to bubble up inside him. He put his arm around her shoulder. 'It'll give you something new to talk about with Iris!'

'That's a rotten, feeble joke!' But she was straightening her nose and pressing her lips together.

He said, 'Of course, Hermia will have to tell them first, it's her pigeon,' and she let out a sudden, wild snort of laughter and leaned against him, shaking. He held her close, stroking her ear. Both of them shook with this unseemly, unsuitable laughter until tiredness quietened them, or perhaps shame. They drew apart and looked at each other, a little shyly.

She said, 'Oh, Charlie . . .'

He said, 'Darling, it's too late. If we don't go to bed we'll never get up in the morning,' and she nodded and sighed.

Lucy said, 'It's half-past *nine*.'

Her grandmother said, 'Well, where's the fire?'

Her voice sounded strange – *smudgy*, Lucy thought. She smiled at Lucy, but her smile was strange too; one side of her mouth lifted up, the other frowning and indifferent. But when she stopped smiling and closed her eyes the strangeness vanished; her sculptured, familiar face rested quietly on the pillow. Only the small frown stayed on her puckered lips, as if she were concentrating hard on something.

'I brought your breakfast up,' Lucy said. 'Mum had to go out in a hurry because Iris rang, and when you didn't come I thought you'd like it in bed.'

There was no response. Standing by the bed. Lucy looked at her grandmother with close attention: the way each hair sprang from the pores of her pink scalp like soft grass, the twitch of her eyeballs under their thin, silken lids, the strong, skeletal line of the jaw through the old, loose skin.

She said, 'You all right, Gran?' and her grandmother's eyes opened at once: darkly brown with a pale circle like smoky glass round the brown, and then yellowish-white with tiny splashes and squiggles of blood.

'Bit of a bad night, that's all,' her grandmother said. 'I'll eat my breakfast in a minute. Who did you say rang?'

'Iris,' Lucy said. 'I don't know what about because Mum took it upstairs, but she said she didn't think she'd be back for lunch.'

She thought her grandmother sighed a little.

She said, 'I can get it, if you're not feeling well. There's cold ham and salad, but I'm going shopping so I can get something else if you like.'

'Cold ham would be fine,' her grandmother said.

'We could have a picnic in the garden, just you and me!'

Lucy smiled, but her grandmother's eyes had closed again as if this was not a prospect that interested her. Lucy felt humiliated, then lonely. She said, 'There's a card from Greg in the post, Aunt Phoebe's taken him to Bognor Regis. That's not very interesting, just the rotten old seaside! She took Toby and me to Africa.'

'You can't always push the boat out,' her grandmother said.

'But Aunt Phoebe's rich.' Lucy hesitated. 'If you have a lot of money, do you have to leave it to your blood relations? I mean, by law?' Her grandmother did not reply and Lucy knew her silence meant that she despised her for asking such a question. She said, 'It wasn't the money I was thinking about.' Her voice faltered and her grandmother opened her eyes and looked at her with an expression that was no more than slightly puzzled, as if she had not altogether understood the question, so that Lucy was comforted, if only a little, and encouraged to ask what she really wanted to know. She said, 'That woman who adopted the little boy? Do you think she ever told him? She couldn't have gone on pretending, could she, not after he was eleven or twelve?'

'I really can't say,' her grandmother said. Her voice wasn't blurred any longer; on the contrary, it seemed to Lucy to be quite hard and dismissing, as if she did not, really, want to discuss this petty matter any further. And then, as if she had discussed it, and it was over and finished with, 'When did you say your mother was coming home?'

'Of course, if one has daughters, one has rehearsed this situation,' Iris said. 'But all to no purpose, it seems. All one's intellectual conceits, all one's balanced, liberal opinions, turn out to be a load of old codswallop! What one feels is just simple and basic. It's so humiliating.'

'Humbling might be a better word,' Maggie said.

'One's education is just no use at all,' Iris said in a tone of comic astonishment, but Maggie felt no impulse to smile. This scene was too ridiculous: she and Iris sitting at opposite ends of a sofa and talking in shrill, amused voices, like neurotic strangers at a cocktail party.

'I'm not so surprised at myself,' Iris said. 'I never saw myself as an intellectual. But what has amazed me is how Angus reacted!' She laughed, showing the whites of her eyes. 'To think a daughter of mine! Never darken my doors again! Like some outraged property owner!'

'Has he actually turned her out?' Maggie asked, awed.

'Well, not exactly,' Iris admitted – it seemed reluctantly. 'It was Hermia who said she would go, in fact, and he made it clear he wasn't sorry. He didn't want her to corrupt her sister, he said.' Iris gave a long, quivering sigh. 'You know, it seems selfish to say so, but I think I was the only one who was really unhappy last night – they were both so angry, it buoyed them up! They're so alike in one way. Once they've made up their minds, they can be very hard.'

'I wouldn't have said Hermia was hard.' Maggie said. 'Quite the opposite.' Was Iris disappointed because Hermia had not wept, clung to her mother?

She smiled slightly, and Iris saw it.

She said coldly, 'I think I know her better. She's compliant on the surface, but underneath she goes her own way. And she and Angus have been spoiling for a row for a long time. He's never forgiven her for failing her A-levels.'

'How absurd,' Maggie said, knowing that it was not. She cleared her throat. 'How does he feel about Toby?'

'Oh, he blames Hermia. Naturally. He told her that she must consider herself entirely responsible.' She gave one of her tinkling laughs. 'After all, Toby has hardly been in a state in which one could expect him to be.'

'I suppose not.' Maggie felt some resentment, but acknowledged it to be misplaced.

'What he said was, he couldn't understand why she had picked on someone like Toby! He said she must be pretty odd herself, to do that!'

Maggie thought, *I must not lose my temper*. She said, with downcast eyes, 'Perhaps they are in love.'

Iris laughed again, like glass breaking. 'Hermia is a great girl for lame dogs, of course.'

'It hardly seems the best way to help him over this particular stile.'

She had meant to be sharp, but her voice shook a little. She thought, *Toby*. Lying in Angus's hospital, alone, undefended . . .

Iris was watching her. She was silent, but her face had softened. Her affection had always needed a show of weakness to stimulate it. Maggie remembered, and then thought that perhaps this wasn't so trivial. She had only to be honestly and unguardedly fearful and sorry, and to let Iris see it, and all would be simple between them . . .

She said, 'Will Angus say anything to Toby?'

'Not unless Toby does to him. And he wouldn't be brutal, anyway. Angus keeps his atavistic behaviour for his family. He exercises his bad temper on me, the way you take a dog out for a walk on a convenient common!' Iris tried to smile, but two perfectly formed tears spilled from her eyes and rolled slowly down her cheeks. Glycerine, Maggie thought, and despised herself. She took Iris's hand and pressed it.

'I'm sorry,' she said, and found that she meant it. It made her feel warmer and gentler. As if some hard crust were dissolving.

Iris smiled and cried at the same time. Her breath came in little, noisy whoops; her fingers tightened on Maggie's. 'I can't help it,' she said. '*I'm* sorry. This is much worse for you, I mean your trouble with Toby . . . But what was so awful, last night, was Angus keeping on telling me that, as if nothing I might feel was of any importance! He said I mustn't make *you* feel guilty.'

Maggie giggled.

'Oh, I know . . . Just another way of getting at me!' Iris blew her nose, reddening the tip. 'Last night, after Hermia had gone, I sat and looked at old photographs; the girls when they were little, and there were some of Toby, too, and it seemed that they had all been drawn away, our children, into some kind of hole or tunnel that had suddenly opened and swallowed them up, and I howled a bit and Angus came down after his bath and said, wasn't this just typical of me, this nostalgic wallowing! I said, what was I supposed to do at this time of night, start ringing up abortionists? And I suppose because that was what he *was* thinking, he started bawling me out like a lunatic. It was all my fault, he had trusted me to look after his children – I'd had nothing else to do, for Christ's sake! – and I had let this happen!'

Maggie wondered if Angus had really said this. But it seemed cruel to doubt it; cruel to Iris, and in a way, diminishing to herself. It was cowardly and distrustful to assume there was a lie in every statement. What did it matter if Angus had been misinterpreted? Iris was her friend. She thought, *old sparring partner* . . .

She said, 'I don't see how you could have prevented it.' And then, 'I suppose none of us have been exactly successful. Perhaps our parents thought the same thing, at one time or another.'

Iris said in a desolate voice, 'You know, in the end, last night when I *finally* went to bed, all I could think was, I wish my mother was alive . . .' She looked at Maggie and within thirty seconds both were laughing.

Maggie said, 'Bloody kids!' She wiped her eyes. 'I see what you mean about the tunnel.' And although she had only said this to express affection, as soon as she had spoken she did see it: their children walking away, shadows against a deeper shadow, growing smaller and less distinct until the darkness swallowed them up.

Hermia said, 'I shall never speak to either of them again as long as I live.'

She sat on Toby's bed, her cloak wrapped round her. He lay on his back, fully dressed in jeans and jersey. He stretched out one leg and wriggled his toes against her thigh.

She said, 'That's a lie. But I shan't *want* to speak to them, not for a long time.'

He grinned at her and after a minute she grinned back, and pinched his toes.

He said, 'Are you in Hugh's flat?'

'I went there last night. Lucky I still had your key. But I can't stay. They'd only come after me, my mother weeping and wailing and my father arranging abortions.'

Toby pulled a face.

'Oh, not for social reasons. He says I only want this baby to give myself a role in life. It's an easy way out, he says.'

Toby smiled.

Hermia said, 'Of course, he may be right. But I don't see it matters. You have to decide to be something. And I would have been a rotten secretary.'

Toby said, 'I'm sorry you had a bad time.'

'Not so bad for me. Worse for my mother. I don't care what he says and she does. She's got nothing else to care about. Her own fault, of course she's let herself be pushed into the part of silly little woman. She thinks it's because it's what my father wanted, but it's her own laziness, really. Too much effort to be a whole human being.'

'Aren't you a bit hard on her?'

Hermia picked bits of fluff off the bedclothes. 'I suppose I'm just showing off.' She could feel his eyes watching her and was afraid they saw too much. She blushed. 'Are you better?'

'I'm allowed out now. Little walks in the park. And they've stopped the E.C.T. I can remember things now.'

Hermia touched the burn mark on his forehead that was fading now. 'Bloody butchers,' she said.

'Doctors are a conspiracy against the laity. Shaw said that.' He paused and added, shyly, 'I did those tests again yesterday. They said I did them all right.'

She nodded professionally (the psychiatrist's daughter). 'My father said he never thought you were schizophrenic. Just those crappy drugs.'

He nodded, not looking at her. He said, with difficulty, 'I don't suppose I'll ever be very competent, though.'

She didn't know how to reply to this. She said, 'Who is?' and laughed gaily.

'You are.' He hesitated. 'I mean you *are*, aren't you? You're all *right*?'

She said, 'I think I shall get a job as a housekeeper, probably to some frightfully rich, lonely old man. Somewhere in the country because that would be good for the baby. I'm not much of a cook, but it's the sort of thing I could learn. I mean, you only have to read a book. And they taught me how to read at school, even if they didn't teach me anything else.'

He said, 'You've got it all worked out, haven't you?' with such flat acceptance in his voice that she felt quite hollow inside. It was one thing to invent a personality to get you through something, quite another when someone else began too believe in it.

Especially Toby ... She felt she had begun to tremble so badly that he was bound to notice it. Part of her wanted to run home and cry and hide in her mother's lap. But she wrapped her arms round herself, under her cloak, and said in her young, clear, light voice, 'Well it's not exactly difficult, is it? There's not much choice. Not that I mind, I mean, I'm terribly glad of it, really, it makes everything so much simpler.' And smiled, very brightly.

He looked at her for perhaps a minute. Then he blinked and said, 'You remind me of my grandmother.' He blinked again, and sighed. Then he sat up and swung his legs over the side of the bed. 'At least I can walk you to the tube station.'

Standing up, he seemed taller than she remembered him being, and terribly frail. She said, for something to say, 'You've grown,' and then, 'Why your grandmother?'

'The way you go on – I'm all right, don't worry about me, take on the world, both hands tied.' He grinned at her, with a sudden look of pride and trust. 'Old indomitable,' he said.

Cautiously, Sara tried to move her left leg. It responded, though it was like moving a log. The side of her face was stiff, but she could twitch the cheek muscle now, as she had not been able to do earlier on, when the child had come in with her breakfast. It was a very minor stroke. If she lay still and waited, perhaps all the effects would pass off. She wasn't afraid, or only of being found out. *So humiliating*, she thought. Suppose she needed to go to the lavatory? This alarmed her so much that she began to imagine she did need to: she recognized this impulse as self-induced fear and dismissed it. Was her brain affected? She began to recite her seven times table in her head. Seven eights, that was the difficult one. Seven eights are fifty six ...

So much trouble teaching Margaret her tables. The child, so clever in other ways, seemed like an idiot, sitting at the kitchen table with tear tracks down her cheeks, weeping and saying, 'I can't do my seven times.' 'There's no such word as can't.' Although it was late and the child should be in bed, she must not give in. She felt so desperate. Like Sisyphus, rolling that stone uphill. If the girl didn't pass into the grammar school, what would become of her?

She would end up behind the counter at Woolworth, clocking into a factory, scrubbing some rich woman's doorstep. But she was so young, you couldn't expect her to grasp the importance. It was all up to her. She thought, 'Even if I make her hate me.' She said, 'You sit there till you know it, my girl, I don't care what time it is . . .'

What time was it? Sara turned her head to look at the clock. Midday. Lucy should be back soon. Poor child, she had brought her breakfast up and she had touched nothing. She must try, before she came back, to eat a little bread, drink a cup of tea . . .

Her leg was heavy and she still felt the stiffness in her face, but she was able to lift herself in the bed. That done, the rest was easier: she poured a cup of cold tea and was glad to drink it; found she could get to her feet and walk to the wash-basin without too much difficulty. She washed her face and cleaned her teeth. There was some pain in her left arm which was going to make it hard to put up her hair, but perhaps that would ease in a little; if it didn't, she could tell Margaret when she came back from her shopping, that she had had a touch of rheumatism this morning.

No. Not Margaret. Lucy had gone shopping. That was an old woman's trick, confusing daughter and granddaughter. She must watch out for that.

Or perhaps she really had meant Margaret? The last thing she wanted to do was to add to her troubles! That would be the last straw for the poor girl; an old mother helpless in bed . . .

Not that she was helpless, thank God. Half-dressed now, and only puffing a bit. If she could be finished by the time Lucy came back, they would have lunch in the garden. The child had suggested it, thinking to please her, and she hadn't answered. She felt guilty about that. It was queer how deeply guilty you often felt about relatively unimportant things. Lying in bed this last hour, remembering Margaret's misery over her seven times table and dwelling on her own frantic anxiety as if it had been some monstrous wickedness to be atoned for! She had frightened her, of course. That had been wrong, to impose her own fear on a little girl. But she must have done worse in her life! Why was it always the small things that rose up to reproach you, when you were ill, or in the poisoned hours before dawn?

Had this been small, though? Fear was a terrible thing. It stripped you naked ...

Had she frightened the child this morning? She had spoken as little as possible and been careful not to smile in case she should make some dreadful, involuntary grimace. Perhaps Lucy had thought she was angry with her? Well, if she had, that was something she could put right. She would say she had been feeling tired and was better now. They would sit in the garden, have lunch in the sun.

She was as tidy as she could make herself. She combed her hair and let it lie loose on her shoulders. She must try to get to the ground floor before Lucy came back: stairs might be awkward, with her dragging leg.

She opened her bedroom door and walked carefully across the landing, put her hand on the banister.

Lucy said, 'Gran,' and she looked down and saw her grand-daughter standing in the hall, her face lifted towards her. There was a man with her, behind her, standing in the open front doorway with his back to the sunlight. Lucy whispered something. Sara couldn't hear her words but the fear behind them pierced her like a sword.

She said, 'Well, what's all this?' and came slowly down the stairs.

The policeman wore plain clothes; a dark, grey suit, very neat and decent. Sara was conscious of how she must appear to him – a careless old woman with dress buttoned askew and ragged, witch's hair. Then she thought, *How stupid, the places he must go into, the kind of sights he sees!* and wished she could see his face more clearly: he sat in the drawing-room, as he had stood in the hall, with his back to the light.

If she could see his face as he spoke, it would be easier to take in what he was telling her. She was so afraid of missing something. Although for most of the time her mind felt perfectly clear, there seemed to be odd patches of foggy confusion, as if a damp cloud had drifted in ...

She understood that Lucy had been stealing. A box of choco-
lates and a tin of talcum powder. The policeman had been
called by the store and had brought her home. He said, 'I must
explain that the decision whether to proceed or not won't be
mine, although it will be based on what I have to say about
her. But we do try, when we can, to treat this sort of thing as a
family matter.' He had a pleasant, even, slightly common
voice.

Lucy was standing beside Sara, leaning heavily against her.
Sara picked up her hand and held it. She could feel the vein
beating in the narrow wrist and closed her fingers protectively
round it. But she was thinking of Margaret. She thought, *that
poor child, what next?*

She said, 'You can talk to me. My daughter won't be home
for some time. Her son is in hospital.'

'Appendicitis can be very nasty,' the man said, surprisingly.
He shifted a little in his chair; watching his shadowed face,
Sara thought he smiled briefly. He said, 'Lucy and I have had
quite a long talk already. I have explained that I will have to
make a report about her.'

Sara felt Lucy tremble. She said 'Margaret', and the child
looked down at her. Except for a slight frown round the eyes,
she was expressionless. *Little potato face*, Sara thought.

She said 'Lucy, I mean,' and managed to laugh, though the
slip had alarmed her. Since she had been left in charge, it
was important she should not be set down as a doddering
fool with her memory going. She said, 'Run along for a little,
dear.'

Lucy hesitated. She looked at the man across the room and
he nodded at her, turning his head so that Sara could see his
profile which was mild and tired and middle-aged and quite
unfrightening. Lucy gave a little, breathy sigh, and left the
room almost silently. But as soon as she had closed the door,
Sara heard her begin to run...

The man said, 'Quite often in these cases, all that is necessary
is to be found out. It's a sufficient jolt, particularly for this
type of child.'

'What type of child?' Sara wanted to say, though she knew
what he meant. Lucy's accent, her parents' comfortable house.

It seemed a superficial judgement to her. But she said, 'I suppose that is true.'

'Not that one should make light of the offence, naturally. The child must understand she has done wrong. But I do find sometimes that with middle-class parents I have to make this point. Unlike most of the families I have to deal with, they tend to take this sort of thing almost too seriously.' He laughed his pleasant laugh and Sara was faintly bewildered. Whose side was he on? The law must have changed since she was young.

'My daughter will be very shocked,' she said, and discovered, as she spoke, that she herself was hardly shocked at all, which surprised and suddenly amused her. She thought, *he knows what he's talking about, he comes from a lower class than Margaret and Charlie, the same class as I do, in fact: we know things that they don't know*, and said, 'You don't have to tell me what children get up to! I used to keep a shop myself. And it's not just the guttersnipes, but the respectable ones! An apple on the side while Nanny was giving the order, or an orange or two. Forbidden fruit.' She chuckled at the aptness of this phrase.

It seemed to make him graver. He said, 'One can't, of course, just accept that. It's too easy. Anti-social behaviour often points to some basic disturbance, even if it's only temporary. In Lucy's case it seems fairly straightforward. The brother in hospital, her parents' natural preoccupation with him, her own less secure status as an adopted child. And of course her age. Has she begun to menstruate yet?'

This did shock Sara. Not the question, but its coming out so pat, like a prefabricated formula. The neglected, adolescent, adopted child. The kind of neat excuse, or answer, or explanation, that her daugher had tried to find for Toby . . .

She said, 'Lucy isn't adopted, that's just some fanciful idea she's got hold of,' but was aware it would get them no further. There was always the lie behind the statement and the reason behind the lie, layer upon layer like the skins of an onion. But people were not onions – how absurd to choose this simple vegetable, she thought, and would have laughed aloud if she had not felt she was moving into what she had already begun to call, familiarly, 'one of my foggy spells,' and been afraid to seem a crazy old woman. Her sight and hearing dimmed and muffled but she could still hear him speaking soberly and sensibly, saying that of course this was a common fantasy and that it did not alter his basic case, in fact it underlined it : the child had felt insecure in the present family situation . . .

She was able to answer, 'I am sure you're right,' 'Yes, that's very true,' to show him she was listening to him explaining Lucy's motives to her, and nodded solemnly as she did so, but inwardly she was laughing. His certainty was so comic! How could you ever really understand why people behaved as they did? Oh, you could guess, make rule-of-thumb assessments, but it was like trying to find your way through some intricate underworld of caverns and passages by the light of one flickering match! The trail was too obscure : it would take a lifetime to follow even one life in all its twists and turns! So wouldn't it be wiser to give up, admit there were no easy answers? More dignified too, she thought; all this poking and prying, taking people apart like clocks. Oh, no doubt this nice man knew his job, maybe there was even some truth in what he was saying, but what did he know about his own life, let alone about Lucy's? What did she, Sara, know about hers, even though she was old and near the finish?

She said suddenly, and in a stronger voice than she had mustered up to now, 'I used to turn a blind eye, of course. What was an apple or two, here and there?'

He didn't answer for a minute. She wondered if she had interrupted him in the middle of a sentence. Then he said, 'Oh yes. In your shop.'

She said, 'My father was a farmer, you know, or would have been, only the family fell on bad times. I often thought I would have liked to live in the country, though. We had a bit of common near, but it was quite a walk and not the same thing when you got there. My father used to say it was bad for people, shut up in towns with nothing to look at but bricks and mortar and cold streets . . .'

He was smiling. Her vision had cleared again, and her mind. She thought, *Thank God for that!* He said, 'As a matter of fact, I'm a countryman myself. I must say I miss it. My wife's a Londoner, though, and if we do ever spend a night out of town she can't sleep. The terrible noise, she says, all those cows and the birds in the morning!'

Sara hoped he wasn't humouring her. Did he realize that towards the end she hadn't been listening? She said, 'What happens now, about Lucy?'

He had a notebook in his hand, though she hadn't noticed him writing in it. Now he closed it and fastened it with an elastic band. He said, 'I think it's very unlikely you'll hear anything further.' He smiled again. 'I'm afraid this must have been rather upsetting for you.'

'I am not upset,' Sara said, and stood up to see him to the door and watch him go down the path: a short, plump man narrow-chested and big-beamed, a little like a pear.

'He's gone,' Toby said. 'I watched him.'

Lucy stood on the muddy bank and walked slowly towards the landing-stage, pale and tear-streaked with leaves in her hair. He picked out one or two and looked at her critically. He said. 'Everyone thinks they're adopted, some time or another.'

'Did you ever?' Lucy's voice trembled, deliberately. Although Toby had listened and been kind, she was not yet entirely certain of his sympathy.

'Not that it's an excuse, of course,' he said, and she knew that he meant this, as the policeman, who had said the same thing earlier, had not. Watching his face as she stumbled out her confession, she had known to some extent what she was doing: pleading the kind of pitiable mitigation that any concerned adult was likely to accept. Toby was a harder nut to crack, but she valued his opinion more. She looked down at her feet and muttered, 'I know that,' acting meekness, but when he touched her hair and said, 'Well, as long as you really do then,' she felt a healing uprush of honest shame and sadness. She leaned against him and cried a little; then he held her away and took her hand and said, 'Who's home?'

'Only Gran. Why didn't you go in?'

He whistled through his teeth not looking at her, and she knew he had been scared to; he had been skulking round outside the house, to get his courage up. She did not examine this, simply accepted it. They went through the gate into the garden and he said, rather rapidly, 'I used to think I knew who my real father was.'

She said, 'What a lie, how could you?' but was envious: she had not thought of this refinement.

'Well. I suppose he must have lived near, or been a friend or something. I know I used to have breakfast with him because I can remember him giving me his bacon rinds. I used to think I belonged to him and he got tired of me or sold me or something!' He laughed; an odd, throaty sound.

'Was he a nice man?'

'I don't know, do I? I just remember that he ran a school bus and I used to think that was a marvellous thing, taking kids to school, especially the little ones, their first time, and then fetching them at the end of the day. Watching their faces, you know, and hearing the things they said.'

This speech found an echo in Lucy's mind. She chased it for a minute but it slipped away. She said, 'Are you better?'

He made no answer, just grinned down at her. But she knew he was still scared. As they approached the house, his hand tightened on hers.

Their grandmother was in the kitchen, getting lunch. Her hair was loose round her shoulders. She looked up as they came in and said, 'Well, I never did. How did you get here?'

'Train,' Toby said.

She said, in her old, grumbly voice, 'I didn't think you flew.'

Toby's mouth was twitching in a tremulous half-smile. 'I took Hermia to the tube station. The main line is next to it, and I thought I might come home for lunch.'

His grandmother looked at him. 'That's a nice girl,' she said.

'Yes,' Toby said. 'Yes, she is.'

Sitting opposite them, Sara thought how alike they were. She had not noticed this before and it puzzled her until she saw what it was that gave them both the same look. The fear on their faces, and in their veiled, watchful eyes.

She felt she could hardly bear it. She wanted to hold out her arms to them, hold them close, say, *Don't be afraid.*

She said, 'What about a cup of tea?' Toby smiled, with

patient irony; Lucy did not respond at all. Sara said, 'The cup that cheers,' and thought, *You old fool, what are you doing, acting this character part?*

She stood up with deliberate, slow movements, filled the kettle, lit the gas. She said, 'Did I ever tell you about my mother and her neighbour, Rosie Hicks?' She watched their faces. They sat still, watching her. She said, 'Didn't I ever tell you that tale?'

'Go on,' Lucy said.

'Well, it's not much really. Rosie was quite a young woman, about fifty, though I suppose you mightn't think that young. But even in those days it was young to die, and she was dying. I don't know what was wrong with her, the doctor said heart, and others said grief: she had buried her husband three months before. My mother had been looking after her; she'd had her bed brought downstairs so she could look out of the window and see a bit of life going by. Then her daughter came to nurse her; she was an efficient girl, but hard. She moved her mother back upstairs and wouldn't let anyone in to see her. "People popping in all the time," she said, "it tires her out." But she couldn't stop my mother. "The doctor says she won't last the day," the daughter said, but my mother took no notice and marched upstairs to where poor Rosie was lying in an ice-cold bedroom, sheet tight across her chest as if she was a corpse already. My mother asked her if there was anything she wanted, and Rosie said she'd like a cup of tea. My mother went down to make it, but when the daughter saw what she was up to, she said, "Oh, I'm afraid mother's not allowed tea, the doctor's forbidden it, it's so bad for her heart." My mother said, "If she's dying, she might as well have a cup of tea first, if she fancies it." So she made the tea, good and strong, and took it up and Rosie drank it. And do you know, from that minute she never looked back? In a couple of days she was up, out of bed and packed her daugher off home. And twenty years later, she turned up at my mother's funeral – she'd moved away and married again, but she must have seen the notice in the papers – turned up in a smart black coat and hat and with a great wreath of lilies. She was living by the sea somewhere, Ramsgate, I think. I said, how nice of her to come, such a journey, and she said, "I owe your mother twenty years of life, what's a few hours out of that." '

Both children were laughing. Sara looked at their sweet, laughing faces and felt tired but content because she had made them laugh for a minute. She said, 'While there's life there's hope, you see. What time do you have to go, Toby?'

'Oh, I'm not,' he said. 'I'm not ever going back.'

Chapter Eleven

He didn't go back. There was no scene. He simply said, to his mother, to his father, 'I'm not going back.' It was impossible to argue with this gentle, withdrawn boy.

Charlie rang the hospital and spoke to the registrar who seemed unsurprised, even pleased. Toby's course of treatment was finished; when a patient chose to discharge himself at this point, it could be counted a good sign. A first, positive step. But they must understand that the next ones might be harder: readjustment to society was often the most difficult stage . . .

'So the ball's back in our court,' Charlie said. This frightened him. He smiled, to disguise his fear, and scratched the side of his nose.

'In his court, shouldn't you say?' Sara said. 'He has to make his own life, you can't make it for him. It's up to him to pull himself together.'

Margaret sighed, with heavy patience. She said, 'Do you really think, mother, that Toby's illness was some kind of failure of *will*?'

'I'm not sure it mightn't be one way of looking at it,' Sara said. She thought, amused, *Why doesn't she say, 'shut up you meddling old fool', and be done with it?* She found that she was quite unhurt by her daughter's sarcastic tone. One of the effects of her stroke seemed to be a new sense of distance, as if, moving nearer her own death and aware of it, she had been lifted on to a calm plateau from which she could look down on her daughter and son-in-law without petty, personal involvement. And yet, though removed, she felt in some ways closer to them than she had ever been: her pity purer, her senses sharper. She was conscious of Charlie's anxiety, his almost physical exhaustion as if he were carrying a heavy suitcase up some endless hill, and knew that in Margaret this same weariness and fear was mixed with a helpless, despairing anger because there seemed to be nothing she could do, no effort or sacrifice she could make, that would put things right for Toby the way she wanted them put right: immediately, now, this minute. Oh, she understood in theory that she must give him time – and, indeed, lectured her mother several times on the importance of not expecting too much, too soon – but it went against her nature. Patience was never her strong point, Sara thought, and this reflection which would once have irritated her, now served to deepen her sad understanding: all that willing energy frustrated, dammed up – or spending itself, rather, against the wall of indifference that Toby had erected round him.

He was meticulously polite; speaking when spoken to, smiling when smiled at. Either this was all he had to offer, or it was some kind of defence. Whatever the cause, he was shut away, cocooned ... At his most natural when he was playing or talking with Lucy; stiffest and most reticent when one or other parent was in the room. Almost as if he were afraid of them, Sara thought, and this surprised her until she saw that although they were diffident and gentle with him, appearing to ask nothing, they were really asking so much. And such impossible things. *Be well, be happy* ...

She said to Margaret, 'He has to find himself before he can *be* anything.'

'I don't know what you mean, mother.'

And Sara did not know how to reply. What could she add to this uncertain intuition? Only that once or twice, sitting alone with Toby and watching him, apparently reading but not turning the pages of his book, a phrase had come into her head as clearly and urgently as if he had spoken it aloud. *I am nothing, I have no place* ...

Growing old, she thought now. Hearing voices, making sudden, cryptic comments, that's what old people do! It alarmed her. She had been keeping an eye on herself, taking care, resting every afternoon. Though she felt no more than a little tired, the remaining stiffness in her leg was a warning. But suppose she was going downhill in other ways she hadn't noticed? *Her mind*. She had caught herself day-dreaming these last few days, sitting back in a chair with her eyes closed and her hands loose in her lap . . .

Margaret cleared her throat. 'Taking drugs gives you a kind of identity. The amiable junkie . . .' She turned from the sink where she was preparing vegetables for supper and smiled almost gaily at her mother. 'Now he's lost that, he has to try to find a new one.'

Sara thought this a foolish remark, but she had seen the pain behind the smile; and when Margaret turned back to the sink the droop of her back and the angle of her bent neck distressed her more than it seemed possible to express. She said, 'I'm sure he will dear, you must hold on to that,' touching her daughter's shoulder but only very briefly because physical endearments embarrassed her, and then went on, speaking unreflectively because of this embarrassment: 'Treating him like a child won't help, though.' And knew as soon as she had spoken that though she felt this deeply and instinctively, she had put in ineptly, chosen, perhaps, the wrong moment to say it, and waited for Margaret's answering anger.

But, 'How else can we treat him?' was all Margaret said.

Toby had been home six days when Sara's neighbour telephoned to tell her that her husband had fallen in the garden and hurt his back. He was in bed and the neighbour was happy to look after him, but he wanted to know when Sara was coming home. He was in some pain.

'I expect he's putting it on a bit,' Margaret said. 'You know what he is.'

Sara did know. But she said, 'Well, I expect he's feeling a bit neglected. It's not unnatural, is it? Though of course he may have done himself a real injury. I shan't know till I get home, shall I? I think, all things considered, I had better go tomorrow.'

She hoped it was not apparent that she was glad of the excuse. She had said she would stay to see Greg when he came home from his holiday, but his return was a week away. And in spite of her disciplined courage, the fear of another stroke made a week seem a long time. Once she was home, she thought, this fear could be put in its proper place: a tedious companion it would be easy to ignore . . .

'*Must you?*' Margaret sounded quite frantic as if it had not occurred to her that her mother would not stay for ever. Then she sighed and smiled. 'It's not just that we like having you, though we do, of course. But you seem to get on so well with Toby. Better than we do, just now.'

From Margaret, the manner of this admission was of some consequence. It was not grudging, but made with sad sincerity. Sara was touched, and longed to comfort her.

She said, 'Well, he seems to enjoy my old stories. Not that they're much, I know; I daresay the truth is, time hangs a bit heavy on his hands.'

'What do you suggest? Basket-work?'

'Something a bit more useful than that.' Sara hesitated, as much to make up her own mind as to wonder how her daughter would take it. She said, 'If you like, he can come home with me. He'll be no trouble, quite the opposite. There'll be a few heavy jobs with your father laid up, and to tell you the truth, I was wondering how I would manage . . .'

She stopped. She had meant only to point out that Toby would really be helpful to her, not a burden, but now it seemed to her guilty mind that she had gone too far, admitted what she had hoped to keep from her daughter. But Margaret seemed not to have heard her, or if she had heard, not to have taken it in. She said, 'I don't want him to think we want to get rid of him.'

'Oh, he won't think that,' Sara said.

But she wasn't sure what he did think. He said, 'I don't mind coming and cleaning out the rabbits if you want me to, but that's about all, isn't it? I mean, what else does grandfather do?'

His faint smile hurt Sara. Or perhaps the hurt had been there earlier when Margaret had shown so little concern, and had only now come to the surface. She said, with a sudden, angry reflex, 'Your grandfather's not *nothing*. There's been too much of that kind of talk!'

He looked astonished. 'I didn't mean . . .'

She said, at once, 'I know you didn't.' But the bewilderment remained in his eyes and she knew she couldn't leave it there. She said, 'And even if you did mean it, it's not your fault. Nor your mother's, come to that; if it's anyone's fault, it's mine. I've let you all despise him. I know he's a funny old man, a bit of a joke, I daresay, with his carry-on about the plumbing, but he's my husband and he's been a support to me all my life. Oh, not in the way your mother would see it, but I never needed a man to lean on as she does, and maybe you get what you ask for from people ... I grant you, he's been a bit of a thorn in my side sometimes, but perhaps that's what I needed, a goad to keep me going!'

He said, 'I don't despise him, Gran, I wasn't even talking about him, really, I only meant, I didn't see what I could do to help. I'm not much use to anyone.'

'Don't pity yourself,' she snapped and then saw that he did not: he honestly believed this. She said, more gently, 'You could be useful to me, for a start. I haven't told your mother and you're not to, she has enough to worry her, but I've not been feeling too well and I'd been thinking, when I go back, he can look after me for a change. And he would have done, you know, just as he'd have done a lot more for me all my life if I'd given him half a chance. But I never did and that was my pride – I was the strong one and I liked everyone to know it!'

She thought, *Truth or remorse? Did I really use his weakness to point up my own strength? If I had been different, would he have been?*

She sat back in her chair and sighed a little. She said, 'If you don't give people a chance you never know ...' but then came to a stop. It seemed that her mind had drifted away from what she had been saying and she had lost the thread. Perhaps it wasn't important, anyway. She said, 'Oh well, that's all past and gone now, what's done is done,' and smiled at her grandson.

He said, 'I suppose I could carry coals and do the garden ...' He swallowed; then his mouth seemed to twitch hesitantly, as if he wanted to say something else. Sara waited but he did not speak, only got up so suddenly and clumsily from the chair he was sitting in, that it slid back across the polished floor and crashed into the bookcase. He returned it to its position – the *exact* position it had been in, and patted the seat cushion like a fussy housewife. Then he straightened up, looked at Sara, looked away, and said in a rather loud, uncontrolled voice, 'Do you think Hermia could come too? I mean, just for a little, until she finds somewhere else to go?'

When Sara had finished speaking, Margaret said slowly, 'Of course I can see how you must feel. I suppose I might feel the same in your place. All I can say is, it wasn't meant to be a cruel deception. We wanted to spare you. Charlie was afraid you'd be so appallingly shocked and upset, and I thought – well, I suppose what it comes down to, I didn't want you to think badly of Toby. That sounds a silly reason, and probably *is*, but it was only one among many. The chief one, that is the one that made us finally decide to say nothing, was that it seemed so unnecessary.'

'Unnecessary?' Sara spoke out of a face of stone. A statue, speaking.

Margaret stared at her, then laughed absurdly. 'Oh, I'm *sorry*. Of course, if she'd gone on with it, we'd have told you eventually. But she's having an abortion.'

She laughed again, nervously. Then the room was silent except for the sound of rain against glass : a late summer storm, blowing against the window.

At last, Sara said, 'Toby does not appear to know this.'

'No. He doesn't.' Margaret spoke in a barely audible voice. Sara saw her look at Charlie.

He said, 'Dear Sara. We have only known since yesterday. Of course he will have to know.'

'Not yet,' Margaret whispered. As if she were praying, Sara thought.

Margaret was sitting on the floor, on her heels. Now she looked at her mother and smiled, with her eyes screwed up. Her expression was kind, but quizzical. Deliberately so. She said, 'What point in telling him until it's over, after all? It would only put a burden on him that he's not equipped to bear. It's Hermia's decision, has been since the beginning. She never expected him to marry her, nor even wanted him to, as far as we can tell. What Toby says is, "She'd hardly want to be lumbered with me as well as a baby," which sounds terribly sad, perhaps, but is so sensible, really. He knows he's not strong enough yet to take that kind of responsibility. Of course, if Hermia had decided to have the baby, we would have helped support it, but I think she only thought of doing that for a very short time. I don't know how much her parents have persuaded her – Iris says, not at all, they only put the arguments in front of her! And once Hermia came to see that it wasn't fair on the child, that it would be a kind of self-indulgence on her part to have it, she made up her mind at once! She's a very conscientious girl.'

'I don't doubt that,' Sara said. Then, more loudly, 'I don't know when I have been so disgusted.'

Margaret sighed, 'Mother!' She gave a small, quickly concealed smile. 'I know this sort of thing is very shocking to your generation . . .'

'Illegitimate babies don't shock me,' Sara said. 'Only your attitude, Margaret.'

She paused, to collect herself. Up to now, she realized, she had spoken out of a very personal sense of humiliation. When she had said, *a cruel deception*, she had meant it: it had struck her to the heart. Since she had deceived her, Margaret could not love her; there was no love without respect and trust. The happiness she had felt these last days, the new sense of expanding, sure affection, was nothing, or no more than an old woman's sentimental delusion. That was all she was to her daughter, an old woman to be humoured.

Her mouth seemed to taste of ashes.

She said, 'I mean your attitude towards Toby. I know you think you're acting for the best, but he's not a baby, he's a young man, grown.'

Margaret was frowning and tracing the pattern on the rug with her forefinger. 'But it's not only him we have to think of, is it? Hermia matters, too! If she'd wanted him to know, she'd have told him. If we tell him now, what purpose is served? If he does nothing, doesn't talk to her about it, he'll feel horribly guilty, and if he does, what agony for *her*! She's made up her mind, poor child, why should she have to go through it all again, with him? And suppose – it's very unlikely, but one can't discount the possibility – suppose he encouraged her to have this baby? What kindness would that be, to anyone?'

'Do you despise him so much?' Sara said.

Her daughter's head jerked up. Sara looked at her steadily.

She said, 'What does Charlie think?'

'I'm not sure,' Charlie said. He was sitting forward in his chair, his eyes on his wife's face. 'As Maggie says, it's so hard to judge what the effect might be.'

'I don't think you should try,' Sara said. 'I don't think it has much to do with it. I was talking about Toby. What you were doing to him.' They were both looking at her now. She felt the trembling start in her hands, and pressed them down in her lap. She said, 'All that matters is that he's a young man and should be given a chance to be one. Whatever choice he makes, he must make it himself. If you don't tell him, you take his dignity away; he won't be a man, he'll be a baby, the baby you love and protect but have no respect for, and he'll know it, and give up, and maybe stay one, all his life . . .'

There was a silence. Sara laced her hands together and massaged the knuckles. *Bags of old bones*, she thought, and said, in that level of her voice that was still quite strong and young, 'If you don't tell him, I will.'

'Oh, I'll tell him,' Charlie said. He stood, stretching himself, and grinned at her; then he put his hand on his wife's shoulder and pressed it, and she put up her hand to cover his and said, 'Will you look in on Lucy first? I expect she's left her window open and the rain's blowing in, that side of the house.' And as he got to the door, 'Try not to wake her.'

He nodded once; then went out. Margaret looked at her mother. A long, unsmiling look.

Sara felt cold. It was a coldness that had begun in her as soon as she realized what she would have to say; and all the time she had been speaking it had deepened and intensified so that now it was like ice packed round her heart. *She will never forgive me*, she thought. *Even if she comes to see I am right, she will never forgive me. Or, if she does, it will be much later, years perhaps, and that will be too late for me . . .*

Margaret said, 'I can't bear it for him.' Then she laughed. 'I suppose you can interpret that two ways. Both are true.' She got up from the floor and went to the window. She closed the curtains. She said, in an ordinary, bright, conversational voice, 'What a filthy night!' and came to sit down again quite close to her mother; not touching her, but leaning against her chair.

She said nothing more, made no sound until Charlie opened the door. Then Sara heard her quick intake of breath.

Charlie crossed the room and sat down. Toby stood in the doorway, looking in. He was wearing his Arab burnous. His face, or what could be seen of his face beneath the hood, was glistening and pale.

Margaret said, 'It's raining.'

Charlie said, 'He can take the car.'

She began to get to her feet. She said, 'Toby.'

'Let him go,' Charlie said.

'I'm afraid she's not here,' Iris said.

She was wearing a silver caftan and looked like a Christmas tree fairy. Beyond her, across the hall, a door stood a little open. A table with lit candles; people talking.

'Her light's on upstairs,' Toby said.

Iris smiled and blushed. 'I'm terribly sorry, Toby. She doesn't want to see you.'

'She didn't know I was coming.'

Iris went quickly across the hall and closed the dining-room door. She stood with her back against it and said, 'I thought you were the cancer research collector. I'm sorry, Toby. We're having a dinner party, or I'd ask you in.'

Toby closed the front door. 'I am in. I want to see Hermia.'

'She's in bed. She's got a cold. She doesn't want to see any-one.' She smiled prettily. 'Be sensible, dear.'

'I don't want to spoil your dinner party.' His mouth was twitching.

Iris laughed.

Toby shouted. 'Hermia!'

Iris glanced nervously over her shoulder. There was a burst of laughter from the dining-room. She said, 'Toby, please . . .'

He said, 'I can yell quite a lot louder, if you really want me to.'

Hermia was lying on the bed. She was fully dressed. Her nose was shiny and swollen. She said, 'How did you get in?'

'Your mother's having a dinner party.'

'What's that got to do with it?'

'I said I'd shout the place down. I thought she might not want everyone to know.'

Hermia sniffed. 'I suppose there's no point in making a public announcement.'

He smiled at her. He sat down in the basket-chair, picked up a book that was lying beside it, and put it down again. Then he stood up and looked at the books on the shelves, moving slowly along and squinting at the titles.

Hermia said, 'I've only read about half of them.'

'More than enough, I should say.' He looked at her and said, in exactly the same tone of voice. 'When are you having it done?'

'Day after tomorrow, most probably. I was going into hospital today but I've got this rotten cold and it's bad for the anaesthetic if you're clogged up.' She looked at him. She said, 'It's no worse than having a tooth out, not so bad, in some ways. Less permanent. I mean, I can always have another baby.'

'How long has it taken you to think up that analogy?' Toby said.

'It was my father's. He was trying to cheer me up.'

'Do you need cheering up?'

She pulled a hideous face at him. Her eyes were pink, like her nose: either her cold, or recent tears.

Toby said in a husky voice, 'I'm quite good with children. It's not much, but it might do for a start.'

'Did you come here to say that?'

He sat down in the chair again, gathering his skirts round him rather primly. 'I wasn't sure. I thought I'd see how you felt first.'

She said, 'Thank you. It's sweet of you. Really, I mean that. But it's not fair.' She began to cry.

He watched her. He said, 'Please don't cry.' Then, 'What isn't fair?'

'*You* know. Not fair to you.' She gave a gasp, felt for her handkerchief under the pillow and blew her nose loudly.

He said, 'Oh for God's sake don't start that.' He got up and peered under the bed and dragged out a suitcase. He put it down on the bed, opened the lid, and started taking things out of the cupboard and throwing them in.

She said, 'Hey! What d'you think you're doing?' But she was beginning to laugh.

He said. 'You're the one it's not fair to, come to that.'

She shook her head and got off the bed. She picked up a hairbrush, looked at it, and put it down again. She said helplessly, 'I can't just *go*. Where, anyway?'

'Hugh's flat, tonight. Or an hotel. I've got some money. Then tomorrow we can go home with my grandmother. You can only pull the plug once a day, but you'll get used to that.' He reached up to the next shelf in the cupboard and pulled down an assortment of garments.

She said, 'Hey, you fool! Those are my old school clothes.'

He said, 'Is your mother likely to come bursting in?'

'I don't know. I don't think so. My father would but she won't have told him. Not with those people there. Why?'

'I want to kiss you,' he said.

He kissed her. He said, 'You'd better see if I've put the right things in the case. I don't really want to stay here too much longer.'

She saw that he had suddenly gone very white. He was shivering; the whole surface of his skin seemed to be shivering, like cracking ice. He saw her watching him and did his best to smile, but it was an effort. She saw what a terrible effort it was.

She said slowly, 'Toby, what are we going to do?'

'I told you.'

'Yes, I know. But we can't stay with your grandmother for ever.'

He said, 'I don't know.' And then stood, shivering and biting his lip and looking so scared that she wanted to put her arms round him and hold him and tell him not to worry, everything would be all right. But she stayed where she was, perfectly still, waiting for him to answer her, and after a little while he stopped shivering and the colour came back into his face. 'I don't know,' he said, and smiled with hardly any effort at all. 'But I promise it'll be better than this.'